MEDICAL MALADIES

STORIES OF DISEASE AND CURE FROM INDIAN LANGUAGES

Edited and Introduced by

HARIS QADEER

THORNBIRD

NIYOGI BOOKS

Published by
NIYOGI BOOKS
Block D, Building No. 77,
Okhla Industrial Area, Phase-I,
New Delhi-110 020, INDIA
Tel: 91-11-26816301, 26818960
Email: niyogibooks@gmail.com
Website: www.niyogibooksindia.com

Editor: Arani Basu
Design: Shashi Bhushan Prasad
Cover design: Misha Oberoi

ISBN: 978-93-91125-75-2
Publication: 2022

Printed at: Niyogi Offset Pvt. Ltd., New Delhi, India

For

Doctors, medical professionals, and frontline workers who lost their lives to Covid-19 and its variants, and for all those who survived

'The clinical gaze is a gaze that burns things to their furthest truth.'

Michel Foucault

The Birth of the Clinic

Contents

Foreword

On the Cusp of Medical Corporatization

One of the most characteristic aspects of work in the literature of the Medical Humanities is the ascendancy and centrality of the physician as a healer. The treatment doesn't always work and loss of life often runs high, but the physician remains the focal point through his or her (primarily his) sufferings on behalf of the patients. Consequently, the patient is at best secondary and often little more than a collection of symptoms that the physician abstracts from the dynamic life they conceal. What this emphasis often results in is a rendering on behalf of the author into an anonymous 'universal' suffering subjecthood for patients (disabled-people-in-the-making) that leaves them as murky existences in the shadow of the physician figure as paramount concern.

I would suggest at the start here that our age is made for work that populates the Medical Humanities (particularly in the West) as the rise of commercial advertising centering on the heroics of physicians and medical staff over-populate television and social media. We see the chronic 'small print' disclaimers made on the audio track about possibilities of mortifying secondary conditions such as heart attack, cerebral hemorrhage, depression, suicide, etc. Sharon Snyder and I have commented elsewhere that this mode of representation might be referred to as the contemporary segmentation of the body into failed and/or failing constituent parts. Thus, parts of bodies can be sectioned off and sold cures/treatments as a critical aspect of selling off the private to the public within neoliberal orders. Further, in the current COVID epidemic age, celebrations of medical heroics are made as cultural thank yous even though they are actually advertisements for corporate medicine and Big Pharma. In these commercial depictions physicians and nurses are the titular protagonists as well and the West assures itself with sentimental narratives of its own overcoming through citation of medical industries. The sentimental narrative of neoliberal medicine is that key enjambment of telling viewers 'they are falling apart' while counterbalancing that message with 'we'll take care of you—just buy our products'.

In this collection, which may be observed to be somewhat removed from Western contexts with its interests planted firmly in India, Haris Qadeer assembles a variety of 'short life' pieces that evoke a wide array of medical contexts and cultural traditions. The multiplicity of India is on display in their portrayal of a variety of medicalized approaches to disability and interrupted health status. The physicians in these works retain their paramount status and thus make the collection recognizable as a gathering of Medical Humanities-based texts. Yet, the patients being treated arrive more developed and often in excess of their diagnostic symptoms. Here, what these stories communicate to the reader is the intimacy of urban and country medical practices and the intimate connection with a less corporatized medicine that characterizes post-industrial cultures such as the UK, US, Australia, Canada, etc. Qadeer's selections avoid the anonymity of so many major traditions within Medical Humanities.

To a significant extent the difference that makes this collection so important as an addition to the field is Qadeer's introduction which provides a compelling history of works on mass death and the deterioration of the social order in the literature of epidemics. The historical scope of Qadeer's commentary extends the more characteristic myopathy of the vast majority of stories analyzed so often by Medical Humanities approaches. The story of medical heroics—unlike, for example, Kafka's *The Plague* that Qadeer analyzes substantively—misses the dynamics of human interaction that medicine so often entails yet is increasingly lost as medicine industrializes and corporatizes delivery of care. Without the investment in a withholding of idealizations of medical deliverers the works of Medical Humanities miss the individuation and wide-ranging historical placement of its works of central interest. This individuation is what comes through in these stories and mark them as departures from the canon of works in the field as most commonly considered.

The next issue that I want to take up is what tensions exist between Disability Studies and the Medical Humanities in order to enable readers to assess the stories to come. The two fields would seem to make comfortable bed fellows on the surface. Disability Studies in the US can be argued to come out of Medical Sociology the close cousin discipline of today's Medical Humanities through the works of Robert Murphy in memoirs such as *The Body Silent* and Irving Zola's voluminous body of work (*Ordinary Lives, Missing Pieces, Meaningful Relationships, Disabling Professions* with Ivan Illich, etc.) not to mention Irving Goffman's work on asylums as total institutions. What all of these works bring to readers' consideration was a shift in focus on the experience of the academician as patient and their downgrading of medical personnel to a more secondary role. Thus, one could argue that Disability Studies was, at least, a counter-discourse to the utopic myth of modern medicine with its cures, treatments, and professionals minus the mortality, poor outcomes, ease of opting for the less successful surgery to save money and lower expectations of expertise, as well as the prison house atmosphere set up by so many medical gatekeepers.

Whereas Medical Humanities work tended to enshrine the myth of the magical medical healer, early Disability Studies flipped the script and focused on an investigator turning their own experience of the medical industry into fodder for critical thinking about failures of medical caregiving and neglect of treatment of secondary conditions. Thus, Disability Studies tends to view 'the medical model' (reduction of disabled persons to sets of medically-interesting, yet deindividuated pathologies) with a great deal of skepticism, with its idealization of medical providers at the expense of the recipients of healthcare, and with its abstraction of individual humanity into the impartial, universal catalog of symptoms to be treated in the future of increasingly bureaucratized, alienated, and under resourced medical industries sold off to private corporations.

In the stories collected here in *Medical Maladies,* one can feel the coming threat of a more corporatized medical practice lurking on the horizon of the still individualized nature of care in India as portrayed. Pathologies are not yet fully abstracted from the dynamic nexus of patients and thus an interaction between physician and patient still play a central role in the delivery of care. Neutrality has not yet been fully adopted as a desirable state of empiricism where individual investment in well being can be placed aside. Disability Studies rightfully worries over the stress on medical 'neutrality' for several competing reasons: 1) neutrality abstracts disability/disease and the humanity of the patient is jettisoned like a stage in the ascent of a rocket into the invisibility of space; 2) 'neutrality' (or lack thereof) often result in Western healthcare in neglect of secondary conditions as if the primary disabling condition is the singular source of all other health situations and thus disabled people often die of inattentiveness to other aspects of their health; third, 'neutrality' tends to disguise responsibility of the medical staff in poor outcomes in the way that Max Weber analyzed decentralization as the primary output of corporatized bureaucracies where no 'one' is answerable to the negative outcomes of corporate labor, product manufacturing, erroneous advertising, workplaces as producers of disabilities among laborers, etc. These are the serious give-and-take concerns at stake in work in the Medical Humanities where disabled people tend to find themselves more commonly subject to the excesses and neglect of medical care in the contemporary world.

Hopefully, *Medical Maladies* can help skirt some of these problems in its variegated attention to subcultural medical treatment and its remaining fingernail grasp on the humanity of the patients as active participants in the healthcare scenario. Much depends on this collection and future work as the Medical Humanities moves to Asia and applies its too easy enshrinement of medical caretakers to those it seeks to turn into objects of care.

David T. Mitchell
Professor, The George Washington University,
Washington DC, USA

Introduction

'The Age of Modern Fiction was ushered in by a virus,' claims David Steel in his essay 'Plague Writing: From Boccaccio to Camus' (1981). He traces the origin of modern storytelling to *The Decameron*, a medieval European text dealing with the Great Bubonic Plague (1346–53) by Giovanni Boccaccio (1313–1375), one of the most influential writers in European literary history. Set in the backdrop of the Black Death, *The Decameron* narrates how the plague ravaged the city of Florence and killed thousands of its inhabitants. The text has an uncanny resemblance to the contemporary pandemic. Steel's comment outlines the influence of the narrative framework of *The Decameron* on the evolution and the growth of techniques of storytelling in fiction and demonstrates how the epidemic influenced and shaped the literary traditions in Europe. For him, the historical circumstances of the Great Plague were 'the direct cause of the storytellers assembling' (Steel 88). Steel studies the literature dealing with different plagues and demonstrates how different authors, from the medieval era to the twentieth century, were preoccupied with the epidemics and fragility of human existence.

The study also brings to light a body of narratives dealing with plagues. Michel Foucault, the French philosopher, also acknowledges a separate existence of the literature of plague, which, according to him, is 'an extremely interesting body of literature.' In a lecture delivered on 15 January 1975, published later in *Abnormal: Lectures at the College de France 1974-1975*, Foucault notes, 'There is a literature of plague that is a literature of the decomposition of individuality; a kind of orgiastic dream in which plague is the moment when individuals come apart and when the law is forgotten' (Foucault 47).

The outbreak of Covid-19 has generated a renewed interest in the relationship between literature and medicine. Scholars and researchers are analysing the literature of plague to understand how epidemics and their aftermaths have been managed in past.

Since ancient times, human beings have adopted various strategies to combat contagious diseases. The ancient Greeks believed in a sacrificial ritual of killing *pharmakos*, a human scapegoat. For them, the killing symbolized the termination of an epidemic from the city. Detention and segregation of susceptible subjects have also been in practice since ancient times. Early references to strategic segregation are in the book of the *Old Testament*. In Leviticus, chapter 13, 'Regulations About Defiling Diseases,' it is mentioned that lepers are unclean, and they must live alone:

> The priest is to examine him, and if the swollen sore on his head or forehead is reddish-white like a defiling skin disease, the man is diseased and is unclean. The priest shall pronounce him unclean because of the sore on his head. Anyone with such a defiling disease must wear torn clothes, let their hair be unkempt, cover the lower part of their face and cry out, 'Unclean! Unclean!' As long as they have the disease, they remain unclean. They must live alone; they must live outside the camp. [Lev. 13]

Temporary or otherwise isolation of diseased bodies has been one of the approaches to curtail the spread of contagious diseases. However, the term 'quarantine' does not appear in the early documents. In *Al-Qanun fial-Tibb* (The Canon of Medicine), 1025, Ibn Sina (980–1037) argued the necessity of a period of forty days of quarantine to weaken the spread of contagious diseases. Quarantine was practiced as a public health measure during the repeated waves of plague that spread across different parts of Europe in the fourteenth century. Historians have estimated that between 1346 to 1353, the plague killed between a third and two-thirds of the total population of Europe, and in some areas almost 80 per cent of the population perished. In the proliferation of the diseased disorder and social chaos, extreme measures were taken by the authorities to curtail the spread. In *Historical Sketches of Quarantine* (1857), Jewell notes that during the plague in 1374, Viscount Bernabo ordered all the infected people to be outcasted from the city of Reggio, Italy. The sick and ailing people were taken to the fields 'to die or to recover' (Jewell 03). During the plague in 1377, the rector of the seaport of Ragusa (Dubrovnik), Croatia, imposed the law of (*trentino*), isolation for a period of thirty days. Later the period of isolation extended from thirty days (*trentino*) to forty days (*quarantino*). The modern-day usage of the word 'quarantine' can be traced back to '*quarantino*'—the law of mandatory isolation of forty days. References to mandatory quarantines to curb the spread of plagues appear in various historical and fictional texts. In 'An Epistle Written Concerning the Plague to Girolamo di Maestro Luca at his Villa,' the apocalyptic spectacle of the quarantine during the 1527 plague of the 'miserable' Florence is vividly depicted:

> The shops are locked, the businesses closed, the courts and the lawyers dragged away, prostrating the laws. Now one hears of this theft, now of that murder: the piazzas and markets, where the citizens used to be in the habit of gathering frequently, are now made into communal graves, and vile dens of thieves. Men go about alone, and in exchange for friends, one meets people infected with this deadly plague. Even if one parent finds the other, or a brother finds his brother, or a wife her husband, each one keeps a safe distance from their relations: and what is

> worse? fathers and mothers spurn their children, abandoning them…I am certain that few shops, where bread is distributed, are still open; but there, the shopgoers infect each other and take-home buboes. (Landon 123)

Mandatory quarantine was imposed by the Ottoman Empire in 1831 in the wake of the first-ever cholera epidemic in Izmir. Quarantine stations were constructed, and Mahmud II issued orders for the establishment of quarantine houses in different provinces of the empire.

In *Discipline and Punishment* (1995), Michel Foucault uses the 'segmented, immobile, frozen space' of a seventeenth-century plague-stricken city to study how under such circumstances, surveillance is exercised by the authorities: 'Each individual is fixed in his place. And, if he moves, he does so at the risk of his life, contagion or punishment' (p. 195). He delineates the measures to be taken against the epidemic. He also mentions 'partitioning of spaces,' 'closing off houses,' 'constant inspection,' and 'registration.' Foucault's description resonates with some of the precautionary measures adopted by various countries, across the globe, as they scrambled to prevent the spread of the Covid -19 and its multiple variants.

Writing Plague

Authors across the world have utilized speculative as well as realist modes to depict the plight and predicament of human beings during epidemics and other similar circumstances. An exploration of literary history from the classical to the contemporary period demonstrates how pandemic literature, written in diverse countries in different eras, has dealt with the relationship of individuals with society in times of public health crisis. One of the earliest works to refer to a plague is Homer's *Iliad*, a poem composed in the eighth century BC. Other classical Athenian works such as Sophocles' *Oedipus the King* and Thucydides' *History of the Peloponnesian War* refer to the health and the moral crisis during the plagues in their societies. Apart from Boccaccio's *The Decameron*, references to the Black Death are also found in other medieval texts such as Chaucer's *The Pardoner's Tale* and William Langland's *Piers Plowman*. Chaucer's poem refers to death as the murderer responsible for the killing of one thousand men by his hand during the plague in the fourteenth century. In the 1720s, after The Great Plague of Marseille, the last of the significant European outbreaks of bubonic plague, many influential texts were written: Daniel Defoe's *A Journal of the Plague Year* (1720) deals with fictional eyewitness accounts of the cataclysmic outbreak of bubonic plague in London in 1665. *The Diary of Samuel Pepys* also contains the author's first-hand account of the plague of London. In *The Masque of the Red Death* (1842), following the traits of gothic fiction, Edgar Allen Poe narrates the tragic tale of a prince named Prospero, who tries to escape a dangerous plague, the Red Death, by hiding in his secluded and luxurious abbey. Inspired by Poe's story,

Jack London wrote a post-apocalyptic novel titled *The Scarlet Plague* (1912) depicting the aftermath of the uncontrollable epidemic, the Red Death. Both Poe's and London's narratives depict pandemics that are capable of wiping out humanity.

In twentieth century literature, plague has also been used as a metaphor by several authors. Albert Camus *The Plague* (1947), a novel based on the 1849 cholera epidemic in the city of Oran, is a metaphoric tale dealing with the Nazi occupation of France. It depicts a virus that spreads uncontrollably from animals to humans and ends up destroying half the population. Camus' *State of Siege* (1948) and Karel Capek's *The White Plague* (1937) are interesting interventions in the theatrical representation of the epidemic. Written as anti-fascist plays, they equate plague with the terror of the Nazi occupation. Both Camus and Capek have used the theme of plague for the allegorical depiction of suffering and disasters. The theme of Gabriel Garcia Marquez's *Love in the Time of Cholera* (1985), a romantic novel, suggests that lovesickness is a literal illness, a plague comparable to cholera. Apocalyptic fiction such as Mary Shelley's *The Last Man* (1826), Stephen King's *The Stand* (1978), and Deon Mayer's *Fever* (2016) speculate dark futures for the human race. While Shelley's novel, the first apocalyptic novel in English, narrates the story of Lionel, the last man to survive a global plague, King's novel deals with the aftermath of an accidental release of highly contagious influenza from a secret American Department of Defence. In his novel, Mayer imagines a future where an airborne AIDS-related virus kills much of the world's population.

Indian authors such as Rabindranath Tagore, Ahmed Ali, Rajinder Singh Bedi, Master Bhagwandas, Kalpish Ratna amongst others have written fiction depicting plagues in India. Tagore's *Chaturanga* (1916) narrates the chaos and commotion in the plague-ridden city of Calcutta, and in *Twilight in Delhi* (1940), Ahmed Ali mentions how Delhi in the summer of 1918 became 'a city for Dead.' Descriptions of the epidemic and innumerable corpses floating in the Ganga in Suryakant Tripathi Nirala's *Kulli Bhat* (1938) resonate with similar situations in contemporary times.

Room 000: Narratives of the Bombay Plague (2015) by Kalpish Ratna (Ishrat Syed and Kalpana Swaminathan) fictionalizes the nineteenth-century bubonic plague in colonial Bombay—the forgotten tragedy of the deadly plague that hit the city in 1896. The title of the novel is borrowed from history. It refers to Room 000, a research laboratory at the Grant Medical College, where the very first successful vaccine against bubonic plague was invented. It depicts how doctors and scientists dealt with the plague: it makes references to Waldemar Mordecai Haffkine, the scientist who created the first successful vaccine against bubonic plague, and Dr Acacio Gabriel Viegas, who diagnosed the first case of plague in Bombay in 1896. Such descriptions of the use of modern scientific methods to control the plague in colonial India reverberate with Pratik Chakrabarti's observation: 'Colonialism provided the first model of using scientific means of pandemic control for the large scale and often coercive regulation of people's lives and livelihoods' (Chakraborti 58). Captain William Listo, a young man from the medical school, devotes himself to finding the cause. Apart from *Room 000*, Kalpish Ratna's oeuvre also includes *The Quarantine Papers* (2010) and *The Secret Live of Zika Virus* (2017)—two interesting texts exploring the different dimensions of diseases and cures. Sidin Vadukut's *Bombay Fever* (2017) is a fascinating intervention in the evolving genre of medical fiction in pre-Covid India. In direct or implied ways, most of the aforementioned narratives resonate with the ongoing coronavirus pandemic ravaging the world.

Medicine and Literature

Can the study of literature be helpful to the practice of medicine? In his seminal work *The Silent World of Doctor and Patient* (1984), Professor Jay Katz narrates the medical condition of Iphigenia Jones, a young patient with a circumscribed breast malignancy. By alluding to the classical Greek myth of the near-sacrifice of the daughter of Agamemnon and Clytemnestra, Katz raises the crucial issue of medical paternalism, and Iphigenia Jones, in his analysis of the text, becomes 'a symbol of the maiming and sacrificing of patients by physicians from antiquity to the present time' (Duffy 22). Katz's work has influenced generations of scholars and researchers who have expressed concerns over patients' rights over their bodies. The Indian-American doctor, Atul Gawande underscores how in the past patients had no say in the matter, and how 'they were regarded as children: too fragile and simple-minded to handle the truth, let alone make decisions. And they suffered for it. People were put on machines, given drugs, and subjected to operations they would not have chosen' (Gawande 210).

Commenting on the complex intersections between medicine and literature, Jane Wood notes, 'medicine and literature [have] looked to each other for elucidation and inspiration'. In their article, 'Literature and Medicine: Contributions to Clinical Practice,' the authors focus upon the relationship: 'Narrative accounts of patients' experiences of illness are regularly considered in medical school courses and in professional reflections on the patient-physician relationship, aging, death and dying, disability, and women's health' (Charon et al.). They also claim that the acquaintance with literary works and 'writing in narrative genres allow physicians and students to better understand patients' experience and to grow in self-understanding, and literary theory contributes to an ethical, satisfying, and effective practice of medicine' (Charon et al.). Fictional depictions of epidemics, diseases, and other health conditions can create awareness about health and hygiene. Literature can play a crucial role in generating awareness about health and society and may persuade readers to contemplate important questions on the intersections of health and humanities.

In the European as well as American literary histories, some of the prominent authors such as Arthur Conan Doyle, William Somerset Maugham, Anton Chekhov, Robin

Cook, and William Carlos Williams hailed from medical disciplines. Similarly, doctor-writers such as Rashid Jahan, Kalpish Ratna, Punathil Kunjabullah, Guruprasad Kaginele have made their mark on the literary map of India.

Medical pluralism in India

Across the globe, India is identified as the birthplace of Ayurveda and Yoga, the ancient systems of medicine and health, and is also known for ancient medical texts such as *Sushruta Samhita* and *Charaka Samhita* produced by early medical practitioners. Other classical systems of medicine such as Siddha, Amchi, and Naturopathy have also been prevalent in different parts of India for centuries. Apart from the indigenous systems of medicine, the country has also nourished foreign systems of medicine such as Unani (Graeco-Islamic), homeopathy, and allopathy on its soil by adopting and adapting them. Medical pluralism has existed in India for centuries but, as Khatri and Joshi claim, 'the healthcare of the masses was always dependent upon the more informal and un-institutionalized sector'. In early times, it was difficult for the common folk to get access to Ayurvedic and Unani practitioners. The practitioners 'easily invariably catered to the needs of the kings, lords, and the elites. There has always been a divide between the folk and professional sectors of medicine, with folk medicine catering to the masses'. As an alternative system, folk medicine has also been existing along with other systems. The presence of magico-religious healers, bonesetter *pahalwans*, street-dentists, snake-bite healers in both urban and rural localities underscores how even in contemporary India, folk healing is a popular alternative system of cure and healing for the masses.

The Unani system of medicine, after arriving in South Asia around the twelfth century, flourished during the Mughal period (Stiedenroth 11). Several Indo-Muslim medical manuscripts such as Abu Bakr Bin Ali Bin Uthman's *Kitab ul Saidana of Al-Beruni* and Muhammad Zakariya Al-Raz's *Kitab-i fi Al-Tibb Al-Mansuri* written during the era, are still relevant to the students and scholars of Unani medicine. In *Islam and Healing*, Seema Alavi argues the existence of 'plural medical culture' (Alavi 11) in colonial India that was sustained by colonialism. She demonstrates how, in the nineteenth century, the Unani system of medicine underwent a tremendous change; and 'a new Unani' (Alavi 11) was created. She comments on the eclectic sources of the new Unani:

> It used the Persian idea of health as individual comportment with Arabic scientistic learning as its intellectual core. To these, it added other knowledges culled from the religious and cultural cosmologies of North Indian society. These included healing through the traditions of the Prophet (*Tibb-i-Nabawi*), and the use of charms produced by fakirs, and talismans, and other such folk remedies. (Alavi 11)

It is interesting to note that different systems of medicine have been influencing each other for centuries. In a similar vein, Charles Leslie, while arguing that Ayurveda and Unani can be studied as the continuation of a 'tradition of syncretism,' explains how both the systems of medicine, 'had been influencing each other for a long time and whose practices were by the nineteenth and twentieth centuries already radically different from the classical texts' (Leslie 356). Professional practitioners who practice Ayurvedic and Unani medicines, according to Leslie, are practicing 'a form of popular cultural medicine'. Several scholars have argued institutionalized training as one of the outcomes of the amalgamation of biomedical knowledge with indigenous medicine—a process that Stiedenroth terms as 'biomedicalization of traditional medicine'.

The roots of the modern/western system of medicine can be traced back to colonialism. It is believed that the Portuguese introduced western medicine in India in the sixteenth century. In his book, Projit Bihari Mukharji comments on the presence of 'western medicines' in the region: 'South Asia had been exposed to 'western' medicine for at least two centuries before the term *daktar* emerged as a socially significant entity. Numerous European medical travellers such as Francois Bernier, Niccolao Manucci, Garcia d'Orta, and John Ovington, visited Mughal South Asia' (Mukharji 1). The East India company brought medical practitioners with them and established medical departments in various parts (Bengal, Madras, and Bombay presidencies) of colonial India to look after the health and the welfare of their military personnel and civilians. Commenting on the medical system in colonial India, David Arnold notes: 'Nineteenth-century India presents us with a medical system that attempted not just to function for the benefit of the colonial rulers themselves (though that was undoubtedly one of its priorities) but also, often ineffectually, to straddle the vastness of a peculiarly colonial divide' (Mukharji 7). The advent of modern medicine (allopathy) in India appears to have created a dichotomy in the medical landscapes of India—a binary between traditional systems of medicine and modern medicine. The homeopathy system of medicine was introduced in the early decades of nineteenth-century in Calcutta (now Kolkata). In 1881, the first homeopathic medical college was established in the same city. Calcutta Homeopathic Medical College played a crucial role in popularising homeopathy in India.

Though scholars of medicine have been writing manuals, treatises, and other medical texts on health and hygiene from ancient times, it won't be wrong to say that the genre of fiction provided authors to reflect upon the issues on health, hygiene, and cure. Thus, from the beginning of the twentieth century—when the genre of short fiction was still in its early phase—several celebrated and less-known authors, wrote short stories dealing with the issues of illness, trauma, health, and medicine. Their writings demonstrate the ethnomedicinal wisdom of different communities, home remedies, plural cultures of medicine, and issues of biomedicalization amongst others.

Medical Maladies: Stories of Disease and Cure from Indian Languages focuses on various contexts of health, illness, patient care, and medical ethics. Stories in the collection deal with different facets of disease and cure in India: How are the different systems of medicines depicted in the genre of short fiction? How are traditional practitioners (*vaids*, hakims, folk healers, midwives) as well as modern doctors and surgeons represented in Indian short fiction? How do doctors incorporate medical knowledge into their narratives? How are the spaces of hospitals, nursing homes, health clinics depicted in short stories? In what ways are the ethics of care and empathy dealt with in the genre of short stories? Who has the right over the patient's body? How are issues of medical paternalism portrayed in Indian short fiction? How do authors narrate the doctor-patient decision-making process in their stories?

The opening story of the anthology 'Quarantine' (translated from Urdu) was written by Rajinder Singh Bedi, a renowned Urdu author associated with the Progressive Writers Association. He is one of the few Indian authors who has dealt with the theme of plague in Indian literature. First published in 1940, the story depicts the fragility of human existence in the face of a fatal epidemic. Dr Bakshi, the narrator of the story, is appointed to oversee the quarantine to prevent the spread of the epidemic in his city. He narrates the story of William Bhagu Khakrub, a sanitation worker of the locality, and his struggle with the epidemic. Apart from death and destruction caused by the plague, the story also outlines Bhagu's commitment and responsibility towards the society. Bhagwandas' 'The Plague-Witch' was first published as 'Plague ki Chudail' in *Saraswati* magazine (1902) and deals with the theme of epidemic, cure, and superstitions. It depicts how certain superstitions pertaining to diseases and cure are rooted in history, culture, and myths, and touches upon the themes of stigmatization and plight of the infected patients.

Different systems of medicine have their particular ways of reading the human body, diagnosing diseases and their causes. Commenting on the difference between Ayurveda and modern medicine, Prakash Desai notes, 'Hindu medicine never became divorced from the rest of life's pursuits, especially not from religious practice, as did medicine in the West' (p. 37). In this collection, Basant Kumar Satpathy's 'A Major Operation' (translated from Odia) and Rajshekhar Basu Parshuram's 'A Crisis of Medical Treatment' (translated from Bengali) deal with the issues of patient's dilemma, treatments, and cure. In both the stories, the authors depict plural medical cultures and their practitioners. In 'A Major Operation,' the titular surgery in question is the traditional way of removing gallstones from the patient's body. The first-person narrative is a dramatic recreation of the entire process from a brief account of the abdominal pain, diagnosis, failed homeopathic and ayurvedic treatments, and finally ending in the recovery of the narrator-protagonist through modern surgery. Parshuram's satirical story deals with the themes of over-medicalization or disease-mongering; it shows how the medicine and treatment industry is capable of exploiting ordinary people. In the story, Nanda Babu, a Bengali widower, falls from a slow-moving vehicle, from which he almost escapes without a scratch. However, on the suggestions of his friends, he visits different medical practitioners: a *daktar*, a homeopath, a hakim, and a *kaviraj*. All of them give different diagnoses for his absent ailment, including a very complicated operation on his skull. All these visits cost him a huge amount of money.

Shankar Raina's 'Whose Turn Now' (translated from Kashmiri), Saadat Hasan Manto's 'Manzoor' (translated from Urdu), Bhabendra Nath Saikia's 'The Cavern' (translated from Assamese), and Zakia Mashhadi's 'Day Care' (translated from Urdu) are set in hospitals and focus on the relationships and friendships that the patients develop at the hospitals. Raina was a practicing cardiologist from Kashmir who wrote stories about patients, medical staff, and caregivers in hospitals. His 'Whose Turn Now' narrates the lives and deaths of a group of patients in the general ward of a hospital in Kashmir. The patients express a range of emotions and feelings towards each other: empathy, love, compassion, and jealousy. The story also deals with Sister Razia, a para-medical staff, and her commitment and compassion for the patients at the hospital. Manto's 'Manzoor' is a patient-centric story dealing with Manzoor, a young boy suffering from coronary thrombosis, a fatal heart condition. It reflects upon the critical care that patients receive, and on the relationships that the patients develop at the hospital. Manzoor becomes a source of strength for Akhtar, a fellow patient, who also suffers from heart disease. Zakia Mashhadi's 'Day Care' is one of the few stories in which the emphasis is on the plight of caregivers. Set in the waiting area of a hospital, the story outlines the ordeal of caregivers. It also underscores how caregivers manage the practical needs of their patients while managing their own lives. The author uses the space of hospitals to critique the religious differences in Indian societies. Saikia's 'The Cavern' narrates the story of Mr Pienar, a social activist, who undergoes heart transplant surgery, a path-breaking intervention in the medical science of his time. Working for an organization that strives to maintain the dominance of the white race in the society, little does Mr Pienar know about the fact that the new heart throbbing within him once belonged to a dark-skinned person, until the wife of the latter reveals the matter to him. This revelation sets forth a series of events that compels Mr Pienar to accede to a strange request made by the woman, i.e., allowing her to listen to his heartbeats. Annie Zaidi's 'Heartless' utilizes speculative mode to tell the story of Ray and Nayan, two young lovers. They hail from an imaginative city where the hearts of its inhabitants are taken out of their bodies before they turned thirty.

The following five stories in the collection deal with questions of ethics and the responsibilities of medical professionals. Premchand's 'Mantra' (translated from Hindi) portrays the dichotomy that exists between the tradition and modern systems of medicine—Dr Chadha, a physician of modern medicine, and the snake-bite healer, a representative of folk medicine. Premchand's depiction of Dr Chadha resonates with M.K. Gandhi's critical view on doctors and the modern system of medicine. Portrayed as a medical antihero, the depiction is different from the usual heroic representations of medical professionals in literature. 'The Surgeon' by Sheeba E.K. delicately captures the inevitability of change and the dynamics of a father-son relationship, and vividly paints, albeit with a tinge of irony, the shifts that have come into modern lifestyle and outlook with the advent of globalization. The story is set in North Kerala and alludes to the caste and class dynamics associated with the medical field and profession. The title of the story is symbolic as it is contrasted with *vaidhyan*, a healer, a practitioner of indigenous medicine, a minor surgeon of yore who also worked miracles. Ultimately, beyond the personal and the professional narratives the story focuses on a painful universal truth: humaneness being surgically removed at the hands of the larger narratives of profit and materialistic comforts. The surgeon, as portrayed in the story, is akin to the idea of a 'villain-surgeon' (Duffy 23). Through her story, the author not only depicts the problems of corruption and medical paternalism but also delineates the adversarial relationship between a doctor and a patient. Bibhutibhushan Bandyopadhyay's 'Doctor Moni' (1937), features a village quack who, despite his passion and dedication, fails to set up a respectable practice and make ends meet. His days pass in starvation in a quaint village separated by miles from his wife for whom he cannot provide. In this short story, the doctor becomes the patient. Diagnosed with loneliness, poverty, and desperation, Moni searches for a cure in nature, in the momentary company of affectionate friends. He meets and befriends Promo, a woman much younger than him, who contracts typhoid and dies in spite of Moni's best efforts to save her. The story ends with Moni sitting alone in the dark at the onset of the monsoon, ruminating about life, fate, tragedy, and deprivation.

'The Gift of Vision' (translated from Bengali) by Rabindranath Tagore narrates in first person the trajectory of Kumu, an unfortunate girl, who loses her eyesight due to the callousness of her soon-to-be-a-doctor husband. Despite that, Kumu chooses to stay with him in utmost devotion. Her husband, to make up for his negligence, vows to remain committed to her rather than wed again. The story reaches its climax at a moment when her husband seems to be less than steadfast to his promise. In a twist and turn of events, Kumu's faith in the sanctity of their marriage remains as her husband refrains from sinning. Through Kumu's predicament, Tagore throws light on the sorry state of the institution of wedlock in colonial India. The correlations between science and religion, between oppression and justice, and between faith and deprivation are carefully illuminated by the metaphors of blindness and sight. 'The Stranger' (translated from Punjabi) by Ashok Vasishth, focuses on a lady doctor who lives her life with conviction and performs her duty with utmost sincerity. The story is a beautiful psychological rendition of the interplay between the past and the present. It focuses on the personal world of a doctor. Amar's English story 'The Final Test' is set in a medical college, and reflects upon the lives of medical students and medical education in mid-twentieth century India.

The anthology includes four fascinating stories dealing with disease, suffering, and female bodies: Rashid Jahan's 'Asif Jahan's Daughter-in-Law' (translated from Urdu), Jeelani Bano's 'A Day in Labour Room' (translated from Urdu), Kartar Singh Duggal's 'The Longing' (translated from Punjabi), and Shirin Shashikant Valavade's 'Narova Kunjarova' (translated from Marathi). In her story, Jahan portrays the unhygienic condition of childbirth in lower-class Indian homes in the early twentieth century. In the story, Kubra, the daughter-in-law of Asif Jahan, is undergoing labour pain and to ward off evil spirits, the women burn incense over her body with dirty clothes. The author, Rashid Jahan, after obtaining M.B.B.S with a specialization in gynaecology and obstetrics from Lady Hardinge Medical College, Delhi in 1929, joined the Provincial Medical Service of United Provinces. In 1931, she was posted to Lady Dufferin Hospital, Lucknow. The Dufferin Fund was founded in 1885 under the patronage of Queen Victoria to focus on the health of Indian women. An integral part of the Dufferin scheme was to train educated Indian women. While the advocates of zenana medical care under Dufferin Fund were content to work within the parameters of purdah, Rashid Jahan's fictional work sought to unveil the mystique that shrouds the female body. The experience of medical practice is central to her work as a writer. Rashid Jahan's specialization in gynaecology made her aware of the complex issues related to pregnancy, childbirth, and their effects on women's health. 'Parde Ke Peeche' (Behind the Veil), Rashid Jahan's contribution to *Angaarey* (1932), dealt with the fragile health of a wife oppressed by domesticity and conjugality. The story 'Asif Jahan Ki Bahu' (Asif Jahan's Daughter-in-Law) adopts the mode of naturalist writing to provide gory details of childbirth and the perils inherent in the traditional practices adopted by midwives. In the story, the dialogue between tradition and modernity emerges from the confined space of women's quarters. The setting of the story in a *zenana* throw light on the doubts and suspicions associated with a lady doctor, especially, because of her association with the colonial institution of hospitals.

In Duggal's 'The Longing,' the conversation between the lady doctor and Rajni, the setting of the operation theatre, the medical procedures surrounding abortion, and the reflection around the moral nature of her action form the essence of the story. For a long time after her operation, Rajni fails to work through the trauma of her abortion. The story underlines how PTSD (Post Traumatic Stress disorder) affects women's physical and mental health. The poignance of the whole situation gets sharpened by the fact that Rajni is unable to conceive after her abortion. Drawing its title from a phrase from *Mahabharata*, Valavade's 'Narova Kunjarova' is a medico-legal story dealing with the dilemma of a doctor. Surekha, an unmarried woman, is accused of the murder of her illegitimate child. In her effort to save Surekha, the doctor elaborates upon the effect of pregnancy on women before the judges. With several references to medical terminologies related to functioning of the female body such as water retention, ovarian tumour, endocrine disturbance, and fibroid tumour, the author conveys the horror of abortion that also doubles up as a remarkable description of the human reproductive system. 'A Day in the Labour Room' (translated from Urdu) by Jeelani Bano is set in a hospital and deals with various medical issues on women's bodies and mental health. The narrator of the story is a lady doctor who contemplates women's health as she attends women patients at a hospital. It also draws attention to questions pertaining to the rights of women over their bodies. These stories outline the complex issue of the depiction of the female body in literature.

The anthology does not claim to cover the entire gamut of short fiction written about diseases and cures in India. Stories from several other languages could not be included because of logistical challenges. The book aims to explore the themes of disease, health, and cure through the genre of short stories and to garner new insights and understanding of literature and medicine in India.

Haris Qadeer

'Illness is the night side of life, a more onerous citizenship. Everyone who is born holds dual citizenship, in the kingdom of the well and in the kingdom of the sick. Although we all prefer to use the good passport, sooner or later each of us is obliged, at least for a spell, to identify ourselves as citizens of that other place.'

Susan Sontag

Illness as Metaphor

Quarantine

Rajinder Singh Bedi

Plague and Quarantine!

Like a fog, the plague descended on the northern plains that lay along the foot of the Himalayas, covering everything in a blanket of gloom and dread. Every child in the city trembled on hearing its very name.

While the plague was terrible enough, the quarantine was more dreadful still. People feared it more than the disease itself, prompting the Department of Health to put out tall posters across doors, streets, and highways that instructed people on ways to keep out the rats. Over time, the original caption 'No Rat, No Plague!,' which appeared on these posters was expanded to include 'No Rat, No Plague, No Quarantine!.'

The people's fear of the quarantine was not without reason. As a doctor, I can say it with some authority that the quarantine claimed more lives in the city than the plague, although the former isn't a disease per se, but rather the name given to an area where those suffering from this infectious pandemic are lawfully isolated from healthy people to prevent further spread of infections. While doctors and nurses were quite well-prepared to handle the quarantine, they could not give individual care to the patients. Separated from their kin and well-wishers, I personally saw many patients lose hope. Many died prematurely just from seeing the unceasing cycle of death around them. It also happened a few times that a person with a minor illness died after getting infected in the germ-filled environs of the quarantine. Due to the excessive number of deaths, the dead were disposed of in a peculiar manner. They were thrown into a heap like corpses of dogs, doused with petrol, and set on fire without following any rites or customs. In the evening, when the flames of the corpses mingled with the fiery rays of the setting sun, the dreadful sight appeared to the patients as if the whole world was on fire.

Also, the quarantine caused many indirect deaths, as people who showed symptoms of the disease were often hidden by family members to prevent them from being forcibly quarantined. As doctors were ordered to inform immediately upon receiving news of an infected patient, people would also hesitate from going to them for treatment. Hence, others would only find out about a house's status as infected on hearing heart-rending cries and wails of its family members, followed by a dead body being brought out.

Those days, I was working in the quarantine as a doctor. The plague's dread had also occupied my mind and soul. After coming home every evening, I would wash my hands profusely with carbolic soap, gargle with a disinfecting mouthwash and drink some nasty stomach-searing coffee or brandy. However, the latter also led to insomnia and made my eyes hypersensitive to light. On many occasions, I had to ingest vomit-inducing medicines just to rid myself of the fear of the plague. At times, when the coffee or the brandy would cause an upset stomach or hot flashes, my mind would senselessly descend into anxious foreboding. A slight itch in the throat and I would jump to the conclusion that these are symptoms of the plague, and I would think, alas, I too will be a victim of this fatal plague! And then…the quarantine.

It was in those days that a neo-convert to Christianity, William Bhago Khakrob, who worked as a sweeper in my street, came up to me and said 'Sir…the unthinkable has happened!...Today, the *ambuasi* picked up a one and twenty patients very close to the locality.'

'Twenty-one people? All in a single ambulance?' I feigned astonishment.

'Yes indeed, a one and twenty…they were taken to the *quentin*…Alas, those poor souls will never come back.'

On further inquiry, I discovered that Bhago would wake up at three in the morning and down a peg or two of the local moonshine, and then as instructed, sprinkle lime powder all over the street in order to prevent the spread of germs. He He also told me that he cleared dead bodies off the streets and ran errands for the dread-stricken people of the area. The plague did not deter Bhago one bit. He firmly believed that death would come to him when it is destined, no matter how much he tries to escape.

In those days, when people were wary of being in the presence of one another, Bhago would tie a turban around his head and face, attentively serving humanity. While his knowledge was limited, he would rely on his experience to advise people on ways to prevent the disease. He would recommend general hygiene, the use of lime powder, and staying within the house. One day, I saw him recommending a liberal dose of alcohol to people. When he came to meet me that day, I asked him 'Bhago, aren't you afraid of the plague?'

'Not at all, Sir…Till death comes, nothing will happen to me. You are a doctor who has healed thousands, but when death comes to me, your medicines and cures will be useless. I hope you don't mind my frankness.' Then, changing the topic, he said, 'so tell me something about the *quentin*.'

I replied, 'Thousands of patients have arrived in the quarantine, and we try our utmost to treat them. But, to what extent, I don't know. Those who work with me are themselves afraid of being too close to the patients. The fear makes their throats and lips go dry. After all, no one goes and talks face to face with the patients, like you do. Neither does anyone work as hard as you do. May God bless you for your services to humankind, Bhago.'

With his head tilted down in embarrassment, Bhago removed the folds of the turban, exposing his face, which was ruddy under the influence of alcohol. 'I am a nobody, Sir. I will be lucky if my useless self is of some use to anyone. Sir, the head padre Laabe (Reverend Mont. L. Abe), who often comes to preach in my street says that Lord Jesus teaches us to sacrifice our lives in the service of others…I think that…'

I wanted to praise Bhago's bravery but was so overwhelmed with my own emotions that I couldn't articulate my thoughts. His confidence and deeds made me envious. Hence, I resolved to give it my all in the quarantine and try and save the lives of as many patients as I could, to try and comfort them, even if that meant sacrificing my own life. There is however a long chasm between words and deeds. My very being quivered when I saw the dreadful state of the patients and the stink from their mouths reached my nose. I couldn't summon the courage to follow in Bhago's footsteps.

However, I made good use of Bhago that day in the quarantine. I tasked him to perform chores that involved getting close to the patients, which he did unhesitatingly. On the other hand, the fear of death, and more so the quarantine, kept me away from the patients.

Looking at Bhago, I thought to myself, had he transcended both the quarantine and death itself?

That day, about 400 patients were admitted to the quarantine, and approximately 250 left for their afterlife.

It was a testament to Bhago's courage that I was able to save many patients. In the graph hanging on the wall in the Chief Medical Officer's room, the survival rate of patients under my supervision was the highest. Every day, I would make an excuse to go to the room and excitedly see the curve steadily approaching the 100 per cent mark.

One day, I had a little too much of brandy. My heart began to palpitate, and my pulse was racing. I began to pace up and down like a madman. I suspected that at last, the plague had got me, and soon buboes would appear on my neck and groin. I became increasingly disturbed and wanted to run away from the quarantine. I quivered with fear. I only saw Bhago twice that day.

Close to the afternoon, I saw him embracing a patient. He was gently caressing his hands. Harnessing all his energy, the patient spoke to him 'Only God knows. I don't wish this plague even upon my enemies. I have two daughters...'

Interjecting, Bhago said, 'Thank Lord Jesus brother, you look well.'

'Yes, thank God, I am better than before. If I am able to leave the quaran...'

He was in the middle of his sentence when his veins tightened, and his mouth started frothing. His eyes turned grey and with a violent jerk, the patient, who appeared healthy to others and especially himself, slipped into eternal silence. Except for Bhago, who was crying silently, there was no one to mourn his death. Had anyone known to him had been there, Bhago would have torn the earth and sky with his lamentations. After all, Bhago was the only 'loved one' of the patients who was present there. He harboured compassion and empathy for every patient. It was he who shed tears for everyone. One day, when he was offering praying to Jesus, he humbly offered his own life for the sins of mankind.

I said to him, 'Yes, this place is worse than hell...I am myself thinking of ways to escape this hellhole...I don't feel good today.'

He replied, 'Sir, what could be more horrifying than what I witnessed today…A patient who fainted under the spell of the disease was presumed to be dead, his body was thrown into the pile of corpses and set on fire. When the petrol was doused and the heap was set on fire, I saw him flailing his arms and legs in the flames. So, I leapt into the fire. Sir!, he was badly burnt, and while saving him, my right arm was completely scorched.'

I looked at his arm and could see the yellowish fat under oozing out. The sight was revolting. I asked him, 'But were you ablc to save the man?'

'Sir, he seemed like a very nice man. However, the world was not able to gain much from his niceness, he was full of pain when he turned his scorched face towards me to say thanks.'

'And Sir …,' he continued, 'after a while, he was in such agony, that never have I seen a patient give up his life in such a horrifying way. It would have been better had I allowed him to burn away. I put him under more agony by saving him. Just now, I lifted his body with my burnt arm and threw him into the same heap.'

Bhago did not say much after that. In between his painful cries, he stuttered 'Do you know what killed him? Not the plague, it was the *quentin*…the damn *quentin*!'

Although the thought of being in this hell together with my friends did bring some relief to the unceasing calamitous atmosphere of the quarantine, the heart-rending cries of man's suffering would tear into the silence of the night. The laments of mothers and wives and the screams of children, which would continue past that hour of the night when even the owl would go silent, created a mournful and depressing atmosphere. I wondered if those who were healthy were so heavy of heart, what would be the condition of those lying sick in their houses, the morose yellowness of the walls seeping into them as if they were stricken with jaundice. On the other hand, there were the patients of the quarantine, who could see the Angel of Death manifest in front of them, and yet clung to their lives the way someone clings to the top of a tree in a flood, watching the fierce waves buffet against his refuge, as if they were trying to slowly submerge him along with the tree.

It was a sense of foreboding that kept me away from the quarantine that day. I feigned an excuse, although it caused me deep anguish and guilt. It was possible that some patients would have benefitted from my presence. However, a feeling of dread had immobilized my soul. Later in the night, I was informed that around 500 patients had been admitted to the quarantine.

I had just finished that god-awful liver-scorching coffee and was about to go to bed when I heard a knock on the door. The servant opened the door, and Bhago came in panting, exclaiming: 'My wife has fallen sick…swellings have appeared on her neck...for god's sake, save her...my breastfed child, just a year and a half old, will also die along with her!'

Instead of showing empathy, I tersely replied: 'Why couldn't you come before? Did the illness start just now?'

'There was only a slight fever in the morning.'

'So, she was sick at home, and you still went to the quarantine?'

'Yes Sir,' Bhago quivered, 'she was only suffering from a slight discomfort, and I thought it was because she hadn't breastfed in a while... besides that, there was no other symptom, and after all, both my brothers were at home to take care of her, and there were so many patients alone in the *quentin*.'

'And you went overboard with your services and kindness and brought the germs home. Didn't I tell you not to go so close to the patients? This is why I didn't go there today. You are responsible for this, what can I do now? You wanted to be a hero, now pay for your heroism...where there are hundreds of patients in the city, there shall be one more... .'

Bhago pleaded 'But Lord Jesus...'

'Off you go Mr Hero...You deliberately jumped into the fire, and now should I the suffer consequences? This is not how sacrifices are made...I cannot help you at this time of the night.'

'But padre Laabe...'

'Get away from here, are you a bloody son of padre Laabe?'

Bhago walked away disappointedly. When I cooled down after half an hour, I felt ashamed. But what was the sense in feeling regret later? My penance lay in humbly apologizing to Bhago for my rudeness and putting all efforts into treating his wife. I changed my clothes and rushed to his house. When I reached the house, I saw Bhago's brothers bringing out their sister-in-law on a cot.

I turned to Bhago and asked, 'Where are you taking her?'

He muttered, 'To the *quentin.*'

'So now the quarantine is no longer a living hell according to you?'

'You refused to come Sir, what option did I have? I thought that at least the doctors will be there to help, and I can take care of her along with the other patients.'

'Put the cot down…The thought of other patients has still not left you…idiot.'

The cot was taken inside the room, and I administered medicine to Bhago's wife to fight the invisible enemy. Eventually, she opened her eyes.

In a tearful voice, Bhago said, 'I will never forget your kindness.'

I replied, 'I am sorry for my behaviour earlier tonight, Bhago. May God reward you for your kindness by curing your wife.'

It was at that very moment that I saw my invisible enemy employ its final tactic. His wife's lips began to flutter. I felt her pulse slipping away. The invisible enemy, so used to winning, once again left me utterly defeated. Feeling sorry for him, I lowered my eyes, turned to Bhago, and said, 'Poor Bhago! You have received a strange reward for your sacrifice.'

He burst into tears.

It was a heart-wrenching scene when Bhaago separated his wailing child from his mother forever. With utter gracefulness, he sent me back home soon afterward.

I thought that Bhago would now retreat into his darkness, unconcerned with anyone else. However, the very next day, I saw him taking care of the patients, saving scores of homes from the darkness that was inflicted upon him…He thought nothing of his own life. I also took inspiration from Bhago and worked with greater resolve. I would visit the homes of the city's poor in my spare time, which had become cesspools of disease owing to their proximity to sewage and filth.

However, eventually, the city's environs became completely free of the disease and its germs. The city was entirely sanitized, and mice were nowhere to be seen. At most, a case or two would be reported, which would be quickly treated, not leaving any scope for further spread.

Slowly, businesses returned to normal. Schools, colleges and offices opened once again.

However, one thing that became prominently noticeable was the attention I received when passing through a bazaar. People were full of gratitude towards me, leading to effusive articles and my photographs being published in newspapers. This praise soon got to my head, manifesting into arrogance.

A grand reception was organised, where prominent people and doctors of the city were invited. The Minister of Municipalities presided over the ceremony, and I was made to sit next to him. After all, the reception was organised to honour me. I was soon swamped under scores of garlands, and as my neck strained under the weight, my character became more apparent. Beaming with haughtiness, I would look across the venue. 'For my great service to humankind, the committee extended its gratitude by presenting me with a modest sum of one thousand rupees.'

Everybody praised my colleagues, but mostly me, and said that countless lives had been saved during the epidemic owing to my efforts. They said that I didn't care whether it was night or day, and dedicated my life to the cause of the nation and its people…that I reached the abodes of the disease and healed those who were on the brink of dying.

The minister lifted a thin stick that was resting on the table's left side and pointed the audience towards the black line on the same graph that was earlier hung on the wall of the chief medical officer, which indicated the wavy curve of patient survival rate. The line showed an overall increase despite periodic ups and downs. Finally, he pointed towards the part of the graph coinciding with the day when all 54 patients under my care were restored to full health. In other words, my success rate was a 100 per cent, as symbolised by the peak of the black curve.

After this, the minister informed the people that in gratitude of his services, Dr Bakhshi (me), shall be awarded the honorary post of Lt Colonel.

The whole hall resounded with applause and praise.

I held my head high and thanked the minister and the audience. In my lengthy speech, I emphasized that not only were hospitals and quarantine zones the nerve-centre of doctors' efforts, but also the homes of the poor. These were the people who were entirely incapable of helping themselves and they were the ones who bore the maximum brunt of this fatal disease. My colleagues and I thus identified this source and wasted no effort in uprooting the disease from its roots. I explained how, after finishing our daily shifts at the quarantine and hospital, we spent our nights at the dreadful homes of the city's poor.

That day, when I, the proud Lt Colonel, returned to my house with my neck squeezed under the weight of all those garlands, and with my hand inside the pocket holding the 100 rupees reward, I heard a voice softly calling out to me.

'Sir, many congratulations!'

As he congratulated me, Bhago kept his broom on the cover of a dirty water tank and untied his turban with both hands. I stood there startled.

'Is it you brother Bhago?' I asked with some difficulty.

'Even if the world doesn't know you, I do, your Jesus does… you are an exceptional student of your padre Laabe, may God bless you.'

There was a lump in my throat when I said that. The haunting image of his wife and child appeared before my eyes. I felt the oppressive weight of the garlands on my neck and that of my stuffed wallet in my pocket. Despite all those honors bestowed upon me, I found myself utterly disgraced and cursed the world for so clearly identifying virtue where it exists.

Translated from Urdu by Amit Julka

A Major Operation

Basant Kumar Satpathy

'Let me tell you this, Bapa! One should never undergo major surgery when one is past 60 years of age. Even if you all have decided to go ahead with the operation and even if a famous surgeon in a modern hospital has agreed to perform the surgery, I do not approve of your decision. I also do not like the condition of this nursing home and the cabin in which you have been put up,' my son, who is a doctor, argued as soon as he arrived.

The operation was to take place at 8 am. the following day. The room adjacent to my cabin had been converted into an operation theatre. The sound of the room being cleaned came through the door. The medicines which had to be taken 24 hours before the operation had been administered to me. I was beginning to feel nervous. 'Everything will be fine. Do not worry.' These encouraging words uttered by my children and grandchildren, and my relatives comforted me.

However, I knew we had not chosen a good private nursing home. But what else could have been done under the circumstances? No beds were available at the government hospital where even emergency patients lay on the floor covered with filth. I was taken to a compromise for a nursing home! It overlooked a stinking pond full of rotting weeds and the area surrounding it was overgrown with grass and littered with garbage. Only a dead man can sleep in peace here among packs of howling dogs and swarms of fleas and mosquitoes constantly bothering one. It seemed as if the suffering they inflicted on my younger son, who stayed by my side, exceeded that of mine. On this bed in the cabin, where I now lay, a nine-year-old girl died of tetanus just three days ago. And, to make matters worse, a boil on my back had not healed completely and it still festered a little. There was a danger of it becoming septic if the surgery was not performed.

I was told that the house, where the nursing home functioned was some doctor's ancestral property. He had gone to England having rented it out to another doctor for a couple of years. For some reason, the famous doctor, who was to conduct the surgery did not seem much interested in the fees he was to receive from me. But, the hands of his diminutive assistant appeared to itch, not to cut me up but to pocket the fees. It seemed as if he would chop me up with an axe at the slightest of nods from his boss. Essentially a nervous person, my thoughts moved in a different direction the moment I heard my son express his reservations about the nursing home. He might be an inexperienced young doctor, but his concern about his father's life would be undoubtedly deeper and more sincere than anyone else's. And, in any case, I had sent a telegram asking him to come and give me his advice. After he arrived, he tried to convince everyone that we were going to do something that would be a grave mistake. As the immediate crisis was over, he suggested that I go with him and receive treatment at the hospital where he worked. All through the afternoon, they held a discussion on the matter. To test my willingness to undergo the operation at this nursing home, my eldest son told me, 'We all have decided that you will undergo the operation here.' My doctor son stood among them, his face wearing a solemn expression.

I lost my temper and said, 'I will not do as you say. I will not undergo the operation here. Will you carry me by force and lay me out on the operation table?' My doctor son said chuckling, 'Father! I have taken leave for only two days. My presence here will not make any difference, because the doctors who will carry out the operation are like my teachers. So, I will not be able to give them any advice. Your eyes would be closed and your pulse would be low. I would be looking at you but you would be unable to utter a word to me. One more thing needs to be thought about. Let us suppose, a world-famous surgeon cuts you open and removes the gallbladder! But what matters more is the post-operative care you receive. But here you will not receive that. Speedy recovery depends on the state of one's mind. If you come with me, everyone will stop worrying about you. You will receive proper care and attention in the hospital where I work, at a very nominal cost.'

No one could muster the courage to communicate our decision to the famous surgeon. In the end, I volunteered to do the job. I said to the doctor, 'Sir, I do not have the good fortune of being operated upon by a surgeon of your stature. I am backing out because I feel terribly nervous. I have decided not to undergo the operation tomorrow. I will go home and return after I feel more confident.' The surgeon, a man of great generosity, told me, 'I will not mind if you decide not to undergo surgery in this nursing home. Out of a 100 patients, two run away from our operation theatre out of fear and nervousness. You are one of those two.'

We left the nursing home immediately. We had to pay 108 rupees for having spent 33 hours there. For each injection the nurse administered to me I was charged five rupees. I had to pay extra money for getting the boil washed with warm water and bandaged and for using the toilet. Some people mildly ridiculed me for leaving the nursing home without undergoing the operation. But I, for my part, congratulated myself for having escaped it with my life. I headed for my son's house at night. On the way, while crossing the station near my house, I felt a keen desire to see my pet dog. But who would fulfill this desire at half past two at night? The relief I was experiencing resembled someone who is to be hanged in the morning, but is informed the evening before that he has been granted indefinite reprieve. There was now no danger of being led to the operation table without undergoing proper tests. My stay at my doctor son's house was a pleasant one. If the need arose, I would go to the hospital; for the time being, I waited for the festering boil to heal.

I was a patient, not a doctor. As the saying goes, 'Today's patient is tomorrow's physician.' Let me first talk about the disease that I suffered from. It took long to get it diagnosed. I was ill with jaundice twice in the space of four years and underwent medical treatment. On both occasions, I recovered but was not completely cured of the ailment. The renowned surgeon, who was to operate on me, had advised my son to get my bowels X-rayed. After two X-rays, the following report came: 'Innumerable tiny translucent objects were detected in the gallbladder.' An enzyme secreted by the gallbladder helps in the digestion of food. This bladder, lying close to the liver, is filled with some sort of greenish fluid called bile. When this bladder bursts inside a rohu fish, this fluid makes its flesh taste bitter. *Kabiraj*s prepare medicines out of this fluid. The gallbladder supplies bile to the liver through a duct. When stones block this duct, bile spreads through the body and one could suffer from jaundice. One might suppose that the gallbladder will have stones if grit finds its way to one's stomach through food. But, in reality, the so-called stones are formed by the body itself.

One can give this ailment a poetic name like, 'Land of the midnight pain,' which echoes 'Land of the midnight sun.' All-day long, one would feel perfectly fine, but when evening falls, one would suddenly experience a burning sensation in one's upper abdomen as if one had a gastric attack. Then the pain begins like a storm raging after a lull and grows steadily and becomes unbearable after a while. At midnight, as the whole world would be in deep slumber, the pain would make me scream, my pet dog would jump up and down the bed feeling utterly helpless. I would open the door, hop on my bicycle and ride along the deserted lanes to the chamber of a retired civil surgeon. Like some patients, some doctors too stay awake at night. He would give me a couple of Gelusil or Diovol or Digene tablets. Returning home I would gult these down with a glass of water and try to get some sleep. Sleep would engulf me around dawn and when I woke up I would feel completely worn-out and drained. I would try to push the excruciating pain that I endured at night, out of my mind.

I did not suffer in this way every day; the pain tormented me once in a while. I had to be very careful about my diet and survived on boiled vegetables, food cooked without spices, buttermilk, skimmed milk, and papaya cooked in turmeric water. I took medicines and supplements such as Liv-52, Isabgol, and tonic carrying pepsin, Horlicks, and Viva. But, as has been said, death will come when it has to come. Sometimes, no medicine will help one get cured of a disease but sometimes even a glass of water will help one to miraculously survive. I was also afflicted with another illness, which doctors called positional vertigo. If I turned on my side and move my head, I would get a terrible sensation. Anything beneath my feet and above my head, would appear to whirl and it would seem as if my bed has sunk into the earth. How would one bring oneself to cope with this? I had to get on somehow by talking to my friends and children, lecturing students in the classroom, and above all keeping my sense of humour alive. Otherwise, life would have appeared unbearably painful. I didn't find a single person who had undergone a similar experience and could share my pain and feelings.

Whenever I fell ill with jaundice, I resorted to taking herbal medicines prescribed by Lakshman Mishra; or else I would take medicines meant for curing indigestion and dysentery. When the X-ray images revealed innumerable tiny translucent objects in the gallbladder, it was clear that the only way out of my problem was an operation. But how could one risk a surgery at 65! Again, how dare one gets operated upon in our hospitals and nursing homes, where people die during simple operations involving vasectomy or hydrocele? Still, undeterred by these risks, people brave operations. They think dying would be better than enduring the agonized throes of death. It would be better to leave the world quietly rather than put so many people to inconvenience at an unearthly hour.

However, surgery was ruled out as it was feared that the aging body would not be able to take the strain. I, therefore, thought I should try ayurvedic cure and met a *kabiraj*, an ayurvedic physician who had received the President's award. Banging the table, he boasted that he would give such medicines that the stones would come out with urine within 21 days. He asked me to take some black tablets with water in which horse gram was boiled. He told me that if I put two drops of this water on the slab of laterite for 21 days, the slab would crack and melt. When the pain subsided completely during the next 21 days, I went to thank and reward the *kabiraj*. He assured me that the stones had gone completely out of my system.

But the very next day, the symptoms of the illness reappeared with a vengeance. Now, I desperately turned to homeopathy. Fortunately for me, a renowned homeopath from Kolkata had set up practice in the town. I was told that he flew to Delhi to treat patients. He was endowed with qualities one associated with powerful deities. If someone came to him with a broken leg, his medicines enabled the patient to walk effortlessly in only three months' time. Someone born blind regained his sight after the homeopath administered to him only half a tablet. Another man, who had a swollen knee, took his medicine, and suddenly the swelling burst noisily, the fluid oozed out and he got completely cured. Such legends were spread about Hahnemann, the founder of the system of homeopathy. When I met this famous homeopath he said, 'I am interested only in the symptoms. It matters little to me whether your stomach is full of stones or splintered glass.' I described the symptoms of my ailment and he informed me that he would cure me of it if I pay him 6000 rupees. 600 rupees would enable my sons to hold my funeral feast with great pomp and ceremony. My death would provide them with an occasion to hold a wonderful feast. Later, I learned that this doctor visited our town only to collect fish, rice of fine quality, and delicious curd and sweets.

The homeopathic globules resembling ant's eggs rarely inspired confidence in me. Nevertheless, carried away by stories of miracles performed by this doctor, one day I went to consult him. After discussing my symptoms and examining me for five long hours, he charged a fee of 500 rupees and took me under his wings. I took the first dose of the medicine and after that my screams brought the house down. When I informed the doctor of this, he told me, 'The medicine at first aggravates the symptoms of the illness and then cures it.' That very night, I decided not to have anything to do with him anymore. A few days ago, I chanced upon him and told him about the surgery I had undergone. He showed a keen interest to have a look at those translucent objects now stored in a glass container.

There was absolutely no improvement in my condition. One day at five in the evening I suddenly experienced an acute pain in my abdomen. Luckily for me, my third son (May he live long!) had come to visit me on that day. He was averse to attending to patients. I do not know what passed through his mind, rather than taking me to a hospital, he went to a telephone booth, called up someone, and brought me to a nursing home by an express train. The doctor said, 'The liver is developing sepsis or will soon do so. So, we must carry out the operation.' The decision was therefore taken to get the surgery done without delay. I was assured that even 80 year-olds, not to speak of those who are only 65, had undergone surgery. Telegrams were sent to everyone in the family and they arrived within 24 hours. However, as I mentioned earlier, I took another train and went to another private hospital. As I was the father of a doctor, I faced no difficulty in getting admitted to the hospital. But I stayed in my son's quarters and went to the hospital only for undergoing tests. Proper arrangements had been made by my son. And it was decided that the operation would be carried out after the sore on my back healed and the eosinophilia count dropped below 24 per cent. Doctor Das was to operate on me along with his assistant, Doctor Ray. I started looking upon them as my saviors. It was not that they were renowned surgeons; in fact, Doctor Das did not enjoy a good reputation as a surgeon. I learned that he borrowed books on gallbladder surgery and started reading them from the day he was asked to operate upon me. He treated me like a VIP patient and constantly tried to boost my morale.

My only experience of undergoing surgery had taken place about 40 years ago, before the invention of penicillin, when Dr Kashinath Mishra removed my hydrocele at Cuttack Medical School. However, the operation was not successful and I had to endure a lot of pain. While I was preparing myself mentally for the operation, the Durga Puja vacation had commenced. Dr Das, like all Bengalis, would never stay away from Bengal during the festive season. He left for Kolkata and the operation was postponed. I found an opportunity to go back home for a few days. I persuaded my son to let me go home on the pretext that I had to evaluate a lot of answer scripts sent to me by the university and he relented. Everyone else in the family told him that once I went back home, I would never return to undergo the operation for I had already run away from one nursing home. I gave him my word of honour and received his permission to go.

My dog was so excited to see me that he peed out of joy. At night it slept by my side, like my granddaughter. I had returned home promising that I would go back after three or four days. But 13 days passed and I was still here. However, I wanted to prove to my children, who had warned that I would never return to the hospital once I came home, wrong and thus bade farewell to my pet dog, my house, and the trees around it. Back at my son's quarters, I was happy to learn that Dr Das had extended his leave. In the meantime, the sore had healed completely, the eosinophilia had dropped to 9-10 per cent. The only issue now was the time my blood took to clot and even this problem was to be resolved soon.

The puja vacation came to an end but Dr Das had not returned. The delay of the operation seemed to give me a fresh lease of life; to my mind, the operation was no different from death. One night, I overheard a conversation between my son and my daughter-in-law, from which I got to know that Doctor Das had come back.

The next day, in the evening, I writhed in unbearable pain for about 15 minutes. My son returned from the hospital around 11 pm. When my daughter-in-law informed him that I was in pain, he said irritably, 'The groans of an old man detained me for an hour at the hospital. Back at home, too I find another old man letting out groans.' He gave me a Baralgan tablet. The pain instantly abated either as a result of the medicine administered or as a reaction to my son's exasperated expression. After dinner, he came to me and said, 'If Dr Das enquires, don't tell him that you experienced pain. Until Dr Das returns, you continue your treatment at home under my supervision.'

The following day, my daughter-in-law took me to the hospital in a rickshaw and put me up in cabin number five. In all likelihood, my son and my daughter-in-law had consulted the almanac and selected an auspicious time and date for the operation. An hour later, my son came and told me that the surgery would be performed on Friday, the day Jesus Christ was crucified! He had decided against bringing me to the hospital in his car because he thought it would be unpropitious if three persons went out together to perform an auspicious task. I was kept overnight under observation. I did not feel as if I was in a hospital. One nurse after another came from time to time to enquire about my wellbeing. The cabin allotted to me was an air-conditioned one.

Before I had set off for the hospital, I piteously asked my son, 'Are you sure your old father will survive this operation?' He assured me, saying, 'This is but a minor surgery. If a half-inch long incision is made on the abdomen, the gallbladder can be effortlessly removed.' My son knew well on what occasion a lie would be appropriate and effective. When Dr Das appeared, it seemed to me as if he was my saviour and had power over life and death. My son, my daughter-in-law, my grandchildren, who took turns to visit me, meant nothing to me at all; for me, Dr Das was incarnated Lord Narayan himself. After asking me the usual questions like, 'How are you doing? How do you feel?' He felt the right side of my chest and said, 'Wash this area between the chest and the navel with soap.' I asked him, 'Will I survive this operation, doctor?' He replied, 'Are you mad, or what? Nothing will happen to you.' I said, imploringly, 'Whatever happens, doctor, make sure I am not taken into the intensive care unit.' Through the glass partition, I could see the ICU and I was convinced that once you were taken there, you never came out alive. Only your dead body was handed over to your near and dear ones.

The countdown began. The surgery was to be conducted 36 hours later. It was 8 am. on Friday; my expedition to the other world would now begin. Jai Jagannath!

My own attitude to the impending surgery amused me a great deal. A man who, while going through unbearable pain pleaded with God to end his life, now desperately prayed to Him to save him from the clutches of death. How powerful is one's desire to live!

On the night of Wednesday, sleep eluded my eyes. For one thing, I was all alone and secondly, I lay in unfamiliar surroundings. My son had given me a book titled *Man-eaters of Tsavo* to read. *Man-eaters of Kumaon* recounted Corbett's experiences of hunting tigers. The former gave a hair-raising account of lion-hunting in Africa. But when the thought of the surgery that was to be carried out on Friday crossed my mind, I did not feel like reading the book. What is the point of gaining knowledge when one's life would be snuffed out only a few hours later!

On Thursday afternoon, herds of specialists descended on me and examined my eyes, nose, ear, tongue, teeth, heart, lungs, etc. They seemed no different from traders closely examining goats and bullocks in a village market before purchasing them. Even a specialist in leprosy came in and looked at my bent finger and pricked it with a pin. I was told that clearances had to be obtained from all the departments of the hospital before the surgery. In the end, came the anesthesiologist to render me unconscious. He patted me saying, 'You are absolutely alright.' Everybody gave the green signal for the operation. Finally, Dr Das and Dr Ray, who would decide whether I would live or die, appeared. It looked as though they were a little unhappy about having to bear the burden of operating upon the father of one of their colleagues. Dr Das again asked someone to wash a part of my body clean. Someone informed me that my son had signed the form in which was mentioned that no one would be held responsible if his father died during the operation. Dr Das, for his part, had stated that he was willing to perform the surgery.

Around 5 pm on Thursday, a barber came, addressed me as grandpa, cracked a few jokes, and removed body hair from the area around the part to be operated upon. I passed my hands over my chest and the abdomen and they felt smooth like a bird's feather.

As a prelude to the surgery, my sensitivity to Penicillin was tested and I was given vitamin-K injection and many more such steps were taken. But I did not let my nervousness overcome me this time. I had resolved not to run away from the operation like a coward. Evening fell. A few relatives who were present tried to divert my attention with jokes and pleasant conversation. *Man-eaters of Tsavo* ceased to interest me. I tried to get some sleep after taking a liquid diet. Everyone left and my cabin grew quiet. The woman who could have brought me solace at this moment in my life had departed from the world 18 years ago. Had she been alive, she would have sat by my side and would have lovingly told me, 'Do not be scared. Look at Lord Jagannath, He will look after you.' Her image seemed to flash before my eyes and then I turned and looked at the framed image of the trinity—*Jagannath*, *Balabhadra*, and *Subhadra*—placed in my cabin. A moment later, a nurse came in, gave me an injection, hung the mosquito net, and said, 'You finish your bath and get ready for the operation by 7 in the morning.' Half an hour before this my grandson had told me, 'Grandpa, your operation will be carried out at 8 am tomorrow. Your name appears on the top of the list of patients to undergo operation tomorrow. So, you have come first in the competition.' I felt restless all night and thought I should have taken a sleeping pill.

I woke up before 5 am in the morning. The Operation Theatre number one, where my surgery was to be carried out, lay on the second floor and it was lit up. Through the window by my bed, I could see a nurse moving about in the ICU. I brushed my teeth and had a shave. I felt amused for I had no job interview to face nor did I have to lecture students in a classroom. This is one of the days when I denied myself the pleasure of having a cup of tea after brushing my teeth. The sweeper came to help me empty my bowels completely. Although, I had not had a morsel of food in my stomach. I took a bath rubbing myself clean. It was a lovely autumn morning. The festival of Kali puja was to be held 10 days later. I combed my hair, wiped my face with a dry towel, and cleaned my earholes with a cotton bud. I wondered why I was grooming myself with such care!

The nurse arrived and asked me to get ready as soon as possible. I went to the framed photo of Lord Jagannath and his siblings and murmured, 'Jaga! I am going to the operation theatre. I am no ardent devotee of yours. After taking bath I fix my eyes on your face for about a minute. I put a flower at your feet if I find one, otherwise, I do not. I have never asked you for anything, not even a handful of sand of the famed Saradha Bali. My death would not make any difference to you at all. Every day, the smoke from millions of incense sticks rises towards you from the Earth. I feel bad about not being able to set my eyes on your face anymore. You might wonder what happened to that old man who used to gaze at your face for a few moments every day. Hail to Jaga!' I looked at my face in the mirror and said to myself, 'How fine does this old face look?' It was seven already and none of my relatives had turned up. It was good that they had not come yet for I should not enter the operation theatre with tears welling up in my eyes. I lay down on the bed, meekly following the nurse's instructions.

She gave me two injections. To me it seemed staying at a hospital meant receiving injections all the time. By the time you leave it, every part of your body would be pricked by needles.

A stretcher fitted with wheels was brought in which could be pulled in all directions. There stood before me four bearers who looked like the messengers of Yama, the God of Death.

'Let me give one more injection, this will be the last one,' assured the nurse. I did not lose my temper. And although she was not good-looking, I liked her because she spoke very sweetly to me and was extremely well-behaved. She treated me like her father. The effect of this injection was different from that of those given to me earlier.

The stretcher was brought up to the level of my bed by the bearers and the nurse asked me to get up. I tried to rise propping myself up with my elbows. I was shocked to find that all energy had drained away from arms. They laid me down on my back on the stretcher, which moved noisily like a bullock cart. I took a last look at the cover of *Man-eaters of Tsavo*, my comb, the mirror, my wristwatch, my pen, the two big eyes of Lord Jagannath, and I recalled the face of my deceased wife. It was as if I was being carried in a chariot. I decided to keep my eyes tightly shut. I thought I should see no evil, but I was aware that people stood on either side of the road, watching my chariot pass, and thought to themselves; this is the old man's last journey.

The lift took some time to reach the ground floor. When it did, they lifted me like servitors carrying the image of

Lord Jagannath and placed me on the floor of the lift. First, the door of the lift opened and I was taken into another room. Here I had to take off the clothes I was wearing and put on new ones. I was not feeling uncomfortable at all. In fact, I was feeling quite fresh and energetic. To me, it seemed as if I no longer had my hands and feet and other limbs. I was now shifted to yet another room, where my body was yielded by one group of people to another. Moments later, another door opened and I realized that, at last, I was in Operation Theatre 1.

Lying on the operation table, I looked up at the reflector of the light overhead, which was not on yet. Two or three nurses were quietly busy arranging instruments for the operation.

Why have not Dr Das and Dr Ray come yet? Let them get done with it quickly. I could think and I could feel and did not experience any physical pain. The light above my head now came on. My son, the doctor, had not come to see me yet. I could not decide what my last words to him would be. Should I tell him about my landed property, bank balance, fixed deposits, etc.?

My body slowly adjusted itself to the profound stillness and the deep silence of its surroundings. I was waiting for the zero hour. For a few moments, I dozed off. I saw a beautiful dream, which seemed real to me. This dream was interrupted when I heard someone calling me 'father.'

The sound of someone calling me 'father' inside the operation theatre was as unexpected as the sight of a pool of water in the middle of an arid desert. I now opened my eyes and looked in the direction from where the sound had come. I saw my son wearing an apron and a mask. He asked me, 'How are you feeling, father?' I replied, summoning the insouciance of an English lecturer, 'Fine, calm, quite composed.' He kept his eyes fixed on me like reminding me of Lord Narasimha waiting to eviscerate the demon Hiranyakashipu (or was he one of the lions in *Man-eaters of Tsavo?*) and Prahlad stood beside him with folded hands. I said, 'My son! I am asking this because I might forget this later. I thought someone came in and handed you a bouquet of roses.' My son must have thought to himself, looking at things from a rational point of view that his father was beginning to lose his consciousness and strange and incoherent thoughts were therefore crowding his mind. I was going to ask him if Dr Das had come. But I could not utter the words. Only a grunt issued from my throat.

It seemed as if time now came to a stop for me. I do not remember when I regained consciousness. Suspended between sleep and wakefulness, I repeated the question I had asked earlier, 'Has Dr Das come?' Flushed with elation, my eldest daughter replied, 'Yes! Yes!' A little while later I asked again, 'Is the operation over?' Someone said loudly, 'Yes, it is!' I inquired again, 'Was anything found?,' 'Yes! A lot of stones,' answered someone. I could not muster the courage to look at my abdomen. 'A very successful operation,' someone remarked. 'How many runs did Pakistan score in the match played in Lahore?' I wondered. Then I asked, 'What time is it?' The answer came, 'It is 2:30 pm.' I felt as if I had lain in deep slumber for a really long time. I experienced no pain. I was drifting in and out of wakefulness. I looked around and realized that I was in another room. A tube had been inserted into my nose and an oxygen cylinder was kept near me. A little blood left in a tube attached through a needle to a vein in my hand indicated that I had been given blood transfusion. Someone said that a Muslim had donated the blood. I thought his blood flowing through my veins will transform me into a tougher and a braver human being. A lot of people stood surrounding my bed and made me feel as if I was a VIP. Slowly, my earthward journey began. Stones extracted from my body numbered 407. Interestingly enough, the monthly pension I received also amounted to 407 rupees. So, it seemed as if for a teacher to qualify for his/her pension he has to accumulate one stone in his/her gallbladder to receive every rupee.

I was like a dry leaf about to drop off to the ground and was beginning to lose the will to live. Just then, it seemed as if a magician filled the stem of the withered leaf with the sap of new life and it now clung to the tree with redoubled vigour. I was told that I would be safe if 48 hours pass without any incident. I survived. Four days after the operation, I helped myself to four pieces of fried rohu fish and had a whole chicken stew for dinner. The stitches were taken out 11 days after the surgery and the person who removed them observed, 'A clean wound.' Only an eight-inch scar was visible. So, it was clear that my abdomen was cut open like a fish and my son had lied to me when he said that only a half-inch long incision would be made in my abdomen during the operation. This is how doctors lie to their patients.

Five days later, the father-in-law of one of my daughters dropped in to see me. He exclaimed from a distance, 'The operation has done you a lot of good, you are in the pink of health! This is for you.' He handed a bouquet of roses to me. This reminded me of the bouquet of flowers of many colours, which I thought an invisible hand gave to my son near the operation table. I was bewildered and wonder-struck.

It was the night of Diwali. Fire-crackers went off all around. I could see the lamps illuminating the terrace of the hospital. I had grown fond of my cabin and the nurses attending to me. Like Alexander the Great, I triumphantly returned home in my son's car after bursting a few crackers. After all, I had defeated death! I headed straight for the Jagannath temple in the outskirts of the town, where evening worship was in progress.

Translated from Odia by Aditya Nayak

A Day in the Labour Room

Jeelani Bano

'Next...'

'So, what's wrong with you?'

She looked at her husband and I realised the situation. She always authorises someone else to speak on her behalf.

All day I stand in the labour room, holding a knife, that cuts a woman's flesh, a pair of scissors, which tear her veins, and drugs which make her lose her consciousness. Dr Reddy is there to prepare the preliminary report of each patient but more often than not he is fed up of these weeping and whining women who come here. So that he chooses to stare at me instead. His eyes remind me of drones, hovering around, buzzing irritatingly. But I ignore them and turn to this patient again.

'Doctor, she is pregnant, four months' down, but she doesn't want the child,' says her male companion. She does not speak a word about what she wants herself.

'How long have you been married?' I ask her opening the register but again she looks at her companion, expecting him to answer for her. Realising the uneasiness that has descended upon both of them I close the register.

'It is too late so let it be.'

'Yes, that is right; let it be.' The woman speaks for the first time, looking happily at the man.

'No doctor no. She is very weak, so I want...,' he stammers, 'er...she wants that...,' he is visibly upset.

Yes, she is very weak. I give the woman another look.

Somehow I think of all those terms and conditions which are put down on a 'Nikah Nama' to be signed while purchasing land, car and women...for this much of dower, in the presence of so and so as witness I say 'Yes' without any compulsion or duress... .

And then comes a shower of blessings and advice. 'May you be blessed with wisdom to understand your duties, to be obedient to your husband...The decision of having or not having children (or their number) will entirely be that of your husband.'

'Sister, take her to the operation theatre, and you sign here, please.' Dr Reddy pushes a form towards the man. Dr Reddy himself is a man so he fully appreciates the agony that a man would be going through on such occasions.

When I entered the room, she was lying unconscious, in complete surrender, which is so typical of women. I see this face of women quite a few times within the span of a day—compulsions of foregoing the rights over her own body. People may play with it the way they want, trample upon it, cut it up into pieces, and throw it away.

After the operation she will come back to her senses but still look groggy. She will try to comprehend the world, which has always been beyond her comprehension, anew. She will feel a kind of dullness prevailing all around as if all the hues of her multicoloured dreams have been washed away by her tears. Now she will find everything empty—right from her womb to the never-ending skies. From now on she will die every minute. She will also go through the agony of dreaming of nurturing this unborn, incomplete child into an authoritative, commanding adult.

'The man who has come with her is not her husband.' The nurse commented.

Perhaps the woman could not explain to the nurse the relationship which existed between her and her companion, the relationship which made the woman offer her body as well as her soul to him and yet could not be given a name. In fact, now it became something to be ashamed of; something to be broken. And that is why the woman is lying on the operation table, unconscious.

I do not say anything in answer; just keep standing with a knife in my hand. Now I have to deactivate that in built scientific laboratory of her system, which moulds, develops and turns out a complete human being.

Once my guide in the dissection hall chided me as I ripped open all the layers of a female body and reached her brain. 'What will you do with her brain? There she does not have anything which she could call her own.' All my classmates had burst out laughing.

'Send it to the laboratory, it is an abnormal case.' I said and put the incomplete blood-soaked foetus in a tray. Dr Reddy came forward and took it in his custody. Now it will turn into a guinea pig, subject to a variety of experiments; people belonging to different branches of science will surround it… opening it up one side, joining it up on the other.

Destroy a man's reproductive powers. Look into a woman's womb first lest she give birth to a woman like herself.

I wash my hands, which are stained with blood and ask the routine question: Who is next?

A woman comes in. A lack-lustre face, a rundown body, and bulging belly. Seeing the agony on her face it is not difficult for me to discern that she is going to deliver her seventh or eighth baby in a short while.

'Write your name here.' Dr Reddy shows the register to her husband who is a healthy, tall, well-built man. Dressed in a fine well-cut safari he seems to be holding some high office. There is another woman who has come with the couple; middle aged, sharp and smart, talking incessantly.

In all probability she is the man's sister. '*Bhabhi*,' she addresses her sister-in-law. 'Chanting the name of Almighty God, go in. This time He will surely grant you a son. Your house will be filled with sunshine.' Then she turns to me and says sorrowfully, 'By God's grace we have everything except a son. My brother is really unlucky in this respect. Doctor, we have come to you with great hopes.' Hearing her babble the patient feels dizzy and slumps to the ground.

'Come on, quick, get a stretcher fast.' Bending over the woman I examine the heartbeats of both the mother and child. I realise she is not in good shape and feel worried about her.

'Oh no doctor, please save my child.' The man too is looking upset.

The child is almost dead. Its waning heartbeats are an indication that it prefers not to be born, than be and face the wrath in its father's eyes.

The overpowering desire of delivering a male child before she breathes her last has made the woman highly agitated. She is trying to say something. There are lots of women whose lips move but voice is not their own.

'Next,' I call out warding off the buzzing droves of Reddy's eyes with both hands.

Three girls enter together. They are young teenagers hardly thirteen or fourteen years of age. They are coming straight from school, wearing same uniform, nervousness… writ large on their face, trying to huddle behind each other. Seeing them Reddy's eyes find a new target.

'Dr Reddy, will you go out of this room for a while?'

Girls of this age usually come with complaints of backache. Unfamiliar faces frighten them and make them feel ill at ease. These girls too were nudging each other instead of coming forward. Then the youngest and rather good looking one of them turned her face towards the wall and started crying.

'Listen girls, you are wasting our time. Come to the point, quick.' The nurse started getting inpatient with her.

Sensing their discomfort, I went up to the girl who was crying.

'Is something wrong? How much time are you overdue?'

She gave me a nervous look, covered her face with both hands and continued crying. Her friends came to her rescue.

'Doctor, Honey did not do anything. The teacher who takes special classes in the evening…he…he…'

'Didn't you confide in your mother or complain to your father?'

With lowered head, Honey kept standing, quiet.

'The teacher says you will get a bad name if you will tell anybody about it. You will also lose the chances of getting married.'

'We have come here without telling anyone.'

'We don't have any money either, doctor.'

'Come to me…,' I beckoned the girl.

She did not move forward but her friend spoke.

'Honey says that she will now die.'

I looked at Honey intently. A young teenager, barely 12 years old, who knows neither a man's love nor the joys of motherhood but has come to acquaint herself with the path that leads to death.

'Honey, why do you want to die?' Before giving anaesthesia, I asked her at the operation table.

'I don't want to live in this male dominated world.' Her answer was simple.

'Stupid girl.' I put my hands on her head with affection.

'All men are not savage. When you grow older you will get a man's love as well as trust.'

Honey vomited on the operation table.

She was trembling with fear and hatred. I slit her open and took out the baby, which hadn't even acquired a shape—the baby of an unwed mother. Now she is going to face divine wrath as well as social stigma, not to mention the legal hassles.

Is Honey a girl of depraved character? Loose morals? Religion and society both are going to ask her questions. Lawyers, judges and spectators will gather in and around the court to have a glimpse of the girl who at a tender age of thirteen went all the way…

What's your name? Where do you live?

I wash my hands, which are stained with Honey's blood and call out… 'Next!'

A blood-soaked woman is brought on a stretcher. A flustered looking man, an ageing mother-in-law and an old man follow trembling with fear.

'She fell from the staircase.'

'A rock fell upon her.'

'No, she slipped in the bathroom while bathing.'

'Is the child in her womb still alive? What could it be, a boy or a girl?' The man is asking again and again. Holding her diary, a lady police inspector barged in.

'Doctor, please help her gain consciousness. I have to record her statement.'

The woman's companions want to leave the room but the door is locked.

I put my stethoscope on the woman's chest. 'Take her away for post-mortem. Why do you bring dead bodies into the labour room?,' my voice is laced with irritation.

'How am I to know as to which of these women is dead and which one is alive.' The male nurse who brings in the stretcher says angrily. 'Bastards! They shove them on us when they are dead.' He is swearing. Outside the ward, people have gathered to get a glimpse of the injured woman.

'She is dead.' They look at each other, satisfied.

Her husband moves towards her, with a sheet in hand. After all he is the one who has to draw the curtain after the final act is played out but he flinches and takes a few steps backwards as he finds his dead wife's eyes staring right into his face. In fact, she stares at all those who come close to her—police inspector, doctor Reddy, relatives, spectators.

'How are we going to perform an autopsy on her? There is no part in her body which is not broken.' The nurse says wearily.

'Her head is spared. Perhaps doctors will open it.'

'No,' Dr Reddy smiles and looks at me. 'Post-mortem is not done on a woman's head.'

'Next…Next…'

But now the bees are all out of my body, stinging. The pair of scissors that I use to cut a woman open fall from my hand. I feel heavily drugged. Swatting the buzzing bees with my hands I shout…

'Next…Next…'

Translated from Urdu by Zakia Mashhadi

A Crisis of Medical Treatment

Rajshekhar Basu 'Parshuram'

It was almost sundown. Nando Babu was on his way back from Hogg's Market. As the tram moved past Beadon Street, it was slowed down by a bullock cart in front. The crossing leading up to Nando Babu's house was still a few minutes away. Just then, Nando saw his friend, Bankoo emerging out of an alley. Overcome with excitement, he called out: 'Bankoo, wait! I am getting off.'

The tram had just started to gather pace, when Nando Babu alighted, with two bags stuck under his arms. As his foot got entangled in the drapes of his dhoti, he lost balance and fell down.

A commotion ensued, and the tram came to a screeching halt. Some co-passengers got down and helped him to his feet, while others peeped out of the windows, assessing the situation—

'He's badly hurt.'

'Give him a glass of milk,' someone said in Hindi.

'Have the legs been hacked off?'

A few others speculated:

'Must be epileptic.'

'Not really. Must be drunk.'

'Or maybe a lunatic.'

'No. He's just a *Bangal*—East Bengali, I guess.'

'Or a countryside rustic.'

Nando Babu wasn't injured, but who cared?

'You really think you aren't hurt? Go home. You will be bedridden for two months.'

Nando's entreaties were not heard. Another old gentleman cut him off, 'There is nothing wrong in doing what is right. I saw with my own eyes that you got hurt, and yet you say that you aren't. Bullshit!'

As Bankoo reached the spot, the upset passengers found their way back into the tram, which subsequently left. Bankoo surmised, 'You must have been dizzy. No need to walk from here. Hey, rickshaw …!'

Nando Babu left in the rickshaw, while Bankoo tagged along on foot.

Nando Babu was forty-year-old, short, well-rounded, and dark-complexioned. He owned a huge house, much furniture and numerous company documents—all handed down by his father, who had worked as a commissariat in the West and earned a fortune. Nando got married young, only to lose his wife after a year. He hadn't married again. His mother had long been dead; the only woman in the house was an aged paternal aunt, who remained occupied with prayers and Hindu divinities. The household chores were taken care of by servants.

Nando wasn't averse to the idea of getting married again, but he was too lazy to try, being occupied with theatre, films, football, and racing. If he was so blissfully happy with friends, how would he find time for marriage? Moreover, he was getting old, and perhaps it was best not to marry again. After all, he was meek, soft-spoken, nonchalant, and exceedingly fond of leisure.

That day, the evening *adda* was on full swing in Nando's big living hall downstairs. Exhausted, he was taking rest, wrapped up in a quilt. Having finished his tea and *papad* (crisp flatbread), his friends were seen socializing over *paan* and cigarettes.

'Don't neglect your health. It's not a good sign to feel dizzy and faint in the cold,' Gupi Babu expressed his concern for Nando.

'I didn't faint,' Nando tried to clarify, 'My feet got stuck....'

'C'mon! You must have fainted. You look feeble. Please go and see Dr Tafadar in the morning. He stays nearby. You won't find a better physician in the city,' Gupi insisted.

Bankoo disagreed, 'I think you should see Nepali Babu. There is no other homeopathic doctor like him. The old man might be a bit ill-tempered, but his knowledge is unparalleled.'

Shoshti Babu, who was cuddled up in a corner, wearing a monkey-cap, and covering himself in a thick shawl and a comforter, chimed in: 'Who travels in a tram at such an odd hour, in this cold weather? If the body loses strength, you will obviously be shaky and fall. Do keep your body warm, Nando.'

Nidhu added, 'Nando da, stop eating coarse rice. Get rid of your ancient mattresses, chadars, and the slow palanquins;

they are good for nothing! You have plenty of money, don't you? Learn to spend it!'

Finally, it was decided that Nando Babu would visit Dr Tafadar in the morning.

Dr Tafadar lived in a colossal building on M.D.M.R. A. S. Grey Street. He owned two motor cars, one of them was a Rover. Given his fame, patients found it difficult to get appointments. Nando Babu had to wait for an hour and a half, before being called in. As he entered the doctor's inner chamber, he found a patient being treated. A heavily built Marwari with a bare torso was standing there. Having measured this patient's belly, the doctor said in Hindi: 'It has grown only by 1¼ inches.'

'Check my pulse too,' the patient demanded.

Dr Tafadar placed a machine around his wrist, and concluded, 'It's perfect!'

'Check my tongue too.'

The doctor peered into his mouth through an opera glass and said, 'This is a minor issue. Come back tomorrow.'

When the patient left, the doctor turned to Nando and said in English, 'Well?'

'Actually, I am in a bit of trouble. Yesterday, while I was getting down from the tram…'

'Compound fracture? Broken bones?'

Nando Babu gave an elaborate account of his problems. He had no pain, no fever; not even breathing or stomach ailments, though he had less appetite since the day before. He was also having nightmares, leading to some anxiety.

Tafadar checked Nando' body parts and asked him to stick out his tongue.

He winced and wrote him a prescription, 'You can now pull your tongue back in. Take these medicines thrice every day.'

'So, what did you see?'

'Very bad,' Tafadar replied in English.

An anxious Nando insisted, 'What has happened to me?

'I will have to observe you for a few more days to come to any conclusion. I fear that it is a cerebral tumour with strangulated ganglia. I will have to make a hole in your skull and operate on your neck to set the nerves right. A short-circuit perhaps.'

'Will I survive?'

'Don't lose hope. I will see you after seven days. I can arrange a consultation with my friend, Major Gossai. Don't eat too much rice or lentils. Stick to egg flip, bone marrow soup, and chicken stew. Feel free to have brandy in the evenings, and drink plenty of ice water. My fee is 32 rupees. Thank you.'

Nando Babu tottered out of the place.

In the evening, Bankoo Babu reminded Nando, 'I had told you not to go to him. He is a leech who makes money by fooling the Marwaris. He will break open your skull.'

'Can't you go to Tarini *kobiraj*, the ayurvedic doctor in our locality?,' Shoshti Babu asked.

'No. If there is really some serious issue with his head, it's better to see a homeopathy doctor, rather than rely on the Ayurvedic ones,' Gupi Babu objected.

'I know you won't listen to me, but you must try ayurveda. This guard I know made a sumptuous concoction. Do you want me to get some for you?,' Nidhu insisted.

Eventually, they settled on homeopathy.

The next day, Nando Babu went to the Nepali doctor's clinic. It wasn't that crowded yet, and he was sent for soon. The huge chamber floor was covered with a carpet. The aged doctor was seated like one of those foxes from Bengali fantasy tales. He was surrounded by a pile of books, gathered on the floor. His chillum kept the entire room smoky.

Nando Babu kept standing after greeting him with folded hands. The Nepali doctor gave him a stern look, 'You may take a seat.'

'Last stage?,' the Nepali asked.

'What?'

'I am not usually consulted unless the patient is nearing his last rites. Am I?'

Nando informed him that that he was in fact the patient.

'How come the allopathic dacoits let you go? What exactly are you suffering from?' the Nepali enquired.

Nando gave a detailed account of his travails.

'What did Tafadar say?,' the Nepali asked.

'He said that I have a tumour in my brain.'

'Do you know what is there in Tafadar's brain? Cow-dung! His horns are hidden by his hat, hoof by his shoes, and tail by his pants. Do you have an appetite?'

'Not since the last two days.'

'Do you get to sleep?

'Not much.'

'Headache?'

'Yes. Since yesterday evening.'

'Left side?'

'I think so.'

'Right side?'

'I think so.'

The Nepali scolded him, 'Answer properly!'

'I think it's in the middle.'

'Any stomach ache?'

'Sort of, but I think it started after I had the roasted chickpeas brought by Nidhu…'

'Biting pain or cramps?'

Nando looked hassled and replied, 'More like twists and turns.'

After consulting a few books, the doctor concluded: 'Take this medicine. First, we need to detoxify your body of allopathy. You know, at the age of five, those people had injected me with quinine; I still get a niggling headache in the evenings. Anyway, I will start your proper treatment after seven days.'

'What is the diagnosis?,' Nando asked.

The doctor frowned and said, 'What will you achieve with that information? If I tell you that you have differential calculus, will you understand anything? Don't eat rice or fish or meat. You can take moong dal juice with roti. No showers. You may drink warm water. No smoking or it will destroy the medicines. Ah! You must be thinking that my medicines in the cupboard are already damaged. Don't worry, there is sulphur-30 in my tobacco. What? Do I need to tell you my fee as well? Can't you see the notice board? It's 32 rupees, plus four for medicine.'

Nando Babu left after paying the fee.

Nidhu opined, 'Why do you have to waste money? We could have used it to watch theatre for five straight days from the private boxes. This old Nepali is a spotted dove, taking advantage of Nando's meek nature. Had it been me, I would have taught him a lesson. If I don't whisk away all his stuff from that almirah, you might as well chop off my nose!'

'I overheard in my office that a well-known *ḥakim* (physician) has just come here. He has also treated the royals. Want to give it a try?' Gupi asked.

Shoshti wasn't impressed, 'You want him to try a healer's medicine in winter? They kill you with juicy concoctions. Tarini *kobiraj* is a much better option.'

Consequently, they zeroed in on the kobiraj.

The next morning, Nando Babu went to Tarini kobiraj's place. The latter was 60 years old, lean, and clean-shaven. Having oiled his body, he squatted on a table, chewing tobacco. This is how he met his patients every day. In a corner, there was a *takht posh* (wooden bed) with a couple of faded pillows for comfort. A pair of wall cabinets were stuffed with medicines.

As Nando greeted the doctor and sat on the wooden bed, the kobiraj asked, 'So, where are you coming from?'

Nando Babu introduced himself.

'Who is the patient? What is his problem?' Tarini asked.

Nando Babu informed him that he was the patient, and gave an elaborate account of his journey so far.

'So, did they drill a hole into your skull already?'

'No. Nepali Babu said that it might be a stone, so I didn't have to go for the operation.'

'Nepali? Who's that?'

'Don't you know of him? Chora Bagan's Nepal Chandra has a M.B.F.T.S in homeopathy…'

'Oh right. You mean, Nepala. When did he turn into a doctor? If I may say this—why visit such amateurs, when you have a learned kobiraj in your proximity?'

'Actually, my friends suggested consulting a doctor, before deciding on an operation.'

'Do you know Jonti Babu, the lawyer from Khulna?'

Nando shook his head.

Tarini continued, 'His uncle had complications in his upper thigh. It had to be amputated by a civil surgeon. Having gained consciousness after three days, he freaked out, "where is my leg? Call Tarini Sen." They called me immediately. I gave him a dollop of Chavanprash. Guess, what happened next?'

'His leg grew back?!'

'Dimwit!,' Tarini abruptly rushed to the next room screaming, 'That cat is licking the goat-milk ghee.' After returning to his position, he said to Nando, 'Let me check your organs. I guess I was right. Were you ever seriously ill?'

'I had typhoid, but that was quite some time back.'

'I knew it! Was it five years back?'

'Almost seven and a half.'

'Five or seven, it's almost the same. Do you feel queasy in the morning?'

'I don't.'

'You do. You just can't sense it. Do you sleep well?'

'Not really.'

'I knew it! You have a stomach illness. Do you have a toothache?'

'I don't.'

'You do. You just can't sense it. Anyway, don't worry. I am giving you some medicines. They will bring relief.'

He then took out a bottle of medicine from his almirah, and started talking to a pill in the middle, 'Don't you jump around! Look, all my pills are alive; they respond every time I call out. Take one each in the morning and the evening. See me after three days, okay?'

'Okay.'

'Nonsense! It's not okay. You also have to compliment the medicine with a mixture of lemon juice and honey. Don't eat rice or salt, only boiled elephant foot yam and catfish stew. Also, drink boiled water, after cooling it down.'

'What is your diagnosis?'

'It's a kind of dysentery.'

A despondent Nando left after paying for the medicines and the kobiraj's service.

'What's up, dada? Done with the kobiraj too?' Nidhu asked.

'No point in getting such useless treatments. Let's travel somewhere for a change of weather,' Gupi suggested.

'Nando should get married and have a family. No point in being a middle-aged bachelor,' Bankoo said.

'Family! God knows how long I will be alive. Why drag a young bride into my mess right now?' Nando reasoned.

'Nando da, buy a motor car, the seven-seater Hudson is perfect for the five of us. A bit of fresh air will do wonders for you,' Nidhu added.

'Actually, the motor and the wife are similar to one another. It's easy to bring them home, but you will be stretched to your wit's end to maintain them. First, a tire blowout, then your wife's acidity, the next day the car's battery may need replacement, and then the child may need your attention. Don't take such a step! You will be hard-pressed. Instead of warming yourself under a blanket in winter, you will have to listen to these grumblings,' Shoshti warned.

'Uncle Shoshti is such a miser; he should have married a bear's daughter to save himself the cost of a blanket!' Nidhu opined.

'Whatever,' Gupi interjected, 'Go to the hakim tomorrow morning, and then we can take a call.'

Nando Babu reluctantly agreed.

Hajib-ul-Mulk Bin Lokman Nurulla Gajan Farullah Al Hakim Yunani stayed on Lower Chitpur Road. As Nando reached the third floor, a lungi-clad person greeted him, 'Hello *babumoshai*! I am *Hakim saheb*-gentleman's *munshi* (secretary). Tell me what's your ailment so that I can explain it to him.'

'I don't know yet. Am I not here to figure that out?' Nando replied.

The munshi insisted, mostly in Hindi, 'At least, tell me about your symptoms. Do you have fever, *pilli*, smallpox or *gheg*?'

'I don't know about any of these diseases. My heart is pounding hard.'

'Now, you are talking,' the munshi concluded, 'So, it's a heart problem. Have you got the *mohor* (gold coins)?'

'Mohor?'

'Hakim saheb doesn't take silver. He takes two mohor. If you don't have them, I can help. It's just for 45 rupees, with a discount of two rupees. You will need this silk handkerchief. It is for two rupees only. You should pay respect to the saheb in the darbar, and offer the mohor on top of the handkerchief.'

Following these instructions, the munshi escorted Nando Babu to the court. The vast floor was covered with carpets. Hakim saheb was leaning against a pillow on a low mattress. He was smoking a *forshi* (hookah). Aged 55, he had long hair and a clean mustache. His trimmed beard had spots of crimson and blue. He was wearing a satin *jobba* (robe), and a skullcap. Some *oguru* (fragrant powder) and *roomi mastagi* were burning in a *dhoop dani* (burner). A spittoon and two silver containers of *paan* and *attar* (perfume) were placed next to it. His minions, seated with bent knees, exclaimed: 'Miracle!' every time Hakim saheb uttered a word. In a corner, a man with a messy hairstyle was making wild gestures, while seemingly playing a sitar.

After greeting the hakim, Nando Babu gave him the mohor. The former picked a piece of cotton from the container of attar, and pushed it into Nando's auricle.

The munshi told Nando, 'You can speak in Bengali. I will translate.'

Following his elaborate account, Hakim Saheb said in Hindi, 'Bring me your head.'

Nando shuddered.

'Don't worry. Show him your head,' the munshi assured him.

Hakim Saheb poked into Nando's scalp and said in Hindi, 'It's the bones. They are flappy.'

'Did you understand? The bones in your head have turned soft,' the munshi explained.

Stroking his coloured beard, the hakim said, 'Bring the *surma surkh*, (the red kohl).'

Someone applied a red powder on Nando's eyelids, 'This will cool your eyes down, and help you sleep,' the munshi reassured Nando. The hakim then called out, 'Rogan Babbar!' Munshi added, 'Hey barber, get the blade.'

Even as Nando objected, 'Hey! What are you doing?,' the barber chopped off his locks—up to two inches—from the scalp, and applied a stinky paste.

'Don't get worried. This is expensive ghee for the head. It will strengthen your bones,' the munshi reasoned.

Nando Babu was stupefied for a moment, then regaining composure, ran out of the house at full speed. The munshi followed him, screaming: 'Wait!'

When Nando's friends came in the evening, they found the living hall to be locked. The servant informed them that Nando was sick. They left, disappointed. Having been restless all night, Nando had vowed never to be led by his friends again. He wanted to take his own decisions.

At 8 pm, he hailed a taxi. 'Keep going straight,' he told the driver. Nando had decided to get off and be treated at a random place, whenever the fare would go up to one rupee. It didn't matter if the doctor practised allopathy or homeopathy, was a kobiraj or a quack, was a Madraji or a *Chandsi* (Ayurvedic practitioner).

Having reached Barabazar, Nando found a signboard: 'Dr Ms B. Mullick.' Nando didn't notice the 'Ms.,' or else he might have hesitated. He pushed away from the curtain, leading to the chamber, and barged inside.

Ms Bipula Mullick was trying to pin the drapes of her sari to the blouse. She was getting ready to go out. She asked in a sweet voice, 'What can I do for you?'

Though caught off-guard, Nando decided to stick to the lady doctor. He appealed, 'I am in deep trouble.'

'Has the pain started?' Ms Mullick enquired.

'I didn't sense any.'

'First confinement?'

'Sorry?'

'First pregnancy?'

Embarrassed, Nando explained, 'I am here for my treatment.'

A surprised Ms Mullick asked, 'Your treatment? What's the issue?'

Having heard the entire story, she inquired, 'Can I know your name?'

'Shri Nando Lal Mitra.'

'Who else is there in your house?'

Nando informed her that he was a widower and had no one apart from an aged aunt.

'What do you do for a living?'

'Nothing really. I am well endowed with the ancestral property.'

'Do you have a motor car?'

'No, but I wish to buy one.'

After asking him a few more questions, Ms Mullick placed her fingers on her lips and pondered for a while. Seeing her shake her head from side to side, an extremely worried Nando insisted, 'Please be honest with me. Is it tumour, stone, or dysentery? Maybe, it's black fever or hydrophobia?'

Ms Mullick roared with laughter, 'You don't have any of these problems. You need someone to take care of you.'

'So, am I mad?'

Ms Mullick suppressed her giggles with a handkerchief, 'Oh dear, no! Why will you be mad? You just need a guardian.'

'I have my aunt.'

Ms Mullick laughed again, 'The idea! No, your aunt cannot do this. I am giving you a medicine, it's a bit sweet and smells of cardamon. See me after a week.'

Nando Babu visited Ms Mullick a week later, and then again after two days. Soon, it became an everyday affair.

One fine day, Nando Babu sent his aunt packing to Kashi for pilgrimage. He then went to the bazaar to buy lobsters, mutton, ghee, flour, yogurt, and sweets. All his friends were invited to the feast. A self-conscious Nando hosted them, dressed in a fine zari-bordered dhoti and silk kurta.

Mrs Bipula Mitra no longer treats anyone except her husband, who is now doing rather well. He has also bought a motor car. Sadly, the daily *adda* has fallen apart.

Translated from Bengali by Rajorshi Das.

Whose Turn Now?

Shankar Raina

(To all those patients with whom my nights and days are spent)

The silence of a graveyard had fallen over the ward. A deathly silence, broken by Salama's occasional howls—as if an owl hooted in the distance. Nabha Chacha came in weeping and fell flat on his bed. His daughter had just died in the other ward. His eyes were red with weeping. Everyone felt for him and a heavy gloom descended on the whole ward. Gula seemed to shrink into the bed with fear. Sister Razia went to Nabha Chacha and putting her hand on his shoulder, said, 'What use are tears now? You have to decide about the body.'

Nabha Chacha's sobs increased. If she could not belong to him when alive, what use was her dust to him?

Salama yelled with all the power of his lungs, 'I knew it. This was bound to happen when you called her daughter with your black tongue! How could she survive your malevolent effect?'

Salama's words seemed to burn a hole in Nabha Chacha's heart and his wails grew louder. Gula felt very bad: how could Salama have the heart to hurt the feelings of the old man with his cruel words? But looking at Salama, Sister Razia felt nothing but compassion. Today his pain was much worse. She went to him, and laying her hand on his forehead, whispered, 'Why do you talk so much, Salama? You will only exhaust yourself. Come, try to sleep. That's a good boy!'

Salama said nothing, as though ashamed of his words. He turned away and began to moan with pain.

All the patients in the ward seemed to have been benumbed, their faces even paler than usual. Nabha Chacha's wails further weakened their morale. Sister Razia was afraid that Salama might say something harsh to Nabha Chacha again. Gently she led him to a side-room. The ward was quiet again. The patients seemed to heave a collective sigh.

Sister Razia tried to forget Nabha Chacha, busying herself in filling a syringe, but she couldn't. Nabha Chacha continued to haunt her thoughts. How fond he was of his Bittan, he was ready to die for her. With his white beard, he looked like the picture of Santa Claus on a Christmas card, craving to give love.

She was terribly moved by Salama's plight. His pain seemed to drain his very life. Cancer had laid its deadly hands on him in the prime of life. Day by day, he seemed to grow worse and his bitterness sharpened with the progress of his disease. He lashed out at everything. There was no one whom his stinging remarks had not wounded till he had antagonised everyone. Sister Razia knew that he was not to be blamed, the terrible pain he suffered constantly had lacerated his soul.

She tried not to let him know how ill he was. But when the fit came on him, he would not even spare her. At this time too he was convulsed with pain. Sister Razia could not bear to see his agony. She gave him an injection of morphine to enable him to go to sleep.

Gula was still dazed with the death of Nabha Chacha's Bittan. It has petrified him. He lay on the bed, coiled like a foetus. Sister Razia could not bear to look at him, a still-closed rose-bud, its stem broken by a gust of wind. He had just entered college when the disease struck, and he had to leave. How he longed to return to college! How pitifully he would look, with what appealing eyes, at Sister Razia, asking her to tell him when he would recover, be able to go to college again. She would try to distract him, but she couldn't take her eyes off his innocent face. Even though reduced to a skeleton, he was still so good looking, a fine, silky down just beginning to make its appearance on his smooth face. He was just a fledgling. Even now he had not been able to comprehend the gravity of his disease. But Sister Razia knew very well that this cruel illness would bring an end to his life any moment.

Every patient in the ward had somehow come to depend on Ama. One word from him was more effective than a hundred drugs. He was the only one who did not talk about his illness. Outwardly he looked quite healthy. In his early youth itself his heart had been affected. And since then, he had found himself in and out of the hospital. The disease seemed to have given him a maturity, his words an exceptional weight, a sensitivity to the needs of others, and the strength to reach out to them. Sister Razia had a soft corner for him, as she had known him earlier. Those days she used to get her clothes stitched from him. Later she had come to know that when stricken, he had been about to be married to Azizi. But the matter ended with diagnosis of his heart problem. The pain of separation from Azizi had further aggravated it, leaving him literally heart broken. Sister Razia had also met Ama's Azizi. After marriage also, Azizi had come to see Ama in the hospital. How lovely she was! But her eyes too were filled with the same deep pain that filled Ama's. But is there anyone here, free from pain? Everyone suffers in one way or another. Sister Razia herself was not too old yet, but she already thought of herself as a burnt-out case, chinar (*Platanus orientalis*) afflicted with dry rot.

Nabha Chacha's wail startled her and the syringe fell from her hands, shattering on the floor with a loud tinkle. Gula woke up and rubbing his eyes sleepily went to the stool near Ama's bed. 'What is it?,' Ama asked. Gula was lost for words. 'It is just—just this dry cold—it is too biting.'

Ama said nothing.

'Nabha Chacha's Bittan is dead too.'

'When was it?'

'A short while ago.'

Ama turned his face to the other side as if unmoved, so many had gone in the last few days—swept away like dust by death. Gula returned to bed and wrapped the blanket tightly, covering himself from head to toe. His heart beat wildly, as if struggling to escape from the rib cage. Today he was in the grip of the terror again. It was advancing towards him menacingly, with open jaws. He left his bed and again sat on the stool near Ama's bed.

'You are not able to sleep, are you? I myself can't seem to,' said Ama.

'Something is happening to me again since yesterday. I don't seem to be able to breathe. My sickness is returning.'

Ama did not reply. What comfort could he offer?

'I shall never recover on this bed. I think I will change it.'

'What's wrong with the bed? You are too superstitious.' Ama rebuked him.

'I can't bear to stay here. This window looks out on to the garden, don't you see? I don't know why they are in such a hurry to burn the dead leaves of that chinar? Look at the dense clouds of smoke! The fire has quite scorched the turf. The sight of the muck and ashes frightens me.'

Ama looked out. The ground was covered with freshly made charcoal and ashes. In the midst stood a mournful looking mulberry tree. All its leaves had fallen. Its branches bare, it was frightening, just like a skeleton. It seemed to him as if it was Salama who was standing there, naked and shivering with cold. Quickly he looked for Salama. He lay there immobile, dead to the world, his ribs protruding sharply through the covering.

When he came here first, the mulberry tree was covered with lush green leaves. The dark fruit hung on it like so many ruby eardrops. The sweet-sour flesh of the mulberry, luscious with juice, just like Azizi's lips. He heaved a deep sigh.

'What is the use of thinking of the past?' Gula spoke as if in a dream, 'but what fun it used to be to walk over the heaps of fallen chinar leaves! Crunch, crunch—And now it is just dust and ashes that fill the air! How can you bear to look out of the window? It frightens me. I am not staying here; I will go to that bed in the corner. Is it vacant?' Gula's face was deathly pale, 'But that bed is unlucky, I remember now.'

From under the blanket, Salama piped in, 'You are right. Did you see anyone recover on that bed? It has eaten up everyone that occupied it.' Normally, neither Gula nor Sula had much to do with Salama, but all three had something in common, they were all in terror of death.

A sharp gust of wind shook the ward. Salama pulled the blanket over his head. Gula sat up and went back to the stool near Ama's bed.

'You might laugh at me, but I tell you I shall never recover unless it snows. I am certain of it. When the snow comes, this muck will all be hidden under it and then you will see how fast I recover—just like that!'

'You are being too nervous. All right, you can have my bed, come.'

They exchanged beds. But lying on Gula's bed, Ama could not rid himself of a vague apprehension. He sat up, walked to the window and leaned almost half of his body out and said, as if to himself, 'The mountains are all hidden, the clouds so low. Oh, it is certain to snow, I can see it coming. Now we all will get well.'

'Oh, it must snow, it *must*. And then I shall go to college,' Gula again felt reassured and went on talking to Ama, who listened attentively. How well he talked, how sweet his words and voice were, like nightingale's! He never seemed to tire of speaking of his college days, of his childish concerns, his young dreams, the excitement, laughter and fun. Listening to him, Ama would also lose himself in dreams. But Salama would seem to have plugged his ears, resentful of it all.

How Salama had changed! They had been admitted to hospital at almost the same time, both with serious illnesses. At that time, they seemed to derive courage from each other. It was only later that they grew distant. What happened was that Ama improved in time. Now he was well enough even to sometimes be able to go to work at his shop. But Salama's condition deteriorated day by day. Pain never released its hold on him, his agony crushing him relentlessly. Well, to each his own luck!

Salama resented Ama's recovery as if it was Ama who had deliberately made him fall ill. 'He thinks he will always remain fit. How he laughs and jokes with Sister Razia!' Though Salama made no secret of his jealousy, he had never hinted of it to Sister Razia. As for Sister Razia herself, she was the same to both of them.

In spite of illness, Ama was still as handsome as ever. How cheerful, how attractive he used to be those days! How long was it? Not too long. Those days Ama used to work in

Master Noora's tailoring shop. The shop was situated on the Amria Kadal bridge. Noora was an expert at tailoring ladies' garments. Ama had an even neater hand at stitching. You could have found a flaw in Noora's work, but not a stitch ever went wrong in anything stitched by Ama. He would be there in the shop, from morning to night, crouching over the machine, stitching away all kinds of feminine outfits. When he worked with fine gold thread on the neckline of a bridal dress, the picture of Azizi's stately neck would rise before his eyes, the colourful designs of printed fabrics would seem to fill the air with fragrance and make him ache with longing for her.

When he saw Azizi after a gap of six years at the *Dargah*, he reeled under the impact. She had grown to full womanhood, her radiant beauty so dazzling that he could hardly focus his eyes on her. And Noora had asked him to begin making preparations for the wedding! But Ama was not ready yet. He did make enough, but his marriage to Azizi was not a trifling matter. Yes, he would marry her, but it would be a truly memorable affair—with full pomp and glory. All his dreams would be translated into reality, and everyone would marvel at the show. He was sure he would find enough work to ensure decent earnings. He had the skill, possessing golden fingers, as you might say. So, he went to see the master tailor in the evening. It was the wedding season and they were under great pressure, swamped with orders and deadlines to meet. He offered to work overtime, through the night too. The master understood the reason for his eagerness to help out very well. He laughed and said, 'You are right, no doubt. But we can't kill ourselves. Do you have the stamina to survive whole nights without sleep?'

But Ama had the confidence of youth, 'But Sir, I am not going to do it forever. It is a matter of just a few days. One has to rise to the occasion, when there is such a pressing need.'

And then it was endless days for Ama—he lost all count of time. He continued to work till dawn after the shutters of the shop came down for the night, stitching clothes and making intricate designs with gold threads. It was backbreaking work, his eyes fixed on the emerging patterns, like painting with grains of sand. Carried away by his enthusiasm, he failed to notice that the effort of taking even a few steps was making him breathless. Driven by uncontrollable urge, he had no time to notice the tell tale signs of a failing heart. It was only when he could not even run the sewing machine that Noora forced him to see a doctor at the hospital. And then he was brought down to earth with one stroke—he had been suffering from heart disease for a long time, and it had only been diagnosed now. When he came out of the hospital after a long stay, there was nothing left, his world had been totally ravaged. Azizi had been married off. The same Azizi, dreams of a shared future—a picture that he had hugged to his heart during the long sojourn in the hospital. He never could be his old self again. His spontaneous laughter was a thing forgotten. His work held no charm for him anymore. He had to drag himself to the shop. But work he had to, in order to survive and he did survive. But was he the Ama that he had been once upon a time, he would ask himself?

Again, he would crouch over the sewing machine, stitching endless clothes for other people's daughters and daughters-in-law, the outfits he had wished to create for Azizi. When he worked the needle with the golden thread over necklines of *pherans*, the needle would seem to pierce his heart, punching a thousand holes in it. But in work he still has no parallel. Under his hands, the clothes would seem to acquire a character. His tailoring skills seemed to become finer with each passing day. Noora found it difficult to handle the flood of orders. There was no one to match Ama's talent in giving a perfect fit to each piece of clothing, throwing each curve of a woman's body into relief.

While taking Jameela's measurements one day, he felt a strange sensation. It was not the first time he had touched Jameela. In fact, he had taken her measurements several times before, but never even raised eyes to her. But how beautiful she appeared to him today! Just like Azizi she looked. Giving a swing to her body, Jameela said, 'Mind you, I don't want any crease or wrinkle to spoil the smooth fit.' Ama stretched the inch-tape with tremor in his hands. Measuring her shoulders, his hands seemed to touch live coals. Jameela's swan-like neck appeared carved out of marble. She turned to him and said, 'It should fit tight in front.' Her veil, sheer as onion skin, had fallen from her head, revealing her full form. How lovely she was! A fever raged within Ama. He could feel the blood boiling in his veins and the veins ready to burst under pressure.

He could not sleep for a long time that night. When he laid Jameela's suit under the needle of the sewing machine, something happened to him. Jameela's eyes danced before him, her translucent neck of a fairy, her burning shoulders and midriff, and his machine beat to the rhythm of Jameela's movements. Whoosh, whoosh, whoosh went the machine, faster and faster, and midriff, midriff, midriff, midriff, his mind chanted the refrain. What the devil was he thinking of, he rebuked himself. But how ravishing Jameela is! The suit felt hot under his touch, as if it already contained the heat of her body. How shameful to think such thoughts after having given everything up! Had the heap of cotton wool been smouldering after all, and ready to go up in flames any moment?

He went on stitching clothes: fair, red, polka-dotted, green, all the colours of the rainbow, firework of colour. He styled them to fit so tight that they would seem like a second skin to the body. Exquisite suits for fairies, for young virgins, for brides with henna-decked hands, the mere touch of which sent a shiver down his spine. The rattle of the machine rang incessantly, increasing in tempo, setting his teeth on edge, it was as if someone ran a sandpaper over his bare skin.

And then before he knew it, he was back in hospital. All hope of survival had left him now. He seemed to have developed an aversion to dreams of a future. With no Azizi as a part of it, life had become meaningless. Why should he carry on with the burden of the ailing heart? The walls of the ward seemed to be closing in on him. Sister Razia alone had understood his pain, and taken it to heart. She took every opportunity to comfort him and gradually he forgot his long illness. A spark had been rekindled in him and now he wanted to live. His lamb-like eyes would follow Sister Razia, who was mother to the whole ward. Sometimes he would even throw a tantrum like a child. Salt was forbidden to him but at his insistence she would give him some stealthily. Occasionally, when free from work, she would sit and chat with him for hours together, and he would forget that he was ill. How warm and affectionate were her words! Ama knew that she too hid God knows how many sorrows inside her. Sometimes she appeared to be more ill than he was. Her youth was long fled and dealing with cantankerous patients day and night, had turned her complexion sickly yellow too. When she walked about in her white uniform, she appeared to Ama like a corpse draped in white shroud, cold like ice—just a walking corpse. One day when Ama went to work in the shop, he brought a suit stitched for her. It was bright maroon in colour. Salama saw him handling a packet over to Razia. A corner was visible and Salama's eyes nearly popped out. Within no time, the news spread to everyone and Ama was so embarrassed that he could not meet anyone's eyes. But he had said nothing to Salama. How could he, to someone so afflicted? He was not bothered about himself, let him say anything, he was not answerable to anyone. But Gula's mind too had been poisoned by Salama, and he once asked him under his breath, 'When is the wedding? With Razia, I mean.' Ama had been speechless for a moment and then whispered, 'How the poor woman is being slandered! As if she could find no one but me.'

But Salama had burst out angrily, 'Why do you hide the truth from us? Do you think we are your enemies? We are not blind—didn't we see you give her the present openly?'

Ama could say nothing. Everyone was embarrassed at Salama's crudeness. And then Salama began to whimper like a dog—his pain had returned. Gula came and sat near Ama. With a pathetic face, he said, 'Salama is very ill, the pain just doesn't go away. You can see he suffers like hell, but his agony makes us lose even the little hope we have for ourselves.'

Ama himself was in despair, he had nothing to say. He knew that Salama's days were numbered. So many of the patients in the ward had died. Whenever someone breathed his last, it would set off a wave of terror in the others. With sinking hearts, they would look at one another, wondering who from the ward would come under the knife next. Ama was overwhelmed with fear and at the same time the urge to live grew even stronger. He tried to console himself, patients even more seriously ill than him had recovered and left the hospital bed, he was in much better shape than them, why shouldn't *he* get well? His glance fell on Salama, and he began to furtively scrutinize the faces of the patients, one by one. Whose turn was it next? When he looked at himself, his mouth went dry with fear.

Gula nudged him, 'Ama Sahib, what are you thinking of?' Receiving no reply, Gula kept quiet.

The orderly switched off the lights and a deathly silence fell on the ward. The ocean of darkness outside seemed to creep in, and the ward was filled with a dense blackness, you could almost feel it with the hand. It seemed to Ama that Gula was slipping away. He was filled with a deep sadness. Even through the opaque darkness, he thought he could see Gula's innocent lamb-like face. He was turning restlessly on the bed. Ama got up and switched on the light. Walking up to Gula's bed, he said, 'Aren't you able to sleep, Gula?' 'Oh, don't get worked up!' Gula was tense with fear—the hunted look of a lamb to the slaughter on his face.

'I think I am going to get worse. See how dark it is outside? How biting the cold? This dry spell must break—a little snowfall…!' He seemed to be mumbling in sleep. 'When will this illness leave me? Will I ever be able to go to college again, see Jameela again?' Gula was lost in dreams.

'Jameela who?'

'She is with me in college. Oh, if you could see her! The vision will light up your world!' Ama asked him to describe her in detail and then said 'Oh yes, I know who you mean, she is a customer of mine.'

'What do you think of her?'

'Oh, she is a beauty, no doubt about it. Perfectly formed in every feature—a golden grain of a girl. In fact, I saw her at the shop the other day.'

'How she grieved over my illness!' again Gula was lost in thought.

'How come she never came to see you here?' taunted Salama.

Gula cringed at the remark, 'How could she come here? In any case, it is none of your business.'

'In fact, I remember now that she asked me about you a number of times that day at the shop,' Ama went on making it up and Salama guffawed, 'Oh yes, of course!'

'If she comes to the shop tomorrow, you must ask her to come here.' Salama could not check himself, 'Trust him to tell her and trust her to come! Why must you clutch at these straws?'

Gula's heart froze at Salama's words, they were so bitter. Ama got up and switched off the lights and silence fell upon the ward. Somewhere in the distance, dogs howled. Ama lay tossing and turning for a long time. A fit of hiccups seized Gula.

When he returned from the shop in the evening the next day, there was chaos in the ward. Gula was having convulsions and the fit of cough was making him wheeze like a blacksmith's bellows. Sister Razia told Ama that Gula's old problem had returned with a vengeance. It was a crisis, and he wouldn't survive unless he was given blood transfusion. But where would he get it from? She seemed to be in a state of panic and Ama gave up all hope for Gula. He went and sat at the head of his bed and was afraid that his own illness would also return.

Sister Razia brought in a bunch of flowers and thrust them in an empty bottle next to Gula's bed. He opened his eyes and stared at the flowers. His eyes glittered, bright as stars. They were all shaken up by Gula's plight. The cold breath of death swept over the ward. Salama too had tears in his eyes and in spite of his own pain, drew close to Gula. 'The poor fellow shouldn't succumb, God forbid,' he thought.

Suddenly Nabha Chacha materialized at the back and after donating a bottle of blood, came and sat near Gula. Raising both his hands upwards, he prayed for his recovery, 'Let me die for you, my boy.' His eyes filled with tears. Nabha Chahcha, so hungry for love!

Drop by drop, the blood went into Gula's veins—drip, drip, drip it fell. By the evening, Gula's condition seemed to stabilize. When he opened his eyes, Nabha Chacha began to hover around him, 'You will recover, my son, you mark my word.'

His words seemed to give comfort to all the patients in the ward and they gathered round Gula. Even Salama felt motivated to ask, 'How do you feel now?' But Gula turned his face away, giving his query no attention at all. Salama felt deeply slighted and mumbled something to himself. When everyone continued to ignore him, he turned to Ama, 'Nabha Chacha is still not content, even after having eaten up that flower-like fairy-child Bittan, and now he is after Gula. Will this bird of ill omen never let go?'

Nabha Chacha recoiled under the searing words. He rose as if stung by a scorpion, 'Yes, it is true. My glance is murderous!' and rushed out of the ward.

Drops of blood fell from the bottle, drip, drip, drip and the icy wind made its own music outside. Gula spoke in a faint voice, 'Ama, when will the snow fall this year?'

Ama comforted him, 'If she comes to the shop, I shall certainly bring her here.' Again, Salama could not contain himself, 'Why must you go on deceiving him with false hopes?'

Ama seemed to be deaf to his words. He tucked Gula in gently and left for the shop. When he returned in the evening, he found the ward silent. The bottle of blood was empty and Gula's pallor was less pale, but Salama was still writhing in pain. Ama came to Gula's bedside and spoke cheerily, 'I met your Jameela and she is on her way here!' Through his groans Salama blurted out, 'Don't be taken in by his words, Gula! He will ruin you too. I feel so bad for poor Razia!'

Gula did not react, it was as if he had heard nothing at all. Eagerly he turned to Ama, 'Is she coming, really? Did you tell her about me?'

Changing the subject, Ama said, 'It isn't so cold today. I think the mountains have already had their first snowfall. It is bound to snow here now.' Gula signed and said, 'Let God heed our prayers!'

Salama screamed, 'It will never snow this year! Why should it? The land has to go to rack and ruin. Everything must be destroyed!'

After this outburst, silence fell on the ward. On the mulberry tree, a gaggle of crows began to caw loudly. Gula was petrified—an innocent babe-in-arms terrified by a bogeyman, the shadow of Death. Nabha Chacha crept back into the room in fear and with a hang-dog look on his face went to Gula's bed, 'My precious one is well now. You have to be ready for tomorrow, for party at Sister Razia's place!' he said, 'Well, Sister Razia turned out to be a crazy one, after all. Who should she go and marry, but the dumbest of them all!'

Ama looked at Salama with a happy look on his face. On his part Salama looked quite shamefaced. And Gula was staring at him incredulously. The smile froze on Ama's face—Gula had still not recovered from the last attack.

At about midnight Gula suffered a relapse. He began to wheeze, short of breath and his chest heaved like bellows. All the patients were awakened by the loud wheezing. But today Salama did not give way to groans and cries. It seemed that by now he had learnt to tolerate pain. His eyes were glued to Gula's face.

Gula's condition worsened. Salama could not bear to look at him. Restlessly he went to him and asked, 'What is the matter, Gula? How do you feel?'

'Oh, I'll be all right.' Salama looked at Gula. He was gasping for breath and he knew that his wish to see the snowfall would remain unfulfilled. A cold shiver ran down Ama's skin and the two exchanged glances. Today Ama too was not his normal self.

A couple of bats strayed into the ward and began to hit the walls blindly.

As the day broke, Ama got up and opened the window and exclaimed with joy, 'God has heard your prayers, Gula it is snowing! There are heaps of snow on the ground, it must have been snowing through the night! All the muck and dust is hidden under it.' Gula moved his eyes. He seemed to draw each breath with a prodigious effort.

'Will you help me to the window too?' Gula tried to sit up, but couldn't. Ama helped him like back and said, 'No need to tire yourself now. Get your breath back first, there is all the time in the world to see the snow.'

'I will get well now, I know. I shall move back to my own bed, so that I can see the fat flakes of snow fall and cover the ground. Jameela should have been here today,' Gula was gasping for breath with each word—the effort was too much for him. A numbness affected his limbs. Ama looked outside the window and said, 'I can see Jameela coming, Gula! There she is, what a lovely silk outfit she is wearing! And how gracefully she walks, with what measured steps!'

'Is she really? Could you take me to the window, please?' Ama did not respond. He continued to look through the window and then said, 'Your girl is still a child, I must say. Look how she plays in the snow! You *are* a lucky guy!'

Again, Gula tried to raise his head, but his body convulsed and he fell down in a heap. Ama touched him and knew that he was dead.

Salama screamed, 'Gula!' and began to weep like a child. All the others were tongueless, only their eyes moved, scanning one another's faces, as if wondering whose turn was next. And Salama continued to gaze out of the window. There was nothing but muck, litter, and ashes as far as the eyes could see. In the midst of the desolation stood the mulberry tree, bare and skeletal.

Translated from Kashmiri by Neerja Mattoo

The Surgeon

Sheeba E.K.

The flight from Dubai was delayed by 20 minutes. He noticed the dark storm clouds gathering as he stepped out of the Karipur airport. As he reached the white Audi car, Anwar was already holding the door open for him. He is like that; on time, every time; has been more of a confidante than a chauffeur, for the past seven years. The mobile tweaked as they were about to enter the main road. It's Dr Ravi Lopez. The thought of going to the hospital had not crossed Dr Ahmad Ali's mind until then. Straight to home, a deep relaxing sleep, clubbing in the evening, and off to Bangalore tomorrow. Four days of each month are spent at the city. And ten days at Dubai. As he saw Dr Ravi Lopez's call, Dr Ahmad Ali had a foreboding that his routine is going to be disturbed. In the two years that this doctor from Karnataka has been practicing as his assistant, he has never been a cause for any inconvenience. He does whatever is assigned to him with certain meticulousness.

'Doctor, please excuse me! This is an emergency,' came the subdued voice of Ravi.

'It's okay. What is it, Doctor?'

'The condition of Raghava Warrier is quite critical! He is not responding to medicines. It's not possible to control internal bleeding. Pulse and BP are going down.'

He went silent for a moment, resumed on not getting any response.

'Doctor, his relatives are suggesting that he be removed from ventilator support. It was never his desire to pass thus, surrounded by all the tubes. Can't we consider that, given the circumstances?'

Dr Ahmad Ali thought for a while. It has been a month since Raghava Warrier, a businessman based in Singapore, has been put on ventilator support. He did not expect him to survive when he returned from his Dubai trip. But, even after 10 days, life is still throbbing within this 79-year-old being. His assets are limitless. No children. It was just two years ago that he returned to his hometown to spend a peaceful life post retirement. It was about six months back, as he was whiling away his time at his Valyam, his ancestral home near Pattambi with his 98-year-old mother, his wife, and his younger brother's family, when a stomach ulcer catalyzed his first journey to the hospital.

A common ulcer. A gift, courtesy his impoverished childhood and the race to build a good life in his youth. It was all under control all this while. But nowadays the pain gets a tad too much to bear. And with BP and Parkinson's giving him company Warrier was in a fix.

It is the obligation of every doctor conscientious enough about the growth of the hospital to remember that it is important to grab on to a patient till his last breath—suddenly, a refrain of the MD, Athikadavan Hamsa Haji, from the mandatory month-end evaluation meetings cut into his thoughts. A couple of random blood tests, X-rays, a scanning here, if possible, an endoscopy there, in some cases, a biopsy. These are the Malayalis who are obsessed with being healthy, yet are quite lazy about maintaining it, always relishing food with high fat and cholesterol content and turn into patients by their own effort and accord—these are the ones who are ever ready to spend money on health care and medical expertise. The grip over Raghava Warrier was, thus, held on with a rigour. Warrier was adamant on consulting Dr Ahmad Ali. They had met at one of the seminars held in Singapore. In fact, after crossing the mighty ocean, Warrier himself came to this hospital, in search of this illustrious doctor, Dr Ahmad Ali. A minor surgery for his stomach ulcer was performed and Warrier slowly transformed into a regular visitor at the hospital, what with the reviews every 15 days and the mandatory checkups each after a month.

The complaint about the pain not receding led to a biopsy test. The test was normal. But it has to be assumed that the body worn out by age and time had to succumb to these tests, which were rather demanding. Now only Warrier remains in the customized critical care unit. It was a known fact that the freezing cold from the air conditioner would bring on pneumonia. But his relatives were there to remind that the temperature should always be optimum and he should never be warm. They helplessly stared at his jawbones jittering, reminded by the crucial fact that in higher temperatures the chances of full-frontal attacks from germs and other bacteria are high. He was shifted to the ventilator just one month back when he couldn't breathe. In short, all the functions of the body were taken over by machines. When he had left for Dubai ten days back Warrier was struggling in that space between life and death. Warrier's relatives were confident that he desired a peaceful death unaided by the tubes, and it seemed to Dr Ahmad that Ravi Lopez was, in a way, lured into the trap by them to call him up.

As they passed Kondotty town market Dr Ahmad Ali gestured to his driver to slow down.

Anwar stopped the car by the road and stepped out. He stepped into the bakery beside the road and bought a chilled bottle of Sprite for the doctor. The water droplets on the surface of the chilled bottle seemed to him like the blooming drops of blood on the surface of the skin on being caressed by the surgical blade. He opened the bottle, took a gulp and looked at his watch. 12.45 pm. He had to reach the hospital within an hour.

'Shall we remove the ventilator support, Doctor?' Dr Ravi Lopez asked again.

'No. I will reach shortly. Prepare the theatre. Set up everything for a tracheostomy.'

Dr Ravi was taken aback. Tracheostomy! It is a medical procedure that involves creating an opening in the neck near the vocal cords in order to place a tube into a person's windpipe to facilitate the entry of air into the lungs. Usually this is done when there is a critical injury to head or face.

'But, Doctor, tracheostomy… But why, Sir! It is 100 per cent certain that he won't be able to survive this procedure. On top of that the patient is quite old.' Dr Ahmad Ali smiled demurely as he recognized the anger in Ravi Lopez's voice.

He was a young Kannadiga. Even though he was a meritorious MBBS graduate he did not show much interest in higher studies. Brilliant, yes! But his conscientiousness was a grave drawback.

'Dr Ravi, do what you have been told!'

The doctor gulped down one more sip of Sprite as he disconnected the call and reclined into the seat.

He was quite busy for a week at the multispecialty hospital in Dubai. Three to four surgeries every day. Most of his patients were obese with generous fat deposits in the lower belly and could hardly walk. These patients who weighed about 180-250 kgs had enough and more money and an unquenchable desire to live. That's precisely the reason why his own life had taken such a turn.

He caressed the seat of his Audi with an urgent sense of motherliness.

During his childhood it was a luxury even to travel even by an auto-rickshaw. Maybe, short trips. Buses, for longer trips. That was Uppa's policy.

He never used to take money from the people who came for anti-venom remedies and treatments. For that precise reason the sense of penury never left the household. Ithatha and Umma never had any complaints.

The car was fleeing past buildings and shops. They were about to reach Pookkottur. Just take a left turn from the Martyrs Memorial and one gets the first glimpse of the ancestral home through the dilapidated compound walls. The mosque where Umma and Uppa rested for eternity was also nearby. As usual, as he passed that way, he felt a sudden surge of emotions in his throat. Whenever he drove past this way, he thought of visiting their graves and offering prayers. But who has the time! He is busy, as always, as usual.

He gulped down what was left in the Sprite bottle as they turned the corner of the Martyrs Memorial.

'You should study hard and become a doctor. Offer free service to the poor.'

Uppa's life was exceptional and it is hard to emulate him. He was a pioneer in indigenous medicine. He was a genius at handling treatment for snakebites. None who sought him out returned disappointed. He was happy with whatever his patients gave him. When a patient poorer than them came he shared it with them.

'Its Chekkutti Vaidhyar's generosity that has taken his children to such heights!' the word spread like wildfire among the locals.

Ithatha is also a doctor, but in government service. She was also married off into a family of doctors.

The second born of Chekkutti Vaidhyar, Ahmad Ali, became the apple of everyone's eye and was plunged into the limelight when he displayed meritorious performance and bagged ranks for both his secondary and higher secondary state board examinations.

'May you become as illustrious a doctor as your father. Don't be greedy for money. It will always destroy us!'

These were the words of Chandrasekhar Sir, the old headmaster, when they went to meet him on securing a seat for pursuing medicine, after a striking performance in the entrance exams. It was Uppa who brought Sir back from the death bed after a deadly bite from a Russell's Viper.

During his medical college years books were his only companion. He was not at all enticed by the parties and exuberances displayed by his privileged classmates. He was the gold medalist from his batch and eventually became a surgeon, just as he had desired. He always had that urge to continue his studies. Uppa wanted him to join government service. He started off his career at the Village Hospital at Manjeri. The strike called by the doctors after a few months was what changed the trajectory for him. In due course he left government service and was lured into one of the prominent hospitals in the medical city nearby and became a prominent surgeon. It was the MD of that hospital who facilitated his training in bariatric surgery abroad. A management that gave him all kinds of freedom. But there was just one exception. Hospital needs profit. Doctors will get a share of the same. England, USA, Netherlands, Switzerland—there's hardly any country he hasn't visited. As he returned from one of his illustrious travels abroad not only did the number of people in the queue outside his OPD increase but all of them looked up to him with a sense of adoration. Surgery became an obsession, an ecstasy for him from then on. No matter who sat in front of him all he could conjure up in his mind was the surgical blade that would graze across the skin. A kind of pleasure is there when the blood drops break out like sweat as you feel the cold of the blade against the warm skin. And the delight from the blood merging with the deep of the red! No other sight would give him that kind of high. Within a short span of time, he secured a national record for the number of surgeries he performed.

Diet with high fat and cholesterol content, a luxurious lifestyle without enough exercise, weight gain beyond one's control, housewives scared out of their wits of losing their beauty, and the NRI Malayalis driven by the intense desire to be cured of diabetes—they all approach him during their short annual leaves. It was indeed a harvest! He could not even come out of the operation theatres on those days. Yes, 90 per cent of the cases that came to him could have been cured without surgery and with a specific customized diet and regular exercise. These were people who were not at all bothered about the side effects of undergoing bariatric surgery. Yet, he never disappointed anyone.

His bank account overflowed. From the paucity embodied by Chekkutti Vaidyar, he rose to the ever-new heights of luxury and exuberance. Most importantly, he didn't want to shrink before the wealth of Zarina. Nothing should be lacking from the life of the only daughter of

Safarulla Khan, the established planter from Kanjirappally. Uppa frowned upon an alliance from a rich girl from the South.

'There is a huge gap in our lifestyles. Do we need such an alliance, son?'

But even though Uppa was a bit disheartened, it happened. It was an alliance brought by colleagues. Her family was affluent, both politically and economically. 'Don't let it go' was the advice he got from all quarters. And in the end the son's desire was fulfilled!

Zarina was a good wife. But she could never become a good daughter-in-law. Uppa's last days were filled with sadness. The death of Umma left him listless. On top of that the mockery he had to face from Zarina's family. The day Uppa passed can never be forgotten.

Uppa passed the day when bariatric surgery was performed on the 40-year-old Abdul Nasser who had come from Saudi for his annual leave. There were three other surgeries that day. For the same reason, not much focus could be conjured up on Abdul Nasser's surgery. There was a strange foreboding and disquiet that was slowly gripping him as he rushed into the next theater after hurriedly sterilizing and performing the asepsis on Nasser. At that exact moment Uppa fell and was rendered helpless in the bathroom, fighting to breathe, all alone, away from everyone's sight and mind.

When I joined for duty after four days I was welcomed by the teary-eyed wife and brother of Abdul Nasser.

'The surgical wound is not healing. There seems to be some infection.' They informed him with a sense of trepidation.

'Please inform the junior doctor. From now on he is in charge.'

Then Dr Ravi Lopez wasn't part of my team yet. My junior was from Tirupati and was someone who was always hooked on to his mobile phone.

Abdul Nasser's uneasiness continued to grow. In order to avoid any complaints, the management intervened and exempted them from paying the room rent. However, there was no further treatment except for the promise that the junior doctor will come and look into the matter. Ultimately, they forcefully availed discharge and went to consult one of the prominent hospitals in Thrissur.

Many days had passed since Abdul Nasser's brother came to visit him at the hospital. He meandered through the crowded OPD with a smile that was tinged with a liberal amount of disgust.

'Doctor must be busy, right! For someone who holds the record for the greatest number of surgeries performed?'

'Please come, we will talk in my office.'

Even if it was suggested politely with the aim of not letting the other patients know, he was not ready to hear any of it.

'Did you go to America and England to learn to kill people? My brother didn't die. You thought you could kill him by filling up his stomach with cotton swabs and threads? It was his children's good fortune that the hospital at Thrissur was able to figure it out on time. They performed a surgery too. And he survived!'

In order to escape his words, the surgeon walked towards the lift.

'Were you sentencing him to death by giving him a free bed here, you hot-shot surgeon?'

His voice reverberated from behind.

'He got his life back, yes. But he cannot go back to the Gulf. He can no longer take up jobs that requires lifting weight. He is now here, at home, doing a small business.'

People were starting to take notice of him and his words.

'They were getting better off. And now, because of you…Don't think that I don't know what to do with people like you…'

I didn't listen to the rest. As the lift slowly went up, I felt a sort of a humming and trepidation in my heart like never before. Had to pay compensations many a time. But, there was the practice abroad from time to time. The interviews in the prominent dailies and newspapers and channels, write ups… all these were enough to attract patients.

'Ali—Almighty is witness to all this. Don't you forget that!'

He remembered how those words uttered by Dr Fazal, his brother-in-law failed to make any impact when they were queuing up to meet the experts when Zarina couldn't conceive even after significant time into their marriage.

Even the healthiest of couples do face some kind of a delay in conceiving, without any obvious rhyme or reason. The only problem is when you look at all this as destiny or karma.

Zarina became pregnant within three months of the start of the treatment. I remember smiling rather vainly when he and Ithatha had come to visit us with savouries as per the custom. Both of them were in government service. Both were quite busy. Yet they didn't have much financial stability. Both of them were simply wasting time.

It was a stroke. Zarina was paralyzed on one side. And from then on, I could no longer bear the formidable depth of his stare.

'Such a condition does not usually come to pass at such an age, Doctor. I don't have to tell you, of all people, about it!' I still remember the rather inhibited words of Dr Hari Kumar, the neurosurgeon.

'I have never seen any patient beyond the age of 65 in this state.'

It was the treatment in England that finally saved Zarina.

When she came back, Zarina was a different person. Always lost in thoughts and in prayers. Immersed in charity work. Luxury was no longer a part of her life. What's unbearable even today is her purdah. How modern a girl she was! But, I didn't go against any of her wishes..

'Ikka-can't you just stop this whole business of making money?' She did ask me one day.

'You know I am a workaholic. Money is not the issue here, Honey.'

I enlightened her with a sweet embrace. And she didn't raise the topic after that.

She helped, rather generously, whoever came home seeking it. The only explanation she had for that was: may their prayers save her husband.

It was only when the car slowed down at the usual traffic congestion near the junction that the doctor realized that they were about to reach the hospital.

It was drizzling. A strange musing that there is a sadness that envelops everything suddenly hit him hard. In that very instant, however, he laughed off the thought.

The Operation Theatre was ready. As the lift was speeding up his heart longed for the touch of the cold steel surgical blade.

'Doctor, only if we get our uncle back. Please do not put him through more pain, otherwise.'

With welling eyes stood Raghava Warrier's nephew in front of him.

'Let's see. Let's try.'

Doctor lifted his eyes upwards for a moment. He did, however, successfully hide a sly smile.

He was sure that Warrier must have almost passed already. Maybe only a few moments were left. The surgery will be done. There will be a small group wailing in the corridor. One side of the critical care unit will be hidden from view as the nurses prepared the body and covered it in a white cloth before handing it over to his relatives. Then to his ancestral home in Pattambi in an ambulance. Body will be kept for public viewing, there will be headlines in the newspapers and news scrolls in the news channels, the ritualistic condolence meetings.

As the blade entered his throat, Warrier's eyes came alive from the deep and sunken sockets.

'Wasn't anesthesia administered properly?' for a moment his hands shivered.

'I don't think there is a need for that anyways,' murmured Dr Ravi, apparently, away from the ears of anyone in particular.

The last moments of Warrier played out as green and red light-dots across the monitor. At that moment a tiny yet dangerous clot that was invisible in Warrier's biopsy report suddenly got transferred into Dr Ahmad Ali's cells. And then, it took on a frenzy and sped and spread across the surgeon's body at a speed dangerously close to inflicting damage to his tissues. Yet, the surgical blades in the hands of Dr Ahmad Ali continued to move in a frenzy, as always.

Translated from Malayalam by Swetha Antony

Manzoor

Saadat Hasan Manto

His condition was quite critical when he was admitted to the hospital. He was put on oxygen support on the first night. The nurse on duty thought that this new patient would not survive till the morning. His pulse rate was unbelievable: sometimes, it was palpitating at a rapid speed, and sometimes, it would stop pulsating for long intervals.

His body was drenched in sweat. Unable to get even a moment of comfort, he would toss and turn from one side to the other. When his anxiety reached an uncontrollable level, he would get up and breathe deeply. His colour was as red as a turmeric tuber; eyes were deep in its sockets, the nose was as cold as a piece of ice, and his body was shivering.

He passed the night in extreme pain. Throughout the night, he was being supplied with oxygen. In the morning, when his condition slightly improved, he went into a deep sleep.

A couple of his relatives came. They sat for some time and then went away. The doctor informed them that the patient was suffering from a heart disease called 'Coronary Thrombosis.' It is quite fatal!

After he woke up, he was administered a few injections. He was continuously experiencing mild pain in his body. His shoulder muscles were stiff; it was as if someone was beating them through the night. Every part of his body was in searing pain, he was not experiencing it because of his sheer weakness. He was quite sure that death was at his doorstep, and he would die in a day or two.

He was around 32 years old. In these years, he had not experienced any relief or rest that he could remember and ease the pain of loneliness. He was separated from his parents as a child. No one knows who raised him! Stumbling through life, he had reached this age and now was employed as a worker in a factory on a monthly wage of 25 rupees, which allowed him to continue with his impoverished existence.

Had he not been battered by the intense pain in his heart, he wouldn't have been able to differentiate between health and sickness—he had never been a healthy person. He had always been suffering from one disease or the other.

He was administered four injections by the evening, but his oxygen support was removed. His heartache had reduced to an extent and he had regained consciousness. Now he could look around and observe his surroundings.

He was in a big ward where many other patients like him were lying on metallic cots. Nurses were busy performing their duties. In the bed next to him, there was a nine- or ten-years old boy wrapped in a blanket, staring at him. His face was glowing red.

'Peace be upon you,' the boy greeted quite affectionately.

'May peace be upon you too,' impressed with his warm demeanour, the new patient replied.

The boy changed his posture under the blanket, and asked him, 'How are you, dear brother?'

'I am grateful to Allah,' the new patient replied tersely.

The boy's face became redder. 'You will be fine soon. What is your name?'

'My name?,' the new patient looked at the boy with fraternal affection and said, 'my name is Akhtar.'

'My name is Manzoor,' he suddenly changed his posture, and called a nurse who was walking by, 'Sister…sister.'

The nurse halted. Manzoor salaamed with his hand. The nurse came near, greeted him warmly and went away.

After a short while, the assistant house surgeon came. Manzoor greeted him: '*Assalamualaikum* (peace be upon you) Doctor sir.' The assistant house surgeon returned his greetings, sat beside him, held his hand, and had a lengthy conversation about the hospital.

Manzoor was curious about every patient in his ward. He was aware of those who were critical and those who were recovering. He knew about those who were being admitted and those who were being discharged. All the nurses were his sisters, and all the doctors were his friends. Among the patients, he referred to some as maternal uncle, some as paternal uncle while the rest were his brothers.

Everyone loved him. Though he looked ordinary he possessed an extraordinary attraction. His face exhibited a glow that worked like a halo around his innocence. He was always cheerful and extremely talkative, and though Akhtar was suffering from a heart disease that vexed him terribly, he was never annoyed with Manzoor.

As Manzoor's bed was next to Akhtar's, he would begin a new conversation after regular intervals. His conversation would depend upon small and innocent sentences.

'Do you have siblings, brother?'

'I am the only son of my parents.'

'Do you still feel pain in your heart?'

'I don't know what heartache is.'

'You will be fine, just drink a lot of milk.'

'I shall ask the senior doctor to give you butter.'

The senior doctor also loved him immensely. During his inspection round in the morning, he would ask for a chair to sit beside him and talk to him about everyday matters.

Manzoor's father was a tailor. He used to rush to the ward for 15 to 20 minutes, every afternoon. He used to bring fruits, feed him in haste, and lovingly pat him on the head before leaving. Donning a burqa, his mother visited him in the evening, and sat beside him for long.

Akhtar connected with Manzoor the moment he greeted him. Their bond strengthened as they conversed regularly. In the silence of the night, when he had time to contemplate, he realized that it was Manzoor's miracle that he was recovering now.

Doctors had given up all hope. He was supposed to count his days on fingertips. Manzoor had informed Akhtar that his pulse was almost missing when he was brought to the ward. In his heart, Manzoor had prayed to God to shower his mercy on Akhtar. It was the result of Mazoor's supplications that Akhtar was pulled out of the jaws of death. But Akhtar was quite sure that he would not live for long, as he was suffering from a fatal disease. Anyway, it is now his heart's desire to live for a few more days, so that he can hold onto his bond with Manzoor for some more time.

A couple of days passed. Manzoor, as usual, used to chatter throughout the day. He was constantly chattering with either nurses, doctors, or cleaners as they were also his friends. Akhtar felt as if every particle in the smelly ambience of the ward was Manzoor's friend. On whichever thing he would cast his eyes, it immediately became his friend.

After a couple of days, when Akhtar came to know that Manzoor's lower body was paralyzed, he was absolutely shocked. But he was also amazed at how Manzoor could remain cheerful despite such calamity. When words burst out like bubbles from his lips, who could imagine that the lower portion of his body was a mere lifeless piece of flesh!

Akhtar never spoke to him about his paralysis. It seemed like a huge mistake to enquire about something of which he was so blissfully unaware. However, someone informed him that one day Manzoor bathed with cold water soon after returning from the playground and his lower body was paralysed.

He was the only child of his parents; they were grief-stricken. Initially, they put him under the treatment of hakims, but to no avail. Then, they resorted to magic and spells but even that was not effective. At last, at someone's advice, they admitted him to the hospital so that he could be given continuous care and treatment.

The doctors had lost all hope. They knew that the paralyzed parts of his body would never be cured but they continued the treatment to console his parents. They were astonished at how Manzoor was still alive! Apart from his lower portion being completely dysfunctional, the paralytic attack had also severely affected many vital parts of his body. They felt pity for him, and they loved him because he had learned the art of perpetual joy from his adverse condition. His innocent mind had invented this strategy to suppress his agony.

Akhtar had another heart attack. This one was even more severe and painful than the previous one, but he dealt it with patience and perseverance. Inspired by Manzoor, he tried to suppress his sorrow and pain and succeeded in it. The doctors were 100 per cent sure that no power in the world could save him this time—but a miracle happened! When the nurse on the night-duty gave the charge to another nurse in the morning, Akhtar's disappearing pulse had become normal… He was alive!

After having battered with a long and exhaustive battle with death, when Akhtar was finally about to sleep, he turned towards Manzoor with his half-closed eyes and observed him to be lost in his dreams. His face was glowing. With his weak and frail heart, Akhtar imagined kissing Manzoor's forehead, and then, he closed his eyes.

When he woke up, Manzoor was chattering with enthusiasm. He spoke to a nearby nurse: 'Sister, please awake brother Akhtar; it is time for his medicine.'

'Let him sleep; he needs rest.'

'No, he is absolutely fine. Please give him his medicine.'

'Fine, I will give it.'

When Manzoor looked at him, Akhtar's eyes were open. He greeted him in a loud enthusiastic voice: '*Assalamualaikum* (peace be upon you).'

Akhtar replied in a weak and frail voice, 'May peace be upon you too.'

'Brother! you slept for a long time.'

'Yes …perhaps.'

'The nurse is bringing medicine for you.'

Akhtar felt that Manzoor's words were strengthening his frail heart. After a short while, Akhtar, himself, started chattering excitedly like Manzoor. He enquired from Manzoor: 'Did you pray for me this time too?'

'No,' Manzoor replied.

'Why?'

'I don't pray regularly…I prayed once and that was enough. I knew that you would be fine soon.' The conviction was evident in his tone.

Akhtar teased him: 'You always tell people that they will be fine. Why don't you get cured and return to your home?'

Manzoor thought for a while: 'I'll also get fine soon. The senior doctor told me that I would be able to walk around in a month. Look, I can slide up and down now.'

Then he made a futile effort to slide up and down under his blanket. Akhtar immediately responded, 'Wow! Mister Manzoor, Wow! One month is nothing. It will pass like this.' Manzoor snapped his fingers and burst out laughing.

More than a month had passed. Meanwhile, Akhtar had suffered from three more mild heart attacks. But his condition had improved, and he was regaining his strength. His muscles had become less stiff, and his pulse rate was normal. Doctors felt that now his life was out of danger. But they were still surprised at his survival!

Akhtar laughed within himself. He knew who saved him. It was neither medicine nor interjection—it was Manzoor! That disabled Manzoor whose lower portion of the body had become dysfunctional, and who was naïve enough to believe his body, which was a huge mass of lifeless meat, was showing a few signs of life.

Akhtar and Manzoor became close friends. Akhtar perceived Manzoor as a messiah who had given him a new lease of life and helped him purge all the dark clouds under whose shadow, he was leading a suffocating life. His misery was transformed into prosperity; he became fascinated with being alive. He wanted to be completely cured at the hospital and start a new healthy life.

He felt anxious whenever he looked at Manzoor whose condition remained constant. The dysfunctional portion of his body was electrically stimulated, massaged daily, and medicines were administrated, yet he showed no signs of improvement. As time passed, he became even more pleasant and cheerful, and Akhtar was concerned and surprised with this attitude.

One day a senior doctor told Manzoor's father to take him home as he could not be cured. Manzoor was told that his treatment would be resumed at his home, and he would be cured soon. Yet, he was quite depressed. He didn't want to go home. When Akhtar inquired about why he wanted to stay at the hospital, Manzoor's eyes welled up with tears, 'I will be lonely. Father goes to the shop; Mother sews clothes at the neighbour's house. With whom will I play and chat?'

'Mister Manzoor, it is just a matter of a few days, you will be fine soon, then you can play with your friends and go to school.'

'No … no,' Manzoor covered his eternally red face with the blanket and started weeping. Akhtar was grief-stricken. He consoled and showed affection to Manzoor.

At last, the words were stuck in his throat; he turned his head to the other side.

In the evening, the house surgeon informed Akhtar that the senior doctor had given instructions for his discharge. He could leave in the morning. Manzoor became quite happy when he heard about it.

Manzoor talked so much that he got tired. He told every nurse, every patient, and every cleaner that brother Akhtar was getting discharged.

He continued with his naïve cheerful chatter till late at night, and then fell asleep. But Akhtar laid awake almost the entire night thinking about Manzoor and his disease. Is there no medicine in the entire world that can cure this lovely kid? He sincerely prayed for Manzoor with all his heart, but he was sure that his prayers would never be answered because, unlike Manzoor, he did not have a pure heart.

He felt depressed at the thought of his separation from Manzoor. He could not believe that he would leave Manzoor in the morning and would start building a new life. Gradually his mind and heart would erase all the memories of Manzoor. Perhaps, it would have been better if he died before the moment Manzoor first greeted him. He was the one who had given him this new lease of life. How could he leave the hospital?

While lost in the thoughts, Akhtar fell asleep. He woke up a little late the next day. The nurses were darting from one place to another in the ward. Turning over his side, he looked at Manzoor's bed. Instead of Manzoor, a skeletal old man was lying there. Akhtar was stunned for a moment. He almost screamed at a nurse who was passing by, 'Where is Manzoor?'

The nurse halted, remained silent for a few moments, and responded in a sad tone, 'The poor lad died at half past five in the morning.'

Akhtar became so depressed that his heart began to sink. He thought that it was his last heart attack. But he was mistaken. He was fine, and after some time he had to leave that hospital as a new patient who was supposed to occupy his bed, had been admitted.

Translated from Urdu by Haris Qadeer

The Longing

Kartar Singh Duggal

'Before I perform the necessary procedures, you can ask any questions that you might have,' the lady doctor said in a straightforward manner.

'No, nothing,' Rajni replied in a subdued voice. 'However, whatever I am doing today, I hate myself for it.'

An eerie silence pervaded the operation theatre for a few moments.

'Aren't you completely convinced with your decision?' The lady doctor eagerly questioned.

'No, I am ready…all that I want to say is that I love her... So what if it is a daughter?'

The lady doctor fell silent again.

'You can start now…,' tears began to roll down Rajni's eyes. 'Doctor, you may begin. I am ready. I am …'

Again, for some moments, there was a strange silence.

'This is called a speculum. I am now going to use this,' the doctor informed her. 'Would you like to see it?'

'No,' Rajni replied while sadly turning her head to the other side.

'Do you have any other questions?'

'Is it going to be extremely painful?' Rajni questioned.

'No, it won't pain much but you will feel a little stress,' the lady doctor explained, feeling sympathetic towards Rajni. When she held Rajni by her arm, Rajni felt her hands were icy cold.

'Now, I am going to put an injection right on top of the uterus,' the lady doctor informed. Rajni lay in an almost unconscious state as if right in front of her eyes, her hundreds of thousands of dreams were fading away in the blue sky, akin to the diminishing visibility of the twinkling stars.

It was at this moment that all the time that she had spent with Partool—right from the time of their love affair, marriage, the first night of honeymoon, his first posting, their new house, her decision to become a mother, her conception—everything flashed before her eyes.

'Don't worry! Now, it will only take five minutes. You will not even feel the pain...,' the lady doctor told her.

Rajni began to remember the past few days. She was so happy when she received the news of her pregnancy. She was ecstatic and could not believe her good fortune. However, what she could not fathom was the reason why Partool was constantly insisting on the 'screening.' All she was preoccupied and concerned with were the thoughts of becoming a 'mother.' Whenever Partool left her all alone in that big house, she longed for a child with whom she could play, whom she could feed, whom she could look after and caress day and night.

'It has just been eight weeks. There is nothing to worry about. No sign of any danger. Had there been a delay of even a week more, there would have been complications...,' the lady doctor went on, trying to boost the patient's confidence.

The train of thoughts carried her back to her husband's repeated insistence on screening... screening ... screening ... only screening ... all the time! Out of love for her husband, she had agreed too. He might just be curious to know whether it is a boy or a girl? What difference does it make?

'The egg is usually placed near the lining of the uterus wall,' the lady doctor continued with her talk: 'We are going to use a procedure similar to a vacuum. The manner in which a carpet is vacuumed. The way roads are cleaned in foreign countries...,' she said in a monotonous tone.

It was a girl child! So what if it was a girl child? Why does Partool's face have sullen expression on it after hearing the news? She was eagerly wishing for a daughter.... There will be a sweet, little daughter who will take care of her future younger brother....

'I hope there is no problem,' the lady doctor asked Rajni with a sense of empathy. Rajni had kept a hand on her chest. She was still trying to come to terms with the painful reality unfolding right before her eyes. Partool was not ready for a daughter. All that he wanted was a son! But how does it make a difference? A boy or a girl—it was their child!

'If you face some problem, let me know. We perform these kinds of cases almost on daily basis. It is as simple as taking a fly out of the ointment.'

She couldn't stop herself from thinking about Partool's behaviour and his stubbornness of wanting to have a son. Despite Rajni's repeated pleadings, Partool did not change his mind. She begged him with her folded hands and went to the extent of saying that she has fallen in love with this unborn girl child of hers. Despite her repeated requests, he remained indifferent.

'Doctor, I have named her Trishna…a word for someone whom the heart desires and longs for…I am going to love her till the very end. She is the apple of my heart, my lifeline…'

'Now…'

As soon as the lady doctor was about to say something, Rajni's mind, once again, dived into memory of her past. He had always been aggressive. In his anger, he often imposed himself on others. On the occasion of learning about Rajni's pregnancy, without her consent, he got an appointment at the welfare centre. After resisting for a long time, eventually, Rajni had to give up before Partool's endless stubbornness.

'Just in case you are scared, that you will not be able to give birth to another child after all this, then rest assured, there is nothing to worry about,' the lady doctor tried to convince the patient calmly.

'This is the safest way of getting rid of an unwanted child…'

Rajni wasn't listening to all this. Her eyes were filled with tears. She did not know what to say…There was darkness before her eyes…She was constantly thinking of Partool. As a newly appointed magistrate, he must now be engaged in attending to some cases in the courtroom. The irony of him being the carrier of justice!

On that specific day, Partool returned home in the evening. Rajni had come back from the welfare centre after doing the necessary formalities. She was still and silent. Partool, almost in a state of ecstasy, pulled her by the arm and kissed her.

'The lady doctor has told me everything,' he said, as he walked into his room, in a state of visible joy, to change his clothes.

Rajni asked a servant to prepare tea for him.

After having tea, he began to prepare to go to the club.

'I don't feel like going today,' Rajni said in a sombre tone.

'You look tired. No worries. However, the doctor was saying that after the cleaning process, Madam was okay.'

'I am okay, my love. Just that today, I don't feel like going.'

Rajni did not go to the club. Throughout the evening, She sat on the lawn in a devasted state and gazed at the sky. She felt as if the sky was very gloomy. A puff of an aroma—at times coming from the left, at times from the right—swayed her. The twinkling rays of the setting sun, like the last signs of hope, appeared to be vanishing into thin air.

When she was tired of sitting outside for long, she decided to come inside for a while and rest on her bed. She began to look at the calendar hung on the wall right before her eyes. She became extremely emotional when she saw the images of laughing and doting kids. It appeared that one out of them would come out of the photo and walk towards her.

She began to cry uncontrollably and said: 'My daughter! My *Trishna*! I long for you!' she uttered these words and looked at the terrace.

She started pleading to the Almighty. She constantly kept on asking for forgiveness from the daughter who could never see the light of the day. In a rather submissive tone, she kept repeating to herself: 'My daughter! Please talk to me. You can give me any punishment that you desire, but please talk to me at least once. Please call me 'mother' at least once. Please forgive me just once.' Days and nights passed, but Rajni could not get over this situation. At times, she hugged her bedsheet, and at times, she caressed her pillow. Her grief was unending.

As she was getting restless, she heard the sound of Partool's car outside. He had returned from the club. She went to the washroom in a state of anxiety. She kept on splashing water on her face repeatedly to assume an air of normalcy.

She came out of the washroom and stood right in front of the dressing table. When Partool saw her, he asked: 'It seems that your eyes have reddened…Is everything okay? You seem to be stressed since morning.'

Then they entered the dining hall while talking to each other.

Gradually, it did begin to seem like Partool-Rajni and their actions were not forgiven by the laws of Nature. They tried once, twice, thrice, four and five times…but Rajni was unable to conceive a child.

Neither could Rajni become a mother again nor could she forget her daughter. After aborting her soon-to-be-born girl-child against her wishes, she got a whole host of religious ceremonies performed. She distributed clothes, fruits, and sweets amongst the poor kids and orphans. None of this though could make her forget the burden of the crime of female foeticide.

Eventually, despite her husband's wealth; the feeling of not knowing what to do with her free time and a situation of an almost nearing mental breakdown, led Rajni to work for a local corporation school. As time passed she became the headmistress of the school because of her long-standing diligence and hard work. Now, in addition to teaching the kids, she also had to manage the administrative roles and other responsibilities of the school. From paperwork to taking care of children's needs to other affairs of the school, Rajni managed everything.

On the day of enrolment of new students, a very interesting incident happened. A young couple had come to get their daughter enrolled at the school. The girl child looked extremely lovely and innocent.

Rajni was not happy with the name of the girl. She asked her parents: 'What is your child's name? If you want to change it, this is the time…This name remains on the school register and stays there forever.' Rajni continued to look at the parents to get a suitable response from them.

The parents got nervous and began to think of a name. Unable to think of a new name, the child's mother looked at Rajni and asked her: 'What is the name of your daughter?'

'Trishna, my daughter's name is Trishna,' replied Rajni with a sense of love and endearment.

'Then you can admit her with the same name. Our daughter too will be called Trishna from today,' said the girl's father.

This became a regular phenomenon. Whensoever a girl child, at the time of her admission in Rajni's school, did not have a proper name, she decided to name her Trishna. In due course, an army of girls in her school were now called Trishna.

They all were Rajni's daughters…There was one or the other girl student in every class with the name Trishna…. They enlivened the environment around her, eased the pain of her heart, and fulfilled the *longing*—her *desire* of having a reflection in her own image. Now she had not one, but many!

Though all of this did not lessen her guilt, it did help her move ahead in life with a sense of warmth in her heart and a glow in her eyes.

Translated from Punjabi by Guntasha Tulsi

Mantra

Premchand

Dusk had fallen. Doctor Chadha was getting ready to play golf. The car stood outside the door and two bearers were seen carrying a palanquin. Behind the palanquin was an old man walking with the help of a stick. The palanquin stopped in front of the dispensary. The old man walked slowly towards the threshold and peeped through the chic blinds on the door. He felt intimidated putting his feet on the clean floor, scared of getting berated. He couldn't gather the courage to speak even when he saw Doctor Sahib there.

Doctor Sahib yelled from behind the blinds, 'Who is there? What do you want?'

The old man pleaded with his hands folded, '*Huzoor*, I am a poor man. For a few days now, my child…'

Doctor Sahib lit the cigar and said, 'Visit me tomorrow morning, tomorrow, morning; I don't see patients now.'

The old man fell on his knees and put his head on the floor and said, 'Have mercy my lord, my boy will die! *Huzoor*, he has not opened his eyes for four days now…'

Doctor Chadha glanced at his wrist. Only ten minutes remained. Taking the golf stick off the hook, he said, 'Visit me in the morning tomorrow, come tomorrow morning; I have a game scheduled for this hour.'

The old man took his turban off and placed it on the threshold. He wept as he exclaimed, '*Huzoor*, please take one look at him. Just one look would be enough! I will lose my son, *Huzoor*, he is the only one left of the seven we had, *Huzoor*. We will die of grief if we lose him, my lord. May you be blessed with a long life, kind sir.'

Such simpleton villagers used to flock there regularly. Doctor Sahib was quite familiar with their character. Whatever one may say to them, they do not pay heed. He slipped the blinds slowly and walked towards the car. The old man ran behind him, repeating, 'Your Honour, do it for good cause! *Huzoor*, have some mercy on the poor and the miserable! I have no one else, sir!'

But Doctor Sahib didn't turn to even look at the old man's face. He sat in the car and said, 'Come tomorrow, in the morning.'

The car left. The old man stood still like a statue for quite a while. He could not come to terms with the reality that there exist such people in the world who could care more for their pleasure, their leisure over someone's life. He was yet to have the piercing realization that the civilized world was so ruthless, so cold. He was one of those old souls, who would always be ready to help in extinguishing a fire, to shoulder the dead, to lift someone's roof, or to settle a strife. Till the time the car was in the old man's sight, he stood still and stared in its direction. He was probably still hoping that the doctor will return. He then asked the bearers to lift the palanquin-bed. The palanquin left for where it came from. He had come to Doctor Chadha after having given up on every other avenue. He had heard great praises about him. After facing disappointment from here, he didn't go anywhere else. He gave up on his luck! On the same night, his lively little seven-year-old boy passed away in the prime of his childhood. He was the only strength of his aging parents. His bright face was the reason for their will to survive. As that lamp doused, their unlit life ahead began to lament in their faces. From their broken hearts came the howling sounds of shattered endearments of old age.

***

Several years passed. Doctor Chadha gained fame and prosperity in abundance, and along with it he also took great care of his health, which was a regular affair for him. It was the result of his disciplined lifestyle, that his agility at the age of fifty could embarrass the youth too. He had a fixed time for each task, and he would strictly adhere to this rule. Often people follow the laws of health when they become sick. Doctor Chadha understood the secret of treatment and abstinence. His child, Sandhya, was also under this strict regime. He had only two children, a boy, and a girl. They didn't have a third child, so Mrs Chadha also looked quite young. The girl was already married. The boy studied in college. His parents' life revolved around him. A model of character and modesty, he was quite passionate, utterly generous, pride of the college, the grace of youth and society. His countenance brimmed with brightness. Today was his twentieth birth anniversary.

It was evening. Chairs were spread across on the lawn. The nobles and dignitaries of the city were on one side, and on the other side, college students were having their meals. The whole area was shining bright with the fancy light arrangements. Means of merriment were also put together. There was to be a short skit, which was written by Kailash Nath. He was also the main actor.

He was wearing a silk shirt, bare-headed, barefoot, and was moving around, hosting his friends. Some would call, 'Kailash, would you come here,' someone else called from another direction 'Kailash, are you going to stay there?' Everyone was teasing him, making a joke or two; the poor one did not get a chance to catch his breath. Suddenly a beautiful woman came up to him and asked, 'Why Kailash, where are your snakes? Would you show me those?'

Kailash shook hands with her and said, 'Mrinalini, forgive me this once. I will show those to you tomorrow.'

Mrinalini urged, 'Not at all, you have to, I will not listen to you today. You put it on "tomorrow" each time!'

Mrinalini and Kailash were both classmates and were in love with each other. Kailash was fond of raising snakes and making them perform and dance. He had kept a variety of snakes. He used to test their behaviour and character. A few days back, he gave a lecture on 'snakes' in the university.

He even showed some snakes' dance! Even the great scholars of Zoology were stunned to hear his lecture! He had picked these skills and learned about this field of study from a well-known snake charmer. He traced people who had such herbs and made all efforts to collect them.

If he ever comes to know even something as small as that there is a person who has some good herbs, it could get him quite restive. He used to make sure that he gets those herbs. This was an addiction. He had splurged thousands of rupees on this.

Mrinalini had visited Kailash many times but had never been so eager to see the snakes. It was unclear why today she was so curious to see the snakes, or it could be that she wanted to demonstrate her authority over Kailash. Nevertheless, her insistence was not well suited for the occasion. She didn't care about the cell getting crowded, or if the snakes would get fidgety because of the crowd, and how bad it would be to tease them at night.

Kailash said, 'No, I will definitely show them to you tomorrow. At this time, I will not be able to show them properly, and there will be no space in the room at all.'

One gentleman teased, 'Why don't you show them, why are you delaying and diverging such a tiny thing? Miss Govind, you must not give up. We will see how he doesn't show them to us!' Another man added more fuel to the ongoing heated conversation, 'Miss Govind is so gullible and naive, that's why you show such tantrums; had it been any other beautiful woman, she would have been annoyed with you on this matter.' A third man took a jibe, 'Ah, she would have stopped speaking with you. Well, this is not fair. And here you are, usually claiming that you can give up your life for Mrinalini!'

Mrinalini noticed that these rogues were putting her under the spotlight, and thus exclaimed, 'All of you do not have to patronize me, I can advocate on my behalf. I do not want to see the snakes-parade right now. Never mind, it's done.'

Their friends ridiculed this. One sahib said, 'Even if you want to see everything, one has to be willing to show it to you!'

Kailash, on sensing awkwardness in Mrinalini's countenance, realized that his denial at the moment had really hurt her. As soon as the feast was over and the singing began, he took Mrinalini and other friends in front of the cell where the snakes were kept and started playing the *mauar.** Then, opening one section at a time, he started to take out each snake. Ah! That was wonderful!

It appeared that those reptiles understood each and everything that Kailash did and could sense his mind. He picked up one snake, placed one of them around his neck, wrapped another around his hand. Mrinalini repeatedly asked him, 'Don't put them around the neck, show them from a distance. Just make them dance a little.' Seeing the snakes clinging to Kailash's neck petrified her. She was regretting, and said nervously, 'I only vainly asked you to show the snakes…,' but Kailash did not listen. Why would

* Musical instrument made from a hollow gourd, used by snake charmers, also known as '*bīn*' or '*pungī*.'

he miss such an opportunity to put on a snake-show in front of his girlfriend!

Then, a friend commented, 'Their teeth must have been broken.'

Kailash laughed and said, 'Only *madaris*, the ropedancers, break their teeth. None of these snakes have their teeth broken. Shall I show them, if you will?'

Saying this, he caught a black snake and said, 'I have no bigger and poisonous snake than this, if it bites, the man will die in no time. And I am not talking about unconsciousness. There is no mantra to cure it. Shall I show its teeth?'

Mrinalini pleaded, 'No-no, Kailash, let it be, for God's sake. I beg you.'

On this, another friend said, 'I do not believe you, but if you say so, I will agree.'

Kailash grabbed the snake by its neck and said, 'No sir, believe it by witnessing it. If you break the tooth and control it, then what? Snakes are very intelligent! If it trusts that this man will not harm me, it will not bite him.'

When Mrinalini saw that at this point Kailash was not going to give up, she suggested ideas to avoid this show. She said, 'Ah, everyone, now let us all move from here. Look, the music has started too. Today I will also sing something.' Saying this, she held Kailash's shoulder and gestured towards leaving, and exited the room; but Kailash was insistent on proving his opponents' assumptions wrong. He grabbed the snake's neck and pressed it vigorously, so much so that its face turned red, and all the veins of its body were distressed.

The snake was not accustomed to such conduct. It could not fathom what was expected of it. It had probably assumed that Kailash wanted to kill it, so it got defensive.

Kailash pressed its neck to open its mouth, showing its poisonous teeth; he gloated, 'Come and see for yourself, any gentlemen who may have been skeptical. Do you believe now or still have any doubt?' His friends came to see its teeth and were shocked. What is suspicion against direct evidence? Kailash loosened the snake's neck and sought to keep it on the ground, but it was furious with rage. As soon as the grip on its neck became lighter, it lifted its head to bite Kailash's finger, and then glided away from there. Blood started dripping from Kailash's finger.

He pressed his finger hard and ran towards his room. There was an herb in the drawer of the table, which could be grounded and applied to even the most toxic venom-bites, and the venom could become impotent. There was a stir among friends. By now the news had spread in the gathering outside. Doctor Sahib ran in panic. Immediately, the area around the finger was tightly wrapped, and the herbs were given away for grinding. Doctor Sahib was not convinced of the herb's effectiveness. He wanted to put a cut across the affected portion of the finger using a scalpel, but Kailash had full faith in the herb.

Mrinalini was sitting at the piano. As soon as she heard the news she ran and started wiping with a handkerchief the blood that was dripping from Kailash's finger. The herb was still being ground, however, by now Kailash's eyes were blinking faster than usual and his lips grew pale. He couldn't manage to stand. He sat on the floor. All the guests gathered in the room. There was a lot of buzz and commotion in the room. Someone muttered something. Others mumbled something else. Meanwhile, the herbs arrived. Mrinalini applied it to the affected finger. One more minute passed. Kailash's eyes were now shut. He lied down and gestured, fanning with his hand. His mother ran and put his head in her lap and an electric table-fan was placed across.

Doctor Sahib bent and asked Kailash, 'How are you feeling?' Kailash raised his hands at a slow pace; but could not speak anything. Mrinalini said in a compassionate voice, 'Will the herbs be effective?' The doctor answered holding his head, 'What do I say, I believed him. Now, even a cut will not do any good.'

Things remained the same for half an hour. Kailash's condition kept deteriorating. Even his eyes were tired, his hands and feet became cold, his face became duller, and his pulse was mellow too. These were all signs of death that had started to surface. There was a furor in the house. In one corner of the room Mrinalini was banging her head, and at the other corner his mother was wailing. Doctor Chadha was held together by his friends, or else he would have killed himself with the scalpel.

A man said, 'If you find someone who can chant healing mantras, it could still be possible to save his life.'

A Muslim gentleman said, 'Sir, even the dead bodies in the tombs have come alive. There are many such miracles known.'

Doctor Chadha said, 'I was foolish that I believed him. A cut or a minor surgery would have worked. I kept telling him, repeatedly, son, don't pet snakes, but he never listened to me! Call them, call some charmer. They can take away everything that belongs to me, I will put all my property at his feet. I will renunciate everything and leave the house; but my Kailash, my beloved Kailash should stay alive. Call someone for God's sake!'

A gentleman among the guests knew a charmer. He ran and called him. But on seeing Kailash, the charmer did not dare to chant anything. He said, 'What can happen now, my lord? Whatever was to happen has happened now.'

Oh fool, why don't you say that what was really supposed to happen, all of that has not happened yet? Why haven't the parents seen their son getting married? Why could Mrinalini's desires not bear any fruit? Were the golden dreams, that made life a source of joy, fulfilled? Did his boat get submerged in pleasure while sailing through the star-lit sea that is life? Rather, what should not have happened has happened.

The field outside was green all the same, the same golden moonlight prevailed over nature like silent music; there remained the same friends and the same people. The same entertainment items stood outside. But where there was a sound of humour, there was now a flow of tears and woe.

***

Several miles away from the city, an old man and an old woman were spending their winter nights in front of the brazier in a tiny house. The old man was drinking coconut water and coughing in between. The old woman was staring at the fire with her head fixed between both her knees. A kerosene lamp was burning on the ledge. There was no cot in the house, nor any bed. There was some straw lying on one side. There was only one stove in this dungeon. The old woman used to collect cow dung and dry wood all day long. The old man used to cut and sell rope in the market. That was their livelihood. Nobody saw them crying or laughing. All their time was spent in trying to survive. Death was standing at their door, where was the time to cry or laugh!

The old woman asked, 'Is there any hemp left for tomorrow, what will you do?'

'I will go borrow ten *ser*** from that Jhagdu Sahu?' the man replied.

'You have not returned the money that he had lent you earlier, why will he lend you more?'

***

'If he doesn't give it, then it's up to him. The grass has not gone anywhere. Won't I be able to cut two rupees worth of it by noon?'

Meanwhile, a man called for them at the door, 'Bhagat, Bhagat, have you fallen asleep? Could you open the door?'

** A measure of the weight of about one kilogram.

Bhagat stood up and opened the door. The man came inside and exclaimed, 'Did you hear, Doctor Chadha's son has been bitten by a snake.'

Bhagat was shocked, he spoke, 'Chadha babu's son! It is the same Chadha babu, isn't it, who stays in a bungalow in the camp area?'

'Yes, indeed. There is chaos all over the city. If you go, you could earn a fortune!'

The old man nodded harshly and said, 'I will not go! It's not my problem! He is the great Chadha. He knows enough. I had gone to him with my dying son, sir. He was about to go to play. I fell on his feet and pleaded to him to take a look at my boy, but he did not even speak properly to me. God witnessed it, heard it. Now he will know what the grief of losing a son is like. He must have several sons.'

'No, this is his only boy. From what I have learned, everyone has given up,' the man replied.

'God is the creator and the breaker. I had tears in my eyes at that moment, but he did not feel any pity at all. I would not have attended to him even if I had been present right at their door,' Bhagat replied angrily.

'Will you not go then? Well, I have told you what I had heard,' the man added rather helplessly.

'Well done, well done, indeed. My heart is at rest now, my eyes are at rest now. That boy must be resting now too! You should go. Today I will sleep peacefully. (To the old lady) Pass me some tobacco! I will smoke some more! Now he will know, that Sahib. All his Sahibi, his lordship, will leave him now. It doesn't affect us. With the death of our son, we haven't exactly missed out on any empire of our own. Where six kids had died, one more passed away. His entire empire has fallen apart now, indeed. It was for his son, that he gathered pennies over the dead bodies, right? What will he do now? I will go to see him once, definitely, I will. But only after a few days, to ask him how he fares,' Bhagat replied stubbornly.

The man left. Bhagat shut the doors, and then he put tobacco on his pot and started to smoke.

The old lady said, 'Who will go out in the cold at this hour anyway?'

'*Arey*, I would not have gone even if it were daytime. Even if he came with his posh ride at my door, I would not have gone. I think of Panna's face all the time. This ruthless one did not even take a look at him. Did I not know that he would not survive? I knew Chadha was not a god, that his gaze wouldn't have dripped any nectar. No, that was an empty head's doing. Now someday I will go and tell him. Why Sahib, say, how are you doing? The world will call me evil; I don't care. Poor men are the ones with defects, right! These rich ones don't have any flaws, they are gods!' Bhagat uttered angrily.

For Bhagat, this was the first time in his life that he had been sitting on such news. Never had it happened in his life of 80 years that he did not run as soon as he would hear the news related to a snake. He never cared for the dark nights of Magh-Paush, the scorching sun, and heatwave of Chait-Baisakh, the rivers and rivulets of Sawan-Bhadon. He used to go out of the house immediately—selfless, self-sacrificing! The idea of a transaction never crossed his mind too. This was not the kind of thing for him. Who can place a value on life? It was a virtuous act. Hundreds of hopeless cases were given life by his mantras; but this time, he could not make it out of the house. He was going to sleep on hearing this news.

The old lady said, 'Tobacco is kept near the brazier. Even today's lot was worth two and a half paise. She wasn't willing to give it to me.'

Saying this, the old lady rested. The old man extinguished the lamp, stood for a while, then sat down. Later, he also laid down; but this news continued to burden his heart. He felt as if he had lost something, as if all his clothes were wet or his feet were covered with mud, as if someone was sitting in his mind reproaching him to go out of the house. The old lady started snoring in a while. Old people sleep while talking and wake up at the slightest noise. Bhagat got up, picked up his stick, and slowly opened the door.

The old lady asked, 'Where are you going?'

'Nowhere, I was just seeing how late it is.'

'It's too late, go to sleep.'

'I can't sleep.'

'Why will you sleep? Your mind is at Chadha's house.'

'What kind of virtue has Chadha bestowed upon me, why should I go there? Even if he comes and begs, I will not go.'

'Didn't you wake up with this intention though?'

'No, I am not crazy that I should sow flowers for those who offered me thorns.' The old man replied.

At this, the old lady fell asleep again. Bhagat shut the doors, came back, and sat down. But his condition was like those who are listening to the sermon, but on the side, music starts playing. While their eyes may be towards the commander; their ears attend to the instruments. The sound of the instrument keeps echoing in the heart too. But one does not get up from their place, in fear of facing embarrassment. Bhagat was influenced by a sense of ruthless rebellion, but his heart kept going out to the hapless young man who was dying at the moment, for whom a delay of even one moment was fatal.

He then opened the doors so slowly that the old lady did not even notice. He came out. At that moment, the watchman was patrolling the village and asked, 'Why are you up, Bhagat? It is so cold today! Are you going somewhere?'

Bhagat said, 'No, where will I go! It is quite late. Well, what is the time anyway?'

The watchman said, 'Must be one o' clock, I think, I was returning from the police station, there was a big crowd outside Chadha babu's house. You must have heard about the condition of his boy; a reptile has stung him. He might be dead by now. If you go, he might get saved. I have heard, they are ready to give up to a thousand rupees.'

Bhagat thought to himself, 'I will not go even if they give me a million rupees. What do I have to do with ten thousand or ten lakhs? Tomorrow I will die, then who is going to use it?'

The watchman left. Bhagat stepped forward. Much like a drunken man, his body movement was not under his control. Bhagat walked recklessly, falling here and there, said one thing, and something else would come out of his mouth. There was retaliation in his mind, and his actions were disconnected from his thoughts. For one who has never wielded a sword, they cannot attempt to do it even when they intend to. Their hands tremble, their bodies do not move at all. Using his stick, Bhagat walked in big leaps and steps. While his conscious mind inhibited him, his subconscious conscience pushed him further. The servant controlled the master.

Halfway to the house, Bhagat suddenly stopped. Cruelty overpowered the venture—I have come so far. What did I have to die for this winter? Why did I not sleep comfortably? I might not have been able to sleep; I could have sung two or four *bhajans*. I have come running so far but in vain. What do I care if Chadha's boy lives or dies! What did they do for me, that I should do anything for them? Thousands die, thousands live. What do I care if anyone lives or dies!

But his subconscious mind had now taken another form. He finally decided that which was very close to cruel—he will not visit as a charmer, he decided; instead, he will go and see what people are doing. He will see the doctor beating his chest and crying and beating himself up, how he beats his own head, how he wails! Those are learned people; they must know how to stay calm! In such a state of violence, he moved forward again.

Meanwhile, he saw two men coming in his direction. Both were walking as they discussed—'Chadha Babu's family is now destroyed, he was their only son.' As these voices reached Bhagat's ear, his steps became even faster. His feet weren't moving much due to fatigue. His head became heavier as if he was going to fall on his face. He must have walked for ten minutes in this state, when he finally saw Doctor Sahib's bungalow. Electric lights were burning, yet there was silence everywhere. There was no sound of crying or mourning. Bhagat's heart started pounding faster. Am I too late? He started running. He had never run so fast in his lifetime. It was as if death was chasing him.

***

It was two o' clock. The guests had all retired from the venue. Only the stars in the sky were left among those who cried. And everyone else was too tired of it. People looked at the sky with great eagerness, waiting for the morning hour, so that the dead body could be put into the lap of river Ganga.

Suddenly, Bhagat reached the gate and called for the Doctor. Doctor Sahib assumed some patient must have come. On any other day he would have turned the person down; but today, he came out. He saw an old man, waist bent, toothless mouth, eyebrows that had turned white. Shaking as he was standing with the help of his stick. He said very humbly, 'Brother, today we have got such a problem that I can't muster words to say something too, could you come again sometime. I assume, at least for a month, I may not be able to see any patient.'

Bhagat said, 'I have heard Babuji, that is why I have come here. Where is the boy? Let me take a look at him. God is a great repairer; he can raise a dead person back from their grave. Who knows, he may still show mercy.'

Chadha said in a distressed voice, 'Come on then, take a look. But it has been three to four hours. Everything is over now. Many charmers have come and gone.'

Doctor Sahib was not hopeful. Yet, he pitied the old man. He took him inside. Bhagat looked at the corpse for a minute. Then he smiled and said, '—It's not over yet, Babuji! If God be willing, then in a matter of half-hour your boy should be back up. You shouldn't lose hope yet. Just ask the palanquin bearers to fetch some water.'

The palanquin bearers brought water and started bathing Kailash. But the pipe stopped working. The number of palanquin bearers was not high, so the guests began filling water from the well outside, in the yard, and passed water to the palanquin bearers. Mrinalini too fetched water in a small beaker. Old Bhagat stood there and smiled as he recited mantras, as if victory was standing right there, right in front of him. Once the mantras were over, he put an herb on Kailash's head, and several times again, Bhagat chanted more mantras.

Eventually, as dawn painted the sky maroon, Kailash's eyes also opened, maroon all the same. Right at that moment, he stretched and asked for water. Doctor Chadha ran and embraced Narayani. Narayani ran and fell at Bhagat's feet and a teary eyed Mrinalini began to ask Kailash,—'How do you feel!'

In no time the news began to spread. Friends started coming to congratulate the family. Doctor Sahib was singing Bhagat's praises, holding him in high esteem. All the people became eager to see Bhagat; but when they went inside and checked, Bhagat could not be found anywhere. The servants said, '—he was sitting with his chillum right here, just about a few moments ago. When we started giving tobacco, he did not take it, and filled it with the tobacco he brought with him.'

As the search for Bhagat went all around, he was rushing home, wanting to reach before the old lady woke up!

When the guests left, Doctor Sahib told Narayani, 'We have no idea where that old man went. He didn't take even a small piece of chillum-tobacco from us.'

Narayani said, 'I had thought, I will give him a huge amount of money.'

Chadha replied, 'I did not recognize him in the dark, but it became clear to me a little later. Once before, he had brought a patient with him. I remember now..., that I was going out for a game and had refused to see the patient. As I am remembering that day, the immense guilt that I feel cannot be put into words. I will make sure that I find him, and I shall fall on his feet, I will ask for forgiveness for my heinous crime. I know, he will not take anything from me, he was born instead to shower prosperity onto others. His kindness will lead me by example, for the rest of my life.'

Translated from Hindi by Kanupriya Dhingra

Doctor Moni

Bibhutibhushan Bandyopadhyay

Thank goodness the heat of the summer had subsided with the advent of monsoon; how tedious was it to survive the summer days! Is there at all a cool breeze in this marketplace, albeit it is surrounded by gardens?

I couldn't do much here either despite living for one and a half years. It isn't just about this village, but have I done anything at all in this life of almost 33 years? I have been an itinerant soul; travelling from one place to another, but neither did I manage to consolidate my practice, nor fetch a steady clientele. Bag anchara, Kalaroa, Simultali, Satrajitpur, Bagan Gaon, how many villages should I keep naming? In none of these settings could my trade last for more than three months. When I came here, to Palashpur, my practice was initially good. I thought God had finally showered His grace on me. But heaven knows what happened after that; it has been months since I have brought a penny home.

In retrospect, I feel that I had a really good time when I worked at Kundu babu's depot in Shyambazar. One of my contacts from my village got me that job. I used to keep their books; my employers loved my handwriting. I lasted there for eight or nine months. During that period, I made the most of whatever Kolkata had to offer—the zoological garden, museums, bioscopes, theatres, Pareshnath's garden, the temple in Kalighat! What a marvel Kolkata was!

After I lost that job, I felt nauseated at the prospect of slaving for others. I thought becoming a doctor would grant me the autonomy I craved for. I talked Kundu babu's house physician into making me his apprentice at his dispensary. I bought and read a couple of books in the vernacular as well. I learned the trade in a couple of months. Ever since then, I left home and wandered from one district to another in this far-off Jashore in search of fortune.

Brahmins did not inhabit this village. There were a handful of lower caste dairymen and oil pressers and the rest were Muslims. There was not a single concrete house in Palashpur; people were mostly poor; most of them lived in straw-thatched huts. This village wasn't that populated either. If you asked me why I came to offer my services as a doctor here, I would cite one of the reasons to be the bi-weekly market for all the nearby villages that was organized in this place. It wasn't really a big deal but quite a lot of people from different villages gathered here on Wednesdays and Saturdays.

At the marketplace square, there were a few straw-thatched huts, one of which was the erstwhile accounts office of the Gangulys of Sobaipur. This accounts office was also a temporary settlement, made of straw and devoid of proper walls. At that time of the year when revenues were to be collected, the zamindar's chief accountant visited this place for a couple of months, accrued the dues, and left. Therefore, nobody really cared about the well being of this hut. It was in a terrible state; there were rat holes all over the floor. The roof wasn't sturdy enough to resist the rain. During storms, one wouldn't be safe in spite of being indoors. I, however, implored their manager to let me stay here.

I lived alone. Like every other village in this part of the world, this village too was full of woods, bamboo groves, and ancient mango plantations. On three sides of the marketplace, there were dense bamboo groves and mango plantations, on the other side there was a jungle, walking through which one would touch the Betrabati river, locally called Betna. Due to the thick forest canopy the marketplace square looked dark even during daytime. As soon as dusk approached, one or two traders, who had shops here, shut their enterprises and went home. Soon the marketplace became gloomy and lonely, fireflies glimmered in the woods, once in a while the rotten stench of the blossoming *ghetkol* flower filled the air, an owl hooted from the branches of the simul tree in the north. I sat alone cooking my rice. At times, I took out my one-stringed instrument and sang to my solitude.

I have not earned a single penny in the past six or seven months. I have advertised extensively in the market that I would charge 25 paise for my service, with an additional paisa per dose of medicine. Yet I couldn't get a patient! To my luck, Mujibur Rahman was a nice man. He had been selling me rice and lentils on credit for months now. That's how I managed to survive.

Last month a case of pneumonia was detected in Damu Ghosh's household in Gowalpara. Mujibur had an influential presence here; I asked him to recommend me. In spite of that, they finally summoned the quack *kabiraj* (herbalist) Abinash Sekra of Balarampur. They had immense faith in his abilities!

I have had my share of trouble with Subhasini as well. Ever since I married her, I dumped her at her father's place. I haven't managed to gift her a decent saree in all these years. A sum of eight or nine rupees is needed to pay for my son's milk. My mother-in-law sends incessant reminders, but where would I get that money? I barely manage to make a living for myself! She was evidently not satisfied with me; she assumed that I was making a fortune by practicing medicine.

No one would believe but I have been surviving only on rice for five months now. Although this is a village, nothing was produced here. Thus, vegetables were extensive; bitter gourds came at two annas a pound, potatoes cost six paise a kg. The fish wasn't priced at anything below six annas. To avoid public knowledge, I would wake up at the break of dawn and walk to the riverside at times to pick up obscure leaves and roots. This is the season of ripe mangoes; so, may be eat one of those with rice. But there have been days when I've consumed rice with only a pinch of salt.

I might not be a qualified practitioner, but how does that matter? Can't one learn medicine by sitting at home and reading a book or two? I have been at it for about seven or eight years now; am I not rich in the experience? Don't patients die even when they're treated by a qualified doctor? Could Doctor Indu of Dhopakhali save milkwoman Bidhu's daughter from dying?

Could anyone explain why malicious rumours were spread that Doctor Moni's medicine kills even the liveliest of men? Maybe I was poor, so nobody took my side; nobody, except Mujibur. He had been selling me essentials from his shop on credit for four or five months now. Otherwise, I would have died of hunger. No one had done even an inch of the favours Mujibur had done for me. I could never repay that debt.

These were absolutely rustic places. The nearest railway station was more than 20 miles away. There was not a single sizeable trading centre nearby; people were grossly uneducated. Rather than calling in a doctor when they were sick, they relied on native, unscientific measures. They preferred to summon an exorcist who claimed they were under the spell of an evil spirit. There was no tradition of seeking proper medical help.

I haven't visited home for one-and-a-half years now. I haven't been home ever since I was in Satrajitpur for a while, before moving to Palashpur. By home, I mean my in-laws' place. It has been a long time since I have had something to reckon as home. To reach my in-laws, I needed to walk 16 miles to the nearest railway station in Navaran. After traveling on a train to Maslandpur, I had to deboard and take a bus to Kholapota. Thereupon, I also had to take a toy train to Hasnabad and finally sail through the Ichhamati river on a boat for six to seven hours to reach my in-laws' place. It cost a sum of three or four rupees. Whenever I managed to earn that much, I sent a money order to Subhasini, although there have hardly been many instances when I have made that much at one go in the past two years. If I didn't transfer money, my wife had to face the caustic wrath of my mother-in-law and widowed sister-in-law.

So, the last time when I was returning from my in-laws, as I finished my meal and was about to take the boat, Subhasini called me to the corner and said, 'Do not keep me here for long. Take me along as soon as you can.'

'Would you be able to manage in those villages?' I asked.

'As if I am living in a metropolis right now! Wherever you live is my city. The endless stream of my sister's humiliating remarks makes me want to hang myself at times, or better, drown myself in the river,' Subhasini replied, sounding frustrated.

'I can understand everything, Subhi. Let me settle in someplace and I would definitely come to take you with me. Do you think I am happy being separated from you? But I am helpless…'

Just as I stepped out of the door, my mother-in-law, as if waiting for her prey, pounced on me and said, 'Don't you dare disappear, son. Our lives are rather pathetic here. I am not well; how can I support so many dependents? I owe a lot of money to the milkman; my daughter spends her days in tattered clothes; how can I bear that sight as a mother? I got her a pair of new sarees; I haven't yet managed to pay for that. You vanish into thin air when you leave, what do I do, what kind of a man does this…' She went on and on!

After that, I haven't visited my in-laws for more than one-and-a-half years now, although whatever little I earned, I mailed it addressed to Subhasini. But, keeping in mind the cost of living, the amount was less than meagre. But what am I to do? I can't seek resort in chicanery or dacoity!

Frankly speaking, I did not have the opportunity of living together with Subhasini ever in my life. Initially, I thought that I would be able to make a living and bring her over. But it has been six or seven years that I am married and I never got that chance. How long could one stay with the in-laws? As the son-in-law, if I spend ten days instead of two, it would be a gross overstay of my welcome! Thus, I left their daughter in their custody and went out in search of a job. My mother-in-law had started to demonstrate clear signs of disgust. I read her hints and moved away smartly. After all, one cannot forsake one's honour!

One day I got to know that there was a vacancy of a teacher in a school in Pankhola. I spend a few hours every day at Mujibur Rahman's shop to talk about life's woes and wonders; he suggested that I should apply.

I got back home and thought about it. I have been practicing medicine for seven or eight years now and haven't quite succeeded to make ends meet. But if I manage to get a permanent job, then, whatever paltry the sum might be, I'd have something stable to rely upon.

I asked around and found out that Srinath Das of Makarandapur was the secretary of that school. The next morning, I set out for Makrandapur.

I crossed the river on a boat by 8 in the morning. A kid was accompanying me. After walking for a while in the fields, he pointed at a banyan tree and instructed, 'Take that road, Babu, the road on the left!'

The sun was right above my head. I crossed a canal by foot and reached a mango grove. The groves were quite dense in this part of the world. After painstakingly finding my way through the grove, I ended in front of a mansion. A lot of courtly architectural marvels crossed my path. Most of them were ancient; saplings had grown on their dilapidated walls. I crossed the village and sat under a banyan tree to catch my breath. I felt thirsty. I should have stopped at someone's place and asked for water. I had to walk past vast meadows now and wasn't sure if there would be any human inhabitation.

I resumed walking again. On my way, there were quite a few villages inhabited predominantly by agricultural workers. But I was a brahmin and couldn't stake the honour of my caste by asking for water in these areas!

I walked past Sundarpur, Chatra, Noldi, Mamudpur…

I ended up in another vast field. It was past noon by then. I was famished, I craved for a meal, at least a gulp of water. Hasn't the district board installed a water pump in any of these villages? Is there not even a pond nearby?

When I finished traversing that long highway and came across a river, it was almost dusk. I discovered that the ferry service office was deserted, the ferry covered in weeds, and absolutely no one around!

What menace! I wondered how to cross the river? I enquired at a peasant village nearby and learnt that the ferry service stopped operating months ago because of the thick outgrowth of weeds. One had to walk for miles downstream to Khalishpur to avail the ferry.

It was too painstaking to walk for miles at this state to board the ferry at Khalishpur. After further enquiry I was told that one could walk for half a mile and reach a simul tree where the river could be crossed by foot.

I walked that half a mile and found the simul tree, but the depth of the water didn't seem any less. I got into the water; its level transcended my ankles and went up to my hips. Gradually up to my chest, eventually I was neck-deep in water. My clothes were wet and soggy. When the water touched my nose, I was tiptoeing my way through. It was dark and desolate around. I was afraid if a crocodile would attack me. There might not be huge crocodiles around, but it wouldn't be surprising to encounter a few fish-eating alligators!

Finally, I managed to reach the other side of the river. There was not a single household around. I couldn't see a trace of light! Two roads diverged in the middle of the field; I wasn't sure which one would take me to Makarandapur. The left one or the right? There was not a single soul around to guide me. Alas, my luck betrayed me. The path I took was the wrong one. I walked half a mile and reached a Bagdi household to learn that I should have taken the other road.

I, thus, returned to that confluence and took the path on the right. That road led me into a jungle. There was a dense outgrowth of mango trees, bamboo plants, and different weeds. I knew this place would be infested with tigers that often preyed on domestic animals. One of my patients once saw the wrath of the paws of such a tiger on his shoulder.

It was getting darker. I was too exhausted to walk. There were ripe mangoes scattered on the path. The mangoes of this region did not fetch much of a price; therefore, nobody bothered to pick them up. I tripped on the mangoes as I walked. At least I didn't step on a snake! My medicinal practices would have promptly ended at that moment.

Eventually, I reached Makarandapur. It was about 9 pm in the night. I took shelter at Srinath Das's household. However, I didn't get the job. My journey was in vain. The next morning, Srinath told me that they wouldn't be hiring anyone this month, perhaps, recruitment would be in October. The school was poorly funded. The district board sends an allowance of ten rupees and twenty-five paise every month and that's all that they rely on. The student fees didn't exceed a few paise; it was not feasible to hire two teachers. Srinath asked to enquire once again in October.

It was a lost case. What would I live on till October that I could wait to apply for the post of a second teacher? The salary was five rupees. The headmaster was paid nine rupees per month.

I returned to Palashpur the next evening after walking for an entire day. I was exasperated. My feet were almost falling apart. Mujibur asked me, 'What happened Doctor Babu?' I told him everything. Then I got into my dark and dingy hut and lit my broken lantern. I washed my hands and face at the river and spread my mat and laid down. I was starving, but I didn't have the energy to cook. I satiated my hunger with a few mangoes that night.

I kept having so many stray thoughts laying in darkness. I had to live all alone; I didn't have anyone to share my miseries with me. Perhaps, this was the worst of my woes. I felt like bringing my wife over. I haven't seen her for so long. At lcast she could take care of me! After I would return from a hard day's work, how I wished she would wait for me and hear what I had to say. At least that could have been a source of happiness. But how would that be possible? What shall I feed her?

It was even darker in the marketplace square. There were just a couple of shops, but the shopkeepers had closed them and gone away. I could see the fireflies glimmering in the darkness of the trees. I could hear bats flapping their wings on the branch of a foreign tree.

It was quite late into the night, but I had trouble sleeping. It was so sultry and humid! I could hear the sonata of mangoes falling on the ground in the orchards nearby as I laid alone.

My life was acquiring more boredom as each day passed. I woke up every morning, walked by the river and then returned to the marketplace square. I limited the length of my walks; what if a patient came by and didn't find me? I remained at my dispensary all day hoping for their arrival.

I open my damned eyes as I sit under the canopy of a majestic tree
I indulge in delusions as I feel I would find your lotus feet
My heart keeps trembling…

Who else could I visit here? There was not a single upper-caste gentleman I could spend my time chatting with in this predominantly agricultural village. My world here was confined to a cycle between my broken shanty of a dispensary and Mujibur Rahman's grocery store. On some evenings I strolled by the lake in Pipilipara and watched how the lower-caste bagdi people caught fish using their clothes from their little boats. I picked up a few herbs and greens for myself on some days. I have been surviving on mangoes and rice since summer. How long could I possibly eat the same thing?

I was not destined for fame. Yesterday, in the other neighbourhood, the oil miller, Bishu's son got bitten by a snake in his mill. I ran as soon as I heard the news. Nobody summoned me; but how could one sit silently upon hearing such a tiding? I bandaged his leg as soon as I reached as I pressed a strip of potassium permanganate on the wound. Meanwhile, their neighbours brought in a quack. The quack came in and ordered to take off the bandage. He performed his usual tricks and the kid was cured. His tricks made no difference; it was my treatment that brought him back to life. But the quack stole the limelight. I don't regret this. I'm honoured that my services managed to save someone's life.

I could put up with hunger. But the boredom of this lonely life was killing me. I sat and dreamt and strived to while away my existential angst.

At times I thought what I might do if I ever hit the jackpot. I would definitely bring over Subhasini and my child. Mujibur had offered me a piece of land by the river; I would probably raise a straw hut there. There would be a garden full of flowers around that hut. In these summer evenings, I would pick some flowers and bring them over to adorn Subhasini's hair. I would speak to the magistrate in charge of this locality and arrange some land for tilling. Once I began to reap the grains, affluence would come by itself.

On an autumn day as I sat in my dispensary, I saw a little girl looking for something near the marketplace square. Our eyes crossed and she stared at me.

I asked her, 'What are you looking for there, little girl?'

The girl replied rather bashfully, '*Ghetkol* roots.'

'What would you do with that?' I asked, sounding rather curious.

'We eat those roots,' she replied.

I wasn't aware of that. If I knew those roots were edible, I wouldn't have had to worry about my entrees. I was aware that there were a lot of *ghetkol* shrubs around the marketplace square, but I didn't know how they looked like. I did hear its name though.

I asked, 'Oh, show me how it looks like?'

The girl replied, 'See there? It resembles a *kochu* plant. But the leaves have three folds.'

'How do you eat it?' I asked.

'Whichever way one likes. You can stir-fry, make it into a curry… Should I pick a bunch for you?' the girl replied.

I wouldn't deny I showed off a bit. How could I eat some obscure root in spite of being a doctor? Even if I do, I would do it out of pity for that unnamed plant. That's the kind of image I wanted to put up.

I said, 'Who would cook that? Does anyone know the recipe here?'

The girl taught me to stir-fry those roots, even picked up a bunch for me.

Before she left, she observed my kitchen and asked, 'Who else lives here?'

'I do.'

'That's apparent. I was wondering who lived with you. Who does the cooking?' she asked.

'Nobody. I do everything myself.'

Probably she took mercy on me upon hearing that, because after that day, whenever she came to the marketplace square to pick up those roots, she would pick a bunch for me as well.

She came in the mornings, at times in the afternoon. On one such afternoon, as I sat by myself, she came and brought some figs for me and said, 'I plucked some from the trees near the pond earlier today. I got two for you!'

I never asked that girl what her name was. She was pretty, had big, dreamy eyes; probably she was eighteen or nineteen years old. She was remarkably fair, a bit uncanny a complexion in these parts of the world. But I could figure out that she didn't hail from an upper-caste household. The other day, I enquired and found out that she was the daughter of Bidhu, the milkmaid. Her name was probably Premlata; they call her Pramo. She had been widowed at a tender age, which was not uncommon among the milkmaids here.

The girl stood for a while and asked, 'Haven't you married, sir?'

'Why would I not marry?' I replied.

'Then why don't you bring your wife over? You wouldn't have to take the trouble of cooking then.'

'Yes, you are right. I'm thinking of bringing her over soon.'

'Are your parents still alive?'

'No.'

'Where's your original home?'

'Far away. You wouldn't know.'

This is how we bonded. Pramo used to visit me regularly, either in the morning or in the evening. She brought figs, bulbous plants, occasionally a round-shaped fruit…whatever she picked for herself, she ensured to get some for me to my delight. At times, she used to stand on the porch and engage in long conversations. That simple beautiful girl picked woods, plucked vegetables, and did whatever she could to dispense her mother's misery. In the same vein, she took it upon herself to make sure that this impoverished doctor had food on his plate. I began to admire her. She tied in a string of empathy, and I thought I reciprocated that. I loved the company of a kind woman in the solitude of the marketplace in Palashpara. Therefore, I was happy whenever she dropped by. Slowly, the frequency of her visits increased. She made excuses to come over, at times without rhyme or reason. She talked her heart out for hours whenever she arrived.

One day I noticed that Pramo recently had been making efforts at grooming herself. I felt that when I chanced upon the well-tied bun of her hair for the first time. She had carefully draped her saree too. One day I observed her smile to be flirtatious, yet bashful. I had never seen her smile like that before. She tried to take care of me in several other ways. She plucked herbs for me, chopped vegetables, did whatever she could. Initially, she used to stand and talk. I found her comfortably sitting at the corner of my porch these days. Her gestures seemed prettier by the day!

There are so many other people in Palashpur. So many people frequented the marketplace square. Nobody had ever cared to show sympathy for the lonely life of this wretched doctor before. My belief that a woman makes the best friend for a man was reaffirmed.

Last spring, she skipped her visit consecutively for a few days. I grew anxious. This had never happened since she had started visiting me. After a couple of days, I was informed that milkmaid Bidhu's daughter had contracted typhoid. I went and inspected. I concluded that it was impossible even for the gods to cure her. But I devoted myself to treat her to the best of my abilities. They lost faith in me after a week and called Doctor Indu. On the very first day, Pramo's face lit up upon seeing me at her bedside. Later on, I heard that she refused to follow Indu doctor's medications. She lost her consciousness six or seven days before her demise.

It has been a few months that I was back to my solitary self. Who would pick herbs and roots and vegetables for me? I was back to my usual diet of mangoes and rice.

Monsoon had set in, and the roads were clogged with water and mud. There were too many mosquitos on the prowl. Clouds gathered above the tallest trees around the marketplace square. It rained for a while and the sky cleared up. Then the clouds gathered again, and it rained more. The drenched roots of the trees looked black as ever!

I sit alone in total silence. It felt as if I had been incarcerated. When it became unbearable, I joined Mujibur at his grocery shop. His store was on the ground level. Kerosine oil, lamp oil, cumin seeds, cheap tobacco, tar, and spoilt mustard oil conjoined to form a weird stench. That stench made me depressed. I felt I was rotting away in this obscure village. Would I ever be liberated from these shackles? I didn't know. Heavens knew what happened to my life. But I felt I would have been able to survive if I had Subhasini and my child by my side.

When I used to live in Kolkata, I remembered once walking through Bhowanipore when I noticed a flock of young ladies coming out of a mansion with books in their hands. They were a mixed-age group of ladies.

I wondered what it was. How come there are so many women here? I thought of investigating.

I later found out that the mansion hosted a women's college.

So many damsels were there in that lot! Their dressing sense was impeccable; some had pretty spectacles on; how amazing they were! On another instance, I was strolling on Debendra Ghosh Road, when I heard a girl singing on the second floor of some rich man's house. I stood by and listened to her. I had never heard such a beautiful rendition. Where would I get the chance anyway? I still remembered the lyrics of her song

Beloved, you did not turn up this morning
The flowers weep; dewdrops gather like tears

Those songs were never meant for rustic folks like us.

After an incessant downpour throughout the day, it stopped raining in the evening. The darkness of the trees blended with the solitude of the marketplace square; it seemed darker than it was. Frogs were croaking in delight. The spot from where Pramo plucked her herbs was inhabited by a choir of chirping crickets. The wind was rustling through the leaves of the huge tree; I could hear fruits fall from the branches in the darkness of the swamp.

I sat alone and pondered in this desolate evening…

Translated from Bengali by Debayudh Chatterjee

The Cavern

Dr Bhabendra Nath Saikia

About 60 press reporters and photographers were waiting with deep anticipation near the flower-garden in front of the main road leading in and out of the hospital. A few amongst them were sitting upon the railing of the garden, a few were sitting on the stairs around the huge statue of Jesus Christ, two of them were reclining against the two large pillars on the car porch of the hospital, some were roaming around in absolute lazy resignation smoking cigarettes. All of them in groups of three to four were discussing, with the solemnity of an expert, with the excitement of winning an argument, and with the enthusiasm to be the prime mover of the *adda*, various issues ranging from bright possibilities of medical science to the uncultivated beauty of wildflowers. The photographers, rendered inactive for a little while in the middle of the conversations, were adjusting the settings of the camera lenses and were zooming through the viewfinders the stairs, and the porch of the road leading in and out of the hospital. The rays of the morning sun were exuding the exact degree of brightness upon the stairs and the porch for photography much to their liking, and they were singing praises of the sun and the sky above for enabling their cameras to capture beautifully the photos of a historic event unfolding before them.

A few times there were sounds of people walking, talking, opening of doors from within the hospital, and each time such sounds were heard the press people got busy, just like passengers waiting on the platform of a station getting suddenly excited by the sound of an arriving train. A few photographers would rush towards the stairs hoping to seize a favourable spot for themselves and immediately there would be commotion among the hundreds of people assembled on the footpath at a distant road. Parents with their kids tucked between their legs would quickly pick them up and would try to draw their attention with their fingers pointed towards the hospital porch, with their expectant gaze fixed in that direction. Even the speed of the cars passing by would slow down for a moment, and every person sitting inside would make haste to cast a glance towards the hospital. But soon everyone realized the falsity behind the sudden excitement; all whether acquaintances or not even laughed at the jocular remarks passed by one or two, and again calmly resumed their waiting for the real event to take place. Many of them lit a new cigarette once this false excitement died down.

In the end however, defeating the vigilance of about 60 press reporters and photographers, the people standing on the footpath were the ones who unerringly signalled the occurrence of the actual event. One could suddenly hear sounds of commotion coming from their direction; the press excitedly looked towards the folks on the street, then followed the trail of their looks towards the veranda of the hospital and instantly ran towards the staircases. A few workers deployed by the hospital authorities immediately created a barricade at the foot of the stairs so as to stall the march of people running inside; the press threatening to break the barriers, started wrangling among themselves to seize the right spot at the front. A movie cameraman managed to sneak out of the hurly-burly ascended about four steps on one side of the stairs and started filming the scenes of scrambling amongst the photographers.

A group of people slowly emerged from within the hospital and advanced along the veranda towards the staircases. Four of them walked in front of the group. On the one side, there was Dr Campbell, the famous medical scientist; on the other side, there was his assistant, Dr Milin; a little behind walked a matron of the hospital; and in the middle, there were Mr and Mrs Pienar. Unending sounds of cameras clicking could be heard followed in the next moment with hundreds of people on the street raising their hands reverberating the surroundings with their cry in unison—'Long live Mr Pienar! Long live Dr Campbell!' The calm and pallid face of Mr Pienar brightened up in the glow of the morning sun; a sense of excitement could now be seen spreading across his face with the words of appreciation and goodwill pouring in from all sides. His lips extended on both sides, casting two linear imprints on two sides of the lips, a slight movement in the wings of the nose; however, it was not known whether they indicated laughter or weeping. In response to the warm behaviour of the press and those on the street, Mr Pienar sought to raise his right hand in appreciation but glanced at Dr Campbell who approvingly moved his head. Pienar waved his raised hand gently as he threw a look towards the crowd, and at once the collective voice of the crowd reciprocated with sheer excitement. Before Pienar could lower his hand, one reporter extended a pencil and his notebook towards his hand; if this famous patient, right after his discharge from the hospital, did the first thing of drawing even a simple line upon his notebook, it was sufficient to enhance the popularity of his newspaper. Requesting him with a calm smile on his face, Dr Campbell slowly pushed aside the reporter's pencil and copy.

A few moments later, a fine-looking white car almost silently appeared to stop at the veranda. Pienar was helped by Dr Campbell and Mrs Pienar at the time of descending the stairs. Just as he was about to get inside the car, one reporter somehow managed to cross the barricade and asked him, 'How do you feel, Mr Pienar?'

Pienar's lips trembled initially; he replied in a choked voice, 'A new life; new world; unexampled!'

The car left the hospital amidst the blissful cheers and clappings of the people. In a little while, the place emptied of people. Even after the departure of the press and the dispersal of the people on the street, a few hospital employees could still be seen lazily loitering around the veranda for a long time. Their minds were replete with a feeling of emptiness that accompanied the parting of a close family friend. An unprecedented atmosphere of thrill and agility centering on this patient had ruled over the whole hospital for the last 118 days. At times, the attention of the whole world was fixed upon this hospital. Each day, over the past 118 days, brought about incomparable respect, pride and success to this hospital. Mr Pienar had left the hospital in a state of complete recovery. An unmeaning sorrowfulness rendered the employees work-shy and inactive for a little while.

Mr Pienar was brought to the hospital just like other patients, that is, in a moribund state suffering from an acute heart condition about four months ago. His situation deteriorated day-by-day, and there was a time when the doctors had begun counting the last moments of his life. But at that very instance, Dr Campbell found an unusual source of inspiration from his long-term commitment to his profession and a trans-human work-energy generated by his uncommon knowledge of medical science, and, most importantly, a still-beating heart in the body of a deceased man of about 31 years. The diseased and dysfunctional heart from Pienar's body was removed, and it was replaced by the one still throbbing with life, just taken out from the body of the deceased person. That was an incident that took place 118 days ago. Having integrated his new heart with the veins and arteries of his body, and made it one with the whole over the last 118 days, today Pienar returned home with Mrs Pienar in a white car amidst the happy cheers and goodwill chants of several hundred onlookers.

To mark this special occasion, Mrs Pienar had freshly decorated their house. New and bright curtains in white were put up; expensive white cloth materials were used for chairs, tables, or whichever furniture required such clothing; even their bed was laid out beautifully with a white sheet. However, these covers and clothing were not plain-looking like those used in the hospital; various kinds of floral designs embroidered with white thread lent a homely hue to the whole arrangement. Mrs Pienar had made all these arrangements as per the instructions received from Dr Campbell in order to ensure that, after spending 118 eventful days in a controlled environment, Pienar was not excited on returning all of a sudden to the homely ambiance among his family members.

A little while after the homecoming, the well-wishers who had assembled in front of his house, upon the request of the police officer and Dr Campbell, gradually withdrew from the place. For getting into an unnecessary feud with the police, two dark-skinned persons were arrested by the police.

The house went silent after Dr Campbell bade farewell. Sitting down on a sofa, Pienar took a deep breath and gently smiled to his wife. It seemed to Mrs Pienar that she had never seen such a smile on her husband's face ever before. It was the smile of a new life, of supreme happiness. Kneeling, Mrs Pienar sat down right near the sofa; she lovingly rested her head upon Pienar's heart and began running her right hand along his arm. She stayed like that for quite a while. Her eyes gradually filled with tears, and soon they flowed down her cheeks. In the quietness of the house, the sounds of Mr Pienar's heart-throbbing seemed like drums of victory signaling the end of a long and tedious battle full of apprehensions.

The first edition of the regional daily, which usually came out of the press in the evening, was released at noon that day. Mrs Pienar collected all the editions of the newspapers that day and handed them over to Pienar. Her husband went through the news stories and laughed at seeing his photo published in each one of them. For several days since then, many newspapers published his story along with his photos clicked in various positions and places within the house or outside in the garden. Mrs Pienar had carefully cut out and preserved stories published in many newspapers in connection with Pienar's health over the last 118 days. She passed all of them to her husband. Going through all of them and engaging in intermittent conversations with well-wishers amongst close acquaintances as well as people from the press, Pienar spent the next few days without any anxiety or discomfiture.

Gradually, the excitement surrounding the event died down. Soon Mrs Pienar decided to resume her work in the office. 'To work?' asked Mr Pienar with a questioning glance at his wife. There were two places where the Pienar couple went for work. The first one was an establishment dealing with the paper business. Many years ago, prior to their marriage, Mrs Pienar was in charge of a small shop selling paper; post-marriage, Mr Pienar invested a significant sum of money in his wife's business. Gradually, their business started expanding and generating good profits. A time came when Pienar left his high-earning government job and concentrated full-time on the business.

They have two sons; they were sent at a very young age to London for studies. Subsequently, several skilled and trustworthy workers were employed in the business establishment of the Pienars. Mrs Pienar was also highly skilled in business management thereby affording considerable leisure time for her husband. Having acquired the benefit of free time, he was soon steeped in the study of political and social sciences. He was prompted by an inner urge to put into practice his wide experience, work-skill, and thought-process acquired through his years of employment as a government administrator. He soon joined a non-governmental political organization engaged in carrying forward the execution of governmental policies amongst the masses. By virtue of his talent and skill, Pienar was soon promoted to the position of secretary in the organization. There was a time when Pienar was drawn towards his wife's paper business; post his assumption of duties as secretary, Pienar drew his wife too towards the activities of the organization. After wrapping up all business-related activities during the day, the Pienars attended meetings of the organization during the evenings. Meetings were held on various subjects, but at the root of all discussions were the prime objectives and principles of the organization—just because a man is born in a place, it does not necessarily entitle him to assume ownership of that particular patch of land.

Therefore, by the act of going to work, the Pienars also meant visiting the office of the organization.

In response to Pienar's question, his wife replied that she would be going to the business establishment. 'What's going on in the organization?' asked Mr Pienar.

'Well, for the last few days, I have received most of the news via telephone. There's nothing new worth the while. Just that during the time of admissions in the Queen's College, a few students from there were sitting on the college veranda along with their parents. They too were demanding admission into the college; otherwise, they would continue sitting there. The police arrived, but before they could do anything, our students in the college, along with the employees and others, came out from the college premises. Sitting there till the evening, I guess they were utterly bored. They must have been hungry as well, so they left the place.' With a smile on her face, Mrs Pienar concluded her statement.

A number of days following the resumption of office work by Mrs Pienar, Mr Pienar made a phone call to Dr Campbell one afternoon. He wanted to go to the office as well, albeit for a few hours every day. With a few words of caution, Dr Campbell permitted him to do so.

On Pienar's first day to the business establishment after recovery, the employees organized a feast in his honour. Even in the office of the organization, a dinner feast was called amidst an occasion of joy and happiness marking his return to work. He was soon attending both the offices more or less regularly.

On his way back home from the organization every evening, Pienar would get down from his white car near a park. The distance between the park and their house was about two furlongs; he takes a slow walk on both sides. This bit of walking was necessary for him. Moreover, the road was almost empty after evening, and one could take a peaceful walk along the stretch.

Once on an evening like this, while walking on his way home, Pienar suddenly had a feeling that someone was calling him in a hushed tone, 'Sir!' A lot of people wished to strike a conversation with him at the slightest opportunity. At times, he had the feeling that everyone here in this world had taken up the vocation of a press reporter. He gradually stopped entertaining their requests.

He went on with his walk; but a little later, the word again struck his ears, 'Sir!'

Pienar slowly turned back to look. At about five to six arms' distance from him, a dark-skinned woman was standing. Now Pienar moved ahead with a feeling of certainty. The woman was not calling him surely. He had no relation whatsoever with this kind of people. He was only thinking about one thing; the colony of the dark-skinned people was located far away from here, then why had this woman come here at such an inappropriate time?

He went ahead, but once again turned back to look at the woman when he was just between two street lights.

Continuing with his walk, he had just reached the point right below a street light when the words fell upon his ears again, 'Sir, would you please…?'

Pienar stopped completely on his tracks and half-turned to look at the woman. She was standing at about five arms' distance. Her pitch-dark face was shining in the bright glow of the streetlight. She was looking at Pienar's face with eyes full of awe and supplication.

For standing right below the streetlight and also for wearing a felt hat upon his head, Pienar's face was hidden under a shadow. It seemed as if the colour of his face had an exact resemblance with that of the woman standing before him. As he looked at her, Pienar suddenly had the feeling that he has seen this woman somewhere before. Yes, he could remember seeing this woman on a number of days waiting at various points on this road. He could also remember her following him on a number of occasions as and when he turned back to look at her.

'Did you say something to me?,' Pienar asked her in a grave voice.

The woman made a gesture of respect by slightly bending her knees concealed under the floral frock and then stood upright. Joining her hands with closed fists and placing them to the middle of her bosom, she spoke with a shivering voice, 'Yes, sir! It was I who had called you.'

'But I cannot seem to recognize you. And I presume I have never been acquainted with you.'

'No, sir! But I do know you. And you would know me too. I am Mary, the wife of Smith.' In a voice mixed with tremendous excitement and eager anticipation, Mary finished her statement in a single breath.

'Smith?' The word came out of its own from the lips of Pienar. Yes, he knew thousands of Smiths; no, he did not know anyone whose name was Smith; or he knew one Smith very well—it was not known which one of these was meant by the nature of his utterance.

'Yes, yes, Smith!' Mary replied eagerly in anticipation. 'My husband, Smith! He was injured in a motor accident. The doctors have transplanted his heart into your body.'

'Oh!' Mr Pienar made an indistinct sound.

'Yes, sir! It was just two months since we got married. We had gone to the National Park on a Sunday. We spent an immensely joyful day there. Look, look at this! This is the last photograph of us that was clicked there with an automatic camera.' Mary continued her speech in a very discomposed manner, and immediately she took out a small photograph from her handbag, moved a few steps ahead and held it up to the unblinking, unmeaning and blank gaze of Mr Pienar. Smith and Mary were sitting holding one another's arms upon a stone by a small river. Smith was bare-chested—his wide, toned, and pitch-dark chest glaring with the sunlight falling upon them. A pale smile spread across his thick pair of lips.

Putting the photograph back into her handbag, Mary continued, 'It was late by the time we were returning home that day. Smith was driving his car at a high speed so as to reach home early. We covered most of the distance unhindered, but right before we entered the city—I cannot actually recollect what happened. I regained consciousness the next day in the hospital. In the meantime, at another hospital, Smith's heart was placed within your body …' Mary's voice choked as she spoke. Rubbing her eyes with her left hand, she at once also rolled behind her ears the curls of her hair that had fallen upon her face.

Pienar was silent and unmoving; he stood still in darkness under the shadow of his hat. He could not find anything to say. After a few more moments of quietness had passed, he asked her in a stifled voice, 'Why have you come to meet me?' The question seemed inconsequential for Mr Pienar to his ears.

'You? I have been observing you every day from a distance. I need to have a closer look at you; I need to have a conversation with you; I need your presence, your company. I have been rendered all lonely, sir. I do not have anyone. But Smith's heart still throbs in your chest. We generally associate feelings and emotions with the heart, don't we? I used to gently caress the part of his chest concealing his heart in appreciation of the wonderful person he was, one with a beautiful mind full of love. Those very heartbeats in your body have still kept you alive. If his heart is alive, then how come my Smith is dead?' With eyes brimming with tears, Mary looked towards Pienar's darkened face with extreme anticipation. 'It is quite late now. I shall meet you later,' the words dropped from the lips of Pienar.

'Meet me?' Mary's eyes brightened up, 'Many thanks, sir! Many thanks!' Looking around her, she again spoke, 'We have a lot of difficulties visiting your locality; I shall nevertheless come to see you. Will you too come to my place, sir?' 'This …this…,' Mary unlocked her purse and seemed to search frantically for something. She then took out a small card and said, 'This is a card bearing the address of our home, in the name of Smith. You may please keep this with you.'

In a somewhat mechanical way, Pienar's hand took the card from Mary's hand and put it inside the inner coat pocket, just near his heart. He then turned abruptly and started walking towards his home. Mary bade him 'good night' from behind in anticipation, and he was heard murmuring something to her in response.

Pienar was feeling stiff in his legs. He felt his head was spinning. Somehow he managed to cover the distance of two furlongs to his home, and upon reaching laid himself down upon a sofa in a state of tremendous weariness.

Shouldn't he have thanked the woman? Shouldn't he have conveyed his lifelong gratitude towards the woman for being able to be alive in this manner? His mind was staring into nothingness; his head seemed to have stopped responding. His mind was still unable to come to terms with the reality. He was feeling restless. He had never thought about the matter in this manner. He was under the impression that the event of his heart transplant was an epoch-marking achievement in the field of human intelligence and workmanship. This new life of his was a living example of the thrilling intervention of science into human life. It was a matter of sheer wonder that the most vital organ in a human body was transplanted onto his own. An epochal and absolutely thrilling event. He knew only this far. However, from whose body was the heart taken out to be transplanted onto his own was a matter he did not feel the need to ponder over. He hardly had the leisure to do so. Nobody, including the doctors, friends, and even the press reporters, had raised this matter before him. Not even the sheer amount of newspaper stories could provoke this thought within his mind. Smith—the name did fall on his ears during some casual conversations; however, such talks had never garnered any serious attention. The name soon disappeared like tablets dissolving in a glass of water. Whenever the thought of a new life came up, he only remembered with infinite gratitude Dr Campbell's divine life-giving powers.

But, as the woman told him today, the heart transplanted within him surely had an owner. This lump of flesh had a throbbing heart associated with it. A lump of flesh, a throbbing heart, a feeling heart. In a way, the owner of this heart had sought his company. What kind of company? What did she want?

Mary's face came floating before his eyes. Her thick and bigger lower lip, broad nose, vivid cheekbones, the upper part of her brows turned inside downwards. The colour of her skin…

Pienar felt very restless. In response to several questions from Mrs Pienar, he only answered in short phrases like 'nothing, nothing has happened', 'why do you need to inform the doctor?'

He could not sleep well that night. It was as if he was repeatedly awakened by the throbbing of his heart. He felt as if the heart within him had sucked for once all the blood from his body; he had become languid and pallid; then suddenly the heart pumped out the blood back to the body like a flash of lightning with full power. The nerves of his body were unable to withstand the full force of the blood; especially the nerves on the sides of his forehead and the ones inside his brain were threatening to be torn asunder; he was writhing in pain. He felt that the heart within him had become too powerful for his half-worn-out body. He could discern the image of a dark-skinned man named Smith floating before his eyes. He had not paid attention to Smith's photograph under the streetlight, but he had a close acquaintance with the community to which Smith belonged. Their broad chests built with tight muscles; the fists of their hands—of what size? of what size? Pienar vainly sought for equivalence of the first of a dark-skinned man's hand. Was it equal to the size of a hand-grenade once collected in the office of his organization? Or was it the size of the distributor fitted inside his capacious white car? Disparate thoughts crowded Pienar's mind. And then he realized that one's fist was indeed equal in size to the person's heart.

Even if it is just for a moment, Pienar actually desired that the circulation of blood within his body, especially towards his head, be stopped.

Pienar's face looked pale in the morning. Standing before the mirror, he stared unblinkingly at his own reflection. Had the colour of his face, the colour of his skin been slowly turning black? Just because of the blood-circulating machine inside his body, was he going to be like Smith and his people one day?

Upon Mrs Pienar's request, her husband was thoroughly examined by Dr Campbell and his associates on that day. Nothing had happened. Everything was fine. In fact, they suggested that Pienar should gradually get back to his normal routine of work.

That day Mrs Pienar took her husband to the office earlier than usual. Pienar had an inkling of doubt in his mind—was he actually taking an active part in the discussion? He shook himself gently and sat upright in the chair. He then started speaking in an unusually loud voice. The other members of the organization were in a discussion to formulate a definite plan of action. However, what they could discern in the words of Pienar was a tone reminiscent of his speeches delivered a long time before. They looked at each other through the corner of their eyes. With an abashed expression on her face, Mrs Pienar indicated her husband to remain silent.

Having spoken excitedly for quite some time, Pienar felt tired. He tried to sit down at ease. But, his heart started beating very fast. With a lot of effort, he tried to pay no attention to the rapid throbbing of his heart but could not hold on for long. In fact, he felt at one time that he did not have the ability to withstand the power of the huge lump of heart that belonged to Smith.

Pienar discontinued his daily habit of going for an evening walk. He was continually tormented by an apprehension of being followed by a dark woman seeking the company of the heart within him. Even at times, he imagined that not only that woman in particular, in fact, the entire community of dark-skinned people had also been following him seeking proximity under the pretext of a throbbing heart. Have they associated the change of his heart with a corresponding change in his attitude towards them?

A few days later, Pienar stepped out anxiously for his evening walk; a little while later, the words fell on his ears, 'Sir!'

It seemed as if Mary had been hiding behind the streetlight on that road every day for ages. She approached Pienar who abruptly stopped in his tracks.

'What do you want?' Pienar roared furiously with the courage of suddenly standing face to face with a tiger.

Mary was taken aback at the outset; however, she soon gathered courage and replied with a tone of supplication, 'I just wish to rest my head upon your chest for once to listen to the beatings of Smith's heart, to experience his presence once more. I haven't experienced that pulsation for so long. His heart still throbs in this world, yet I cannot listen to that; this is too painful to bear, sir. Unbearable pain!'

'What arrogance!' roared Pienar for the second time as he excitedly turned away with the intention of refilling his empty rifle with bullets.

Now Pienar did not have the strength to tell Mrs Pienar that nothing had happened to him. He waged a war with his own self for an hour after reaching home, and finally revealed, with a weary voice, the story of the woman to his wife. Told her that the woman intended to rest her head upon his chest…

Mrs Pienar rose hissing like an angry snake. What would she do now? Should she call up at the organization's office? Or Dr Campbell? She roamed about anxiously around the whole house.

Later that night, the two Pienars were lying abject upon their wide bed, made one by putting together two smaller beds side by side. Who was asleep, who lay awake, none was concerned about the other. Mrs Pienar felt a strong burning sensation in her head. Looking once at her husband's chest with half-opened eyes, she again shut her eyelids. Did she discern the rhythmic vertical movement of her husband's chest in the dim light? She did. The heart was distinctly throbbing, moving up and down rapidly. It seemed as if there was a huge pump instead of the heart operating within the chest. During the course of their long-married life, she had often felt the pulsations of her husband's heart; however, this unnatural movement seemed so irksome now! How alien was this lump of flesh within him? Whose heart was it that had taken centre stage within someone who was so dear, so loving, and so close to her? What was her affiliation with this alien heart? Mrs Pienar's nose crinkled with a tremendous sense of self-pride and aversion.

It was in the middle of the night, amidst deep silence, Mrs Pienar heard a dreadful thumping sound coming from within her husband's heart. The sound grew louder with every passing minute—louder and louder and louder. And after a while, the sound resembled that of the musical instruments played by the company of men as part of the final rites of a dead body and filled the deep caverns of Mrs Pienar's ears. She sat up on the bed.

Two days later, Mrs Pienar separated the two beds. She pushed her own bed to the other side of the long bedroom. She explained to her husband that she was a bit unwell, and her presence nearby may disrupt his sleep at night, which was unacceptable.

Disrupt his sleep? Pienar's heart had a mischievous laugh within. When did he sleep?

Mrs Pienar's attempts at a rational explanation went in vain. Mr Pienar could somehow feel deep down in his soul that his wife had started detesting him. She was scared of him. Had his external appearance changed in the meantime to the extent of scaring people at night? He could further recollect—people in the office of the organization, in that of his own business establishment, and even those on the streets had started murmuring things about him from a distance. They looked at him with a peculiar expression on their faces. Such looks were intolerable for him.

Pienar felt like keeping himself away from the company of such people. He started feeling scared of their looks. And then he was constantly reminded of another look, that of none other than Mary. Beseeching, helpless and tearful eyes. He was scared of that look as well, but that look was not of disgust, that look was not of one who was terrified. All of a sudden, Pienar felt like he should meet Mary. Where did she stay? How far did she stay? Lying upon his own bed at one corner of the long bedroom, he looked towards the other one at the opposite end and thought—at least not this far hopefully!

Rummaging through the pockets of his coats, Pienar, at last, discovered the card bearing Smith's address. He tucked the card inside the inner chest pocket of the coat he was wearing and left his house in a chauffeur-driven car.

Eventually, Pienar's white car reached the colony of the dark-skinned people situated far away from the city. The car halted in front of a house; and immediately boys and girls, men and women both young and old, and a lot of others surrounded the car. Suddenly, there were screams of 'Pienar, Pienar' from amidst the crowd. The shutters and doors of houses were flung open; a few faces glanced out of the window; and a little while later, quite a few people came out running on to the streets. Within a short time, the entire street was filled with hundreds of people. They made the whole locality reverberate with their cries of 'Pienar, Pienar.' Lost in an unknown ecstasy, a few of them even seemed to break into some kind of dance around the car. A few inspired ones put their hands through the open window of the car and desirably pressed Pienar's chest. With every push, the card bearing Smith's address was pressed closer to Pienar's chest.

In response to this cordial welcome of the hundreds of people around, Pienar for once felt like raising his right hand

and slowly waving at them. Wanting to raise his hand, he took a compassionate glance all around him; it was as if he was seeking somebody's permission. However, there was none to approve of his action. His chauffeur was sitting and staring ahead with a grave look upon his face. Apart from that, there were only dark skins everywhere and nothing else. As if struggling against the downward momentum of a very heavy burden, Pienar started lifting his hand in a very weary and exhausted manner. At last, the hand was raised, and it was waved slowly. With great enthusiasm, the collective cheer of the crowd conveyed their greetings to the raised hand of Pienar. Pienar experienced a strange pain within himself. All of a sudden, he started fearing these people as well. It seemed as if the colour of their skin had literally taken the form of darkness and was closing onto him from all sides.

He instructed his chauffeur to start the car. The car had stopped right in front of Mary's house. Amidst the huge gathering of people, she seemed to have lost her way at the very doorstep of her own house. She was weeping to herself all the while as she clutched a part of the car.

The story of Pienar's visit to the forbidden territory fell on the ears of Mrs Pienar. Fixing her look straight upon her husband's eyes, she asked, 'What is this?'

Like a gullible child charged with an offense, Pienar remained silent.

The following day witnessed a large number of people from the organization flocking into Pienar's house. Many of them asked Pienar a lot of questions, subjected him to interrogations; many others tried to convince him in a variety of ways—the heart is just one of the many organs in the human body, just like a machine; a machine exactly resembling the distributor of a motor vehicle. The civilization and value-system of a person are not exchanged in return with this machine. The heart installed within Mr Pienar's chest could rather have been of steel. Just because the human heart could be fashioned out of steel, it does not entail that steel will become as valuable as gold; these are vain thoughts. Pienar should keep in mind that a group of people influenced by erroneous ideas must not tarnish the efforts and endeavours of a civilized race. It would be a matter of great regret for having to explain these things to Pienar, a one-time secretary of the organization.

The present secretary of the organization wrote to Pienar the following day and asked him to stay home for a few days. Similarly, Dr Campbell also informed him in writing, 'He is advised complete rest for a few days.'

Complete rest? Sitting alone in his room one day, Pienar uttered these words to himself. What kind of rest is referred to as complete rest? Having had to confine himself all alone in that solitary room, he realized that the whole race had subjected his disgustful life to this imprisonment. The notable votaries of human knowledge and the work ethic had confined him to isolation. A woman who had once considered his life as her own now maintained distance from him while staying in the same house for the fear of these heartbeats falling on her ears. And as for himself, he was still not aware of the actual nature of the machine that created these throbbings, despite nestling it within his own chest. So torturous! When an organ from one's own body is so estranged from the rest, it became very painful to bear the separation.

'Too narrow, too narrow,' Mr Pienar started murmuring to himself. 'Our chests are too small to accommodate the lump of flesh that is surrounded by the aura of the *heart*. Too narrow a space. That is possibly why I have felt such excruciating pain. Had the heart been nothing but merely a machine, then it would probably have occupied a narrow space. Had it been made of steel; a much narrower space would be required.'

Pienar stood up. The world-famous, pioneering patient, Pienar started moving about anxiously within the room. 'The world's greatest handicapped, poorest among the poor, utterly lonely, a living being without a heart,' uttering these phrases as if raving to himself, Pienar ran down his fingers through the hair. After standing still for a while, he quickly changed into a proper dress. He again tucked Smith's address card into the chest pocket. He then placed a revolver inside his pocket. It was given to him by the organization.

Mrs Pienar had taken the car and the chauffeur to the office. So Pienar walked for a distance and then boarded a taxi, and, finally got down at the doorstep of Mary's house.

'Sir!' Mary screamed in disbelief.

Mr Pienar seated himself down upon a chair. In a somewhat discomposed voice, he spoke, 'You ardently desire to listen to the throbbing of Smith's heart, don't you?'

Mary's eyes sparkled for a moment. 'Yes sir, Yes!' she replied.

'Come, come! Rest your head upon my bosom. Listen to the sounds of the heart beating to your heart's content. Come!' Mr Pienar reclined on the chair.

Mary was rendered speechless as she fixed her look on Pienar's face. He again summoned her aloud, 'Come!'

'Why are you behaving like this, sir? What has happened to you?'

'I do not have time to respond to your questions. I have very little time in my hands.' Pienar replied in a detached tone. A little while later, he suddenly spoke in a voice of supplication, 'Come, Mary come; the later it gets, the more I shall suffer. Look, my hands are wet with perspiration!' As he uttered the last words, he took the revolver out from his pocket.

'What?' Mary screamed in horror, 'Are you going to kill yourself?' She ran towards Pienar and embraced him. Then kneeling down, she pressed her head hard against Pienar's chest. 'No, no, please don't do anything of this sort! You know, you know already that you cannot kill yourself anymore. At most, you could only end up killing Smith. Please do not destroy that piece of heart in this manner. Wherever you stay, howsoever you stay, please keep my Smith alive within you!' Mary started imploring him fervently in a confounded manner. Then she silently laid herself down in a moribund state while keeping her ears close to Pienar's heart.

At one point of time, Mr Pienar came out of Mary's house. He left his revolver behind at her place.

As Pienar walked along the road in darkness, three persons followed him silently at a distance.

The following day, Pienar's dead body was found lying in the park near his house.

An urgent secret meeting was convened that night in the office of the organization. Dr Campbell was sitting with a grave face amongst a number of people. A pen and paper lay in front of him. A member was explaining to him, 'Look, Mr Campbell! Tomorrow morning, the press people will surround you with questions. Therefore, your statement must be prepared this very night. You have received the greatest award in this world. It will take a number of years for people to discern any error in your formulation. However, whatever you pronounce tomorrow, people shall respectfully accept it. Can't anything be said to have happened in this way, doctor? Say, a pump made to pump out water cannot be used to pump out oil. If anybody does that, then it is possible that the pump will operate for a few days initially, but it will stop functioning soon after. The machine inside Mr Pienar's body might have stopped functioning precisely for the same reason.'

The person pushed the white sheets of paper lying on the table towards Dr Campbell.

Translated from Assamese by Dhurjjati Sarma

Narova Kunjarova

Shirin Shashikant Valavade

After a busy evening shift at the government hospital, I came home to the doctors' quarters in pitch darkness. It was the usual—power cut. What else can one do during a power cut but lie down? That's what I did. A short while later I heard a commotion outside.

An agitated female voice was demanding to see the doctor. Manjula, my ever-protective maid was replying equally forcefully that the doctor was sleeping and could be seen the next morning at the hospital. 'Go home now and come back tomorrow,' Manjula said, her tone softening a little, but the woman was insistent.

'Who is it, Manjula?' I called out, resigned to seeing another patient. 'What does she want?'

Manjula waddled in, grumbling, 'Just come to trouble you, these people. Won't let you rest for five minutes even.'

'It must be important. She wouldn't come at this late hour, otherwise,' I said to her. 'Tell her to sit in the hall. I'll come in a minute.'

A frail anxious looking middle-aged woman was sitting in the chair by the door. She wore a plain white sari, no jewellery, but a frown. I wondered why she had come so late at night, in the dark and alone. As soon as I walked in, she scrambled to her feet and said, 'Namaskar doctor,' in a tremulous voice.

I waited for her to compose herself but she kept fidgeting and blinking as if she was debating what to say and how much. After a few minutes, I asked, 'Has someone been admitted in the hospital? Is that what you have come to see me about?'

She shook her head. Then slowly she spoke, 'I have come to you for something quite different, doctor.'

She swallowed a couple of times and then began, 'My name is Indu, doctor. Do you remember the police case that was referred to you yesterday? About a young girl Surekha? I am that girl's brother's wife.'

I recalled the incident clearly. Two police officers had brought a young 20-year-old girl to me and said that she had been charged with the murder of an illegitimate child. Surekha was unmarried, they said, and when they found the decomposed body of a ten-twelve-day-old infant in the lane behind her house, she was the prime suspect. They wanted me to examine her and submit a report.

Surekha more than lived up to her name. She was pretty, with fine features, dark curly hair, and a good figure—enough to attract male attention. She had looked at me like a terrified doe—her large eyes pleading with me. To save her? Or was she saying please try to understand what I am saying?

Every time I have to deal with a medico-legal case, I recall my professor's words. He had warned us as students, 'Always remember, never do a slipshod or incomplete investigation. Be thorough when you conduct an examination. Write a detailed and accurate report. If you don't, you will be trapped when you have to present yourself in court. Facing a cross-examination is trickier than walking a tightrope. And if you are not careful the legal system will get you. So even though you may come across as cold and heartless, when you handle a medico-legal case you will benefit in the end.'

It was not easy for me to be detached that day. But I knew that if I let my sympathy rise to the surface I could get involved, which could lead to complications.

Surekha was too frightened to speak so I didn't ask her anything. I did a routine examination. I found signs of a delivery that could have taken place two or three weeks' back. A pregnancy in advance of seven months, and evidence of lactation too. I wrote down all the facts in my report and decided to put Surekha out of my mind till the case came up in court.

And now this woman had turned up to plead on Surekha's behalf.

'Why have you come here now? My report has already been sent to the police,' I said trying to hide my displeasure.

'I know, doctor, that's why I have come. Your report is going to have very serious consequences for Surekha,' she said in a voice thick with emotion.

'I only wrote what I found in my examination,' I said matter-of-factly. 'Do you mean to say it is not true? Your girls go and get themselves in trouble and then you come and beg and plead with the doctors to save them. Why didn't you keep an eye on her in the first place?' I was really angry by then.

Tears streamed down Indu's cheeks. She looked at me as if she was transported to a time in the past. Almost as if she was talking to herself, she mumbled, 'A cruel trick fate has played on us.'

Deep sobs racked her body for a couple of minutes. But then she controlled herself and proceeded to tell me what had happened. 'Doctor, a grave injustice is being committed here. I want it to get exposed. That's why I have come to you.' Her voice was strong and steady by then.

'What do you mean? I don't understand,' I said. 'Are you telling me Surekha is innocent?'

'No doctor, I am not saying that. I know she is at fault. But it is a small mistake. Let me give you the background. Seven-eight months ago, my son fell critically ill. My husband and I spent all our time at the hospital with him. Surekha was alone at home with her father. At that time my younger brother came to stay with us. He could not resist Surekha's charms and one day when my father-in-law had gone out, he violated her. The poor girl was helpless against the hefty young man and though she struggled she could not push him away . She was terrified and said nothing to anyone. Soon my son passed away and I was drowned in my grief. I spent several months in my father's house. When I returned from there, I noticed the change in Surekha. On questioning her I found out what had happened. Six months had passed since the incident. I was livid. But what could I do against my wretched brother? The shameless rascal had a young wife and a baby daughter…'

Indu was limp with exhaustion by this time. She took several deep breaths before continuing, 'My husband advised me to take Surekha to Mumbai. Everything was taken care of discreetly and we returned a fortnight ago. I hoped that once we got Surekha married, the matter could be forgotten. But God works in strange ways. Obviously, someone who bore us a grudge, who wanted to shame our family, had found out that Surekha was pregnant and they threw a dead baby outside our door and then reported it to the police. These things are not uncommon, you know doctor,' she sighed.

After a pause, she continued, 'I have come alone, in the dark night so no one sees me, to seek justice from you. Tell me doctor, how much of the blame would you put on Surekha? My good-for-nothing brother gets away free but Surekha is punished for life…'

'Well even killing an infant is a…' I deliberately tried to intimidate Indu.

She silently drew out a card from her purse and held it out to me. It was an OPD card from our hospital with a case number on it. 'You can check the case papers, doctor. The senior doctor had examined Surekha exactly one month ago and certified that she was six and a half months pregnant. We went to Mumbai soon after and three days later Surekha was free of her burden.' She stopped and looked at me strangely. 'The infant the police found was a full-term baby, that's what the doctor's report said. Then how can it be Surekha's child?'

I sent Manjula to the hospital to get the papers from the OPD. Since OPD duty was by rotation it was fairly easy for a nurse to access case papers.

Everything Indu had told me was true. Which meant that it was not Surekha's baby that had been found. In that case, Surekha could be charged with abortion or termination of pregnancy. The punishment for this was relatively light. But she was actually being charged with infanticide, which meant a life sentence.

Did Surekha deserve to be punished for a crime she did not commit? I was bound by the law. But could I still find a solution for her?

Indu wanted me to reassure her. 'God isn't asleep, is he, doctor? Won't he come to her rescue through your efforts?' she asked.

I felt sorry for Indu. After all the tragedies she had faced one would have thought she would have no faith left. But here she was imploring God, invoking him to wake up from his slumber.

'Let me think about it,' I said to her. 'If I can stay within the law and do something for her...' I tried to sound reassuring though I had little hope myself.

Indu perked up a little. 'I feel so much better after having told you the truth, doctor,' she said as she walked out with a distinctly lighter step.

I lay awake for a long time thinking about Surekha. Finally, I got out of bed, went to the study, and reached for Mody's book on jurisprudence. I hoped I would find something to clear the confusion in my mind. It was ironic that I was now consumed with the desire to help Surekha when I had just submitted a report that could incriminate her. But after hearing Indu's story I was determined to ensure that the culprit did not escape and the 'sanyasi' did not get hanged, as was almost certain.

My eyes flew over the pages of the textbook and I found a couple of examples cited there that could help Surekha. But much would depend on how the questioning and cross-examination went in the courtroom. We'll see what happens when the time comes, I told myself and put the book away.

The next day I spoke to one of the senior doctors about the case. 'In such instances, it is best to speak the truth. Only then are you safe,' she advised. After a few moments, she added, 'I am absolutely sure that a full-term baby cannot be Surekha's.'

Several weeks later the case came up for hearing and I was required to go to the court to give evidence. My mind was in an uncharacteristic turmoil that morning.

The sepoy announced, 'Doctor...*hazir ho*!' in a stentorian voice. I stepped into the witness box and took the oath to speak the truth and nothing but the truth. I answered all the routine preliminary questions about name, profession and all that. The report I had submitted was read out. Then the legal counsel asked what had come to my notice the day I had examined Surekha. The clerk diligently typed out every word I uttered. In the silent courtroom, the only sound that was heard was my voice and the *khat khat* of an old typewriter. So many eyes were trained on me. Indu and Surekha, their entire being concentrated in their ears, waited anxiously to hear what their god was going to say through my words.

When the report was read out and the public prosecutor stated his case, the judge granted Surekha's lawyer permission to cross-examine me. He stood up slowly and walked up to me. Our eyes were locked. In his I glimpsed a flash of hope, of faith. In a quiet voice he began, 'Doctor, almost all the signs that you noticed in the course of your examination of this patient are also seen in a condition known as fibroid tumour, isn't it? In your book of jurisprudence, it says, "Most of the above signs may possibly be simulated by the passage of a large fibroid tumour per vaginum". Do you agree with this statement?'

I had hoped with all my heart that Surekha's lawyer would raise this point. I was so relieved when I found he had picked it up. I took the book he held out, went over the lines I had read over and over again at home, and said, 'Yes.'

'That's all Your Honour,' he said. He had succeeded in planting a doubt in the judge's mind that Surekha could possibly have had a fibroid tumour.

The judge allowed himself a tiny smile as he glanced from the lawyer to me. He read the marked sentence in the textbook before handing it to the public prosecutor saying, 'Read it. If you wish to ask any questions, you may.'

The shock of white hair on the public prosecutor's head bore testimony to the years of experience in the courtroom. He skimmed over the page of the textbook. I played out the questioning in my mind. I was fully expecting him to say—'Doctor, the book says most of the signs, not all the signs. If we take into account most of the signs, a few signs still remain. These few signs are not evident in a case of fibroid tumour, but they are definitely seen in a woman who has given birth to a child. Is it not so, doctor? Could you please tell us what those few signs are and if you found them in this case?'

And on that one point, all the defence I had so carefully built up would crumble. I would have no choice but to tell the whole truth—'The few other signs are white stretch marks on the lower abdomen and milk secretion from the breasts. Both of these were seen in Surekha's case.'

I continued to play out the scene in my head. The public prosecutor would then say—'Is it possible for these specific signs to appear in any other condition?'

My reply would be—'The white marks are possible in instances of water retention or ovarian tumour. Similarly, milk secretion is sometimes caused by endocrine disturbances.'

The prosecutor could ask—'However, in these conditions, the signs you have classified as most and all internal signs will not be visible, is that right? For example, changes occurring in the uterus and the cervix, and vaginal discharge?'

I would be forced to say—'What you say is right. The remaining few signs are noticed in water retention, ovarian tumour or endocrine disturbance, but the other signs will not be present.'

'In effect, you are saying, doctor,' the prosecutor might remark in a heavily sarcastic manner, 'that in this woman you found all these major signs as well as the minor, less important ones. That is to say all the signs of pregnancy, in this case. Am I right?'

I would have had no choice but to say yes and prove conclusively that Surekha had given birth. Despite my every wish to help her I would not have been able to do anything for her. An innocent girl would pay the price…

If that happened, I would present the senior doctor's OPD case paper to the judge and use it to establish that Surekha could only have delivered a premature baby, not a full-term one. While she would have been acquitted of the charge of infanticide, she would have been accused of undergoing an abortion. Of course, her lawyer could ask me for proof that it was a forced abortion, not a natural one. But that would cause scandal and humiliation. People would say, 'You can't clap with one hand you know!' Because by our arguments we would have established that an unmarried girl had become pregnant.

I came out of my reverie when I heard the public prosecutor speak. What was he going to ask me about the fibroid tumour now? He had finished reading the lines that were pointed out to him in the textbook on jurisprudence. Then looking the judge straight in the eye, had declared calmly, 'I have nothing to say on this.'

A wave of disbelief swept through the courtroom. The opposition stand had faltered. Surekha's lawyer sighed with relief. The judge stared at him. Holding his gaze, the public prosecutor said, 'I just want a clarification of one statement made in the doctor's report.'

'Proceed,' ordered the judge, obviously curious to find out more.

My heart began to thud. Now what? He had said nothing on a vital point, what was he going to ask now?

Like an examiner viewing a student, he watched me. He seemed somewhat anxious, almost as if he was afraid that I would not handle his question properly. 'Doctor,' he said, 'if in this case, you saw signs of a fibroid tumour, why at the end of your report did you say that there were clear indications that the patient had undergone a delivery?'

For a minute I was stumped. I had not paid attention to this point. Involuntarily my eyes turned to Surekha. Was I going to let her down at this stage?

I took some time to think, to gather my thoughts. And then the words slipped out, 'What I wrote was absolutely correct. There were definite indications of delivery having taken place. But I did not specify whether a child had been delivered or a fibroid tumour, because I did not know. In obstetric terms, delivery means expelling per vaginum–through the vagina. It could be a child, a fibroid tumour, a placenta, or anything else.'

'There you are!' Surekha's lawyer jumped up with joy. Tears of happiness and relief flowed down Surekha's cheeks.

The judge looked at me kindly. Somewhere Indu was raising her hands to her god. As for the public prosecutor, his expression was inscrutable. I just could not figure out what was going through his mind, no matter how hard I tried. I had given Surekha's lawyer a point to defend her, that it was a fibroid tumour and the child that had been found was not Surekha's. The compassionate judge would give her the benefit of the doubt and acquit her for lack of conclusive evidence. He would simply be reiterating his stand that it did not matter if ten guilty persons escape so long as one innocent victim is not punished.

I came out of the courtroom, my head buzzing with doubts. I had not taken the OPD case paper out of my purse. No one had asked me whether I or anyone in the hospital had examined the girl. Was it really my responsibility to provide answers to unasked questions? Should I have given the OPD papers to the judge? If that would have resulted in Surekha being punished, then why she alone? Why not the man who had forced himself on her?

The statement uttered by Yudhisthira about Ashwathama, '*Narova kunjarova**,' came to mind. It was a blatant half-truth. I too had said, 'She did deliver, but I don't know if it were a child or a fibroid tumour.' And that was the truth.

A few months later I moved to Delhi and Surekha and her story were soon forgotten.

---

* The phrase 'Narova Kunjarova' is taken from Mahabharata. It is Yudhishthira's tricky reply to Dronacharya's question regarding the death of Ashwatthama.

A few days ago, we were invited to a reception. There were many eminent people present. I moved around talking to friends, greeting acquaintances and colleagues, when I saw a distinguished-looking elderly gentleman approach me. His face looked familiar but I could not place him.

'Doctor Shubha Rao, isn't it?' he said.

'It is Mrs Shubha Nayak now,' I laughed. 'This is my husband, Dr Nayak.' After a pause, I said, 'I'm sorry I cannot remember your name.'

'I have aged, haven't I,' he said with a smile. 'I used to be the public prosecutor in Belgaum. After I retired, I came to live here in Delhi. We met once in the courtroom many years ago. I embarrassed you by asking an awkward question, didn't I? We lawyers do enjoy bullying you doctors … sometimes!' he chuckled.

'It came to me in a flash then. The Surekha case! Where is that girl? Do you know what happened to her?' I asked him.

'She was married soon after that and is a happy family woman now.'

'That day, you spoke like a seasoned lawyer. I admired your confidence. I still remember your last reply. Just as well. Otherwise, an innocent victim would have gone to jail. You know how it is in these small towns…people are always making a false allegations against each other to settle scores.' He cleared his throat and continued, 'I also knew that the child was not Surekha's. You can't hide such things in a small town. She may have escaped punishment for infanticide but she would have definitely been charged for illegal abortion. We had no choice but to save her.'

My eyebrows shot up in surprise. 'We?' Swallowing a couple of times, I added, 'You mean you knew...' I couldn't keep the surprise out of my voice.

He smiled, handed me his visiting card, and said, 'Come over some time.' Then he turned away, leaving me to ponder over his enigmatic words, '*Maunam sarvartha sadhanam*'—Silence always serves.

For a long time, I stood there thinking everyone lauds the Goddess of Justice, who is blind like Dhritarashtra. But who acknowledges the pujaris at her temple who, just like Gandhari, choose to blindfold themselves?

Translated from Marathi by Keerti Ramachandra

Day Care

Zakia Mashhadi

The crowd there was always dense. People jostled as if free gifts were being distributed. But could the faces of those who come to receive free gifts look like the ones seen here? Here, the faces were pinched, gloomy and wrought with fear. Fear of death. Fear of a long period of troubled life; drain of finances, apprehension of losing near and dear ones. Losing own precious life. That young girl with agony writ large in her beautiful eyes was sitting patiently, waiting for her name to be called. Someone had put a kerchief on the chair next to her indicating that the seat was not vacant.

'May I sit here?' someone asked. The voice was soft and gentle yet it made the girl start. She remained quiet though. Her body felt numb. The question was repeated, this time with a gentle hand on her shoulder. Perhaps the touch had a silent language, a language that penetrated right into the heart. The girl lifted her eyes and looked at the woman. She was much older, around forty.

'Please be seated. Someone was sitting here. You could leave when he comes back. No need to ask me,' she replied this time as if with some effort. The woman pushed the kerchief to one side and lowered herself gingerly in the chair. The hall was air conditioned; in fact, the entire building was but the throng corroded its efficacy. Smells of sweat and medicines mingled and became a regular feature of the general ambience. The woman thought that there was another smell, swirling in this large area that was distinct from the rest. She had never experienced anything like this anywhere before though she was middle-aged and had seen enough life. It was the smell of death …death that tiptoed around—silently, stealthily. Today too, a stretcher was pushed close to the wall. The man lying on it was marking his time. Many tubes were jutting out of his veins, giving false hopes to his relatives while he himself prayed silently for his sufferings to end. The atmosphere was insufferably stifling. The fellow who had kept his kerchief on the chair hadn't returned yet. The woman felt somewhat guilty for appropriating someone else's seat and also a sense of insecurity. The man could come any minute. She would be obliged to vacate the seat. But won't he be leaving the seat himself as soon as the name of his ward was called out? We are all waiting for our respective calls; she thought ruefully. The hollowness that churned her stomach made her turn to the girl sitting next to her.

'Who is ailing?' she asked.

'My husband,' the reply was as short as the question.

'Oh, you are married; don't look at all. Your husband too, must be very young then, tch tch,' her voice revealed genuine concern.

The girl heaved a sigh. Like a faint trace of lightning showing through the dense clouds her dark eyes glistened with tears. She kept quiet. Only her eyes spoke. So many spoke at a time but no one heard anyone. Their hearts were heavy as lead; an unfathomable anxiety made them so. Every now and then, in the midst of this queer mixture of din and quiet, the uniformed hospital guard, who, usually stood at the doorway would come forward and call out a name using his mike. Patients who were done with their chemo for the day would have to be discharged and taken out by their attendants. Also, their papers, complete with the date of the next chemo, could be obtained from the medical counter. On some occasions the attendants would be called because of some additional medicines that were required or some which were found missing from the prescribed kit. His booming voice would engulf the din that was there in the hall. From amongst the harassed looking faces the one whose name was called out would start to get up.

Rokiya Khatun…Rokiya Khatun…the mike rattled.

A tired looking, bearded man, wearing a coarse crumpled kurta looked this way and that. From his appearance he seemed to have come from some nearby village. But the magnificent metro city did house people who looked to have come from villages or small towns. They built plush offices and bungalows for the rich and powerful and pushed hand carts to provide easy access to fruits, vegetables and other essentials. Recently the city was decked up like a bride as it was hosting the Commonwealth Games. A whole lot of these people toiled day and night to make the place fit for those who would wallow in the luxury of five- and seven-star hotels. Their job done they were driven out of the precincts of the VIP areas because if they were not, they would have looked like patches of leucoderma on the face of the bedecked bride. So it was not really easy to guess by physical appearance whether someone came from the suburbs or was living in the metro.

After waiting for a few seconds, the guard left the mike on his stool and came right into the crowd. 'Who is Rokiya Khatun, hurry up please. Why don't you people heed the announcement. It is sheer waste of time,' he shouted out. Though he was loud his voice was laced with a kind of gentleness and sympathy. In the same hospital the nurses and ward boys of other departments were not as courteous and sympathetic. They explained the prescription and other related instructions only once and lost their tempers if further queries were made by the patient or their attendants. The usual retort was: Are we here only for you. Can't you see the crowd waiting for their turn? A little more mumbling if the query was considered stupid. Once an exasperated patient said, 'Sir, wouldn't it have been better to explain once more instead of chiding for so long?' Sir gave him a fierce look and moved away. The poor fellow went around asking people to tell him the number of times he had to take his medicines and when he had to come for his next injection. It took a lot of effort to find a person who was educated enough to read the prescription and also kind enough to explain. To some extent one could empathise with the staff too. They worked under great pressure and the poor folks who thronged this famous government hospital were mostly uneducated. They, sometime, did give trouble to non-medic staffers. To begin with the sheer number of people who visited the hospital on a daily basis was a trial for their nerves.

Conditions were same here too but the staff was exemplary in its dealings. They knew well that the patients who came here were booked for their journey beyond. Survival rate was very low, like that of grains which came out whole from the grinding stone. As the famous saying goes—'No one can destroy the one whom God protects.' But God seemed to protect only a few from amongst those whom He afflicted with the dreaded disease.

Scooping a little girl with large, sad eyes in his arms the bearded man got up. The emaciated girl was about three to four years old but looked slightly younger. 'Yes, seems our turn has come. They want our little Ruqaiya Khatoon.' 'Yes, yes, I meant that only. Hurry up.' The guard threw an affectionate glance towards the girl. Pressing the record file under one arm he held onto the child firmly and started walking in long strides. Even in his consternation he did not forget to plant a kiss on his little girl's cheek and mutter under his breath, 'Sister must be getting angry. I am late. I wonder how guard sir pronounces the names. I could not recognize my own child's name.'

'What a little beautiful girl she is!' The older woman commented. Some people lose words when they are unhappy while some try to unburden themselves by talking. The woman was reticent by nature but in her agony, she felt her heart would burst if she did not vent her feelings.

The younger woman who was sitting with her head bowed looked up suddenly and blurted, 'My daughter is almost the same age.' Tears betrayed her voice.

'Oh, who is looking after her?'

'My mother. She lives in another city. Here because of her father's illness, I could not look after her properly. She was rattling around, neglected. She had to be left in some one's care.'

It seemed that in this alien land where everyone was preoccupied with their own plight, sympathy from unexpected quarters made the girl lose her cool. Tears rolled down her cheeks.

Controlling herself she asked, 'And who is ailing in your family?'

'My eleven-year-old son, he is here for chemotherapy.'

The younger woman was shaken. For a woman it is difficult to decide who is more important for her—husband or children. She thought of her daughter whom she did not forget even for a moment.

'Where is your husband?' she wanted to carry on.

'He is with the child. Has taken him out for a while. Actually, we came early. His chemo is scheduled for the second session.' Silence again spread its wings between the two women. The hall reverberated with sounds.

After a long pause the older woman spoke again. 'He is our only child, was born after 12 years of marriage. We had tried all kinds of treatment, visited shrines of all faiths, even magic potions and talismans; nothing happened. When all hopes were dashed and we resigned ourselves to God's will, the child happened out of the blue. We thought God had bestowed us with the most precious gift. But for what? To teach us the lesson that His will is supreme and that we should not insist on something that has not been destined to us?'

The younger woman felt shaken from inside. Only child! That too after so many years of waiting. A precious child. But isn't every child precious? Her own daughter left with her grandmother for better care.

The older woman continued: 'We are strict vegetarians. But when doctors advised a high protein diet for him, we started giving him non-vegetarian food. First, we bought it from hotels but then we were cautioned against the quality and hygienic way of cooking so I started cooking at home. For the sake of the child the religion was cast aside. Now right from eggs to chicken, I cook everything at home. To gain expertise I joined cookery classes. Thank God he relishes the dishes. I have the utmost gratification in looking after him, being at his disposal all the time. And I will keep on serving him as long as God grants me the pleasure of it,' she spoke slowly but with emphasis on every word. Her voice did not betray any emotion though. Her face too remained expressionless. Her grief had reached the height where everything dissolves into nothingness, grief included.

The younger woman did not know how to react. As if unmoved by the misery of such magnitude she kept staring into nothingness. The older woman pointed at two figures coming from the left. 'There they are. Father and son. It is past 12. Our turn should be coming in a while.'

Now the younger woman looked at them, walking. The child did not look sickly except for a yellow tinge in his dark eyes and a shaven head. He was tall for his age and so far hadn't lost his good build. His hair loss could be due to chemotherapy. Women with shaven heads covered with scarves was a common sight here. Another common sight was a mask to protect a body weakened with chemotherapy from any further infection. The younger woman felt a lump in her throat and looked the other way. Just then the mike made a rattling sound. The guard holding it threw a cursory look at the papers in hand and called out, 'Akhil…Akil… oh not Akil, it is Akheel…attendants please come forward, Akheel's attendants…'

The older woman jumped to her feet. 'Come child, your turn has come at last.'

The younger woman too, got up with the same impatience. 'No, he is asking for Aqeel's attendant. Aqeel is my husband going through his chemo. Something must have cropped up, I wonder what.' She sounded alarmed. Not bothering about each other, both women took long strides and surged toward the guard. A bit confused, he looked at the papers again and said, 'One at a time, please. Akhil's attendants should come.' Controlling the stammer caused by confusion, this time he had tried to pronounce as clearly as he could.

'Yes, it's us, my Akhil, we had been waiting since early morning.' She held the hand of her young son and almost ran toward the door leading to the wing for treatment. The younger woman tried to fall in step. In fact, she wanted to reach first.

Who was it, Akhil Pandey or Aqeel Ahmad? Harassed and tired, the two women looked at the guard. The usual uninterrupted bustle continued in the Day Care section of B.R. Ambedkar Cancer Hospital of All India Institute of Medical Sciences.

Translated from Urdu by the author

The Gift of Vision

Rabindranath Tagore

I heard that a lot of Bengali maidens have to find husbands all by themselves these days. I accomplished that feat as well, albeit with a little help from the gods. I observed a lot of rituals and worshipped Lord Shiva right from my childhood.

I got married as soon as I turned eight. But, because of the sins of my past life, I was deprived of my husband in spite of the holy vow. The three-eyed goddess snatched away my vision. I didn't have the fortune of seeing my husband till my last breath.

My life was in flames ever since I was young. At 14, I gave birth to a stillborn. I was almost dead; but why would the one destined to endure pain die so easily? The lamp meant to burn throughout the night is never low on oil; it achieves nirvana only when the sun rises.

I did survive but due to the weakness of my body, or the sorrow of my mind, or whatever the reason might be, my eyes contracted a disease.

My husband was studying medicine then. He became enthusiastic whenever he got the delight of implementing his newly acquired knowledge. He took my treatment upon himself.

My elder brother was studying towards his law degree at a college then. One day he came over and shunned my husband, 'What have you done! You've almost ruined my little sister's eyes. You must consult a better doctor.'

My husband replied, 'How better would a better doctor be? I know all the medicines needed to treat this.'

My brother was infuriated, 'So you mean to say that there's no difference at all between you and the senior most professor of your college?'

My husband replied, 'You are a law student; how much do you know of medicine? If you ever get into a legal battle over your wife's property after your marriage, would you be consulting me?'

I thought to myself that whenever kings clash, the pawns are the ones that suffer the most. My husband got into a skirmish with my brother but both sides blamed me. If my brothers gave me away, then why should they be concerned about my well-being? My mirth and agony, my ailment and rejuvenation, pertained to my husband's desires.

The other day, the bitterness between my husband and my brother regarding the mere event of my eyesight reached new heights. My eyes were secreting water but, on that occasion, their flow increased. Neither my husband, nor my brother could figure out the real reason.

One evening, when my husband was still in college, my brother arrived with a doctor. The doctor diagnosed me, warned that the infection would worsen without proper precaution, and prescribed a few drugs. My brother ordered for their purchase without any delay.

Once the doctor left, I pleaded to my brother, 'Have mercy on me, dear brother! Do not interfere with the ongoing treatment.'

I dreaded my brother ever since I was a child; I never expected that I would speak back to him. But I did understand that the initiatives my brother took bypassing my husband would bring more distress than good.

Even my brother was surprised by my audacity. He remained silent for a while and said, 'Fine, I won't bring a doctor anymore. But do abide by whatever he prescribed.' My brother taught me to use the medicines once they arrived and went away. Before my husband got back from college, I threw all the vials, cotton, and tablets into the well.

After the skirmish with my brother, my husband's enthusiasm increased twice over. He changed the dosage almost every day. I put on an eyepatch, subsequently spectacles; I took eyedrops, applied ointments, partook stinking fish oil and almost puked my intestines out; tolerated whatever I was told to do. My husband used to enquire how I felt. I told him it was better than before. It must be getting better, I convinced myself. When the secretion increased, I thought I was getting better. When the secretion stopped, I thought it was a sign of recovery.

But after a few days the pain worsened. My vision got blurry and my sinews started aching. I could hardly hold myself together. Even my husband grew restless. He was looking for an excuse to consider a second opinion.

I advised, 'What's wrong in consulting another doctor just to honour my brother's wish? It saddens me that he is not pleased at the course of affairs. You would be leading the charge; the other doctor would be at your service.'

My husband said, 'You're right.' On that very day, he summoned a British doctor. I am not sure what they talked about but I thought that the doctor admonished my husband. I saw him stand silently with his head bowed down.

When the doctor left, I held my husband's hand and said, 'Heaven knows from where you fetched that white idiot? You should have got an Indian practitioner. How would he know better than you about my eyes?'

My husband hesitated for a while and said, 'There must be a surgery for your eyes.'

I pretended to be angry and said, 'You knew right from the beginning that a surgery was required. But you didn't tell me. Do you think I would be afraid of that?'

My husband got over his embarrassment; he said, 'How many mighty men would not be unnerved at the thought of an eye surgery?'

I jokingly remarked, 'A man might be with his woman.'

My husband turned gloomy and said, 'You're right. A man can only be proud.'

I tried to dispense his gloom and said, 'Do you think you can match up to us in pride? We win on that front as well.'

Meanwhile when my brother visited, I called him aside and said, 'Brother, I was following that doctor's instructions and my eyes were well. But one day I made a mistake and anointed the medicine that was supposed to be orally consumed. Ever since then my eyes deteriorated. My husband suggests I go into surgery.'

My brother replied, 'I thought your husband's treatment was going on. I was disappointed and stopped visiting.'

I said, 'No, I was secretly following that doctor's instructions. I didn't inform my husband because I didn't want to hurt his feelings.'

One has to tell so many lies if one is born a woman! I cannot hurt my brother's sentiments, nor can I disrespect my husband. One has to be a mother and coddle the child; one has to be a wife to take care of the child's father. Women need to deceive so much!

At least the deceit paid off. Before I went blind, I saw my brother and my husband reconcile. My brother thought that the accident happened because of the secret treatment. My husband thought that he should have listened to my brother right at the onset. Two repentant hearts grew closer in regret. My husband started asking for my brother's advice; my brother began to humbly agree with whatever my husband opined.

Finally, upon their conjugal decision, one day a British doctor arrived and operated on my left eye. My weak eye could not endure that. Whatever bleak vision that was left eventually diminished. Subsequently, the other eye also got engulfed in darkness. The image of the well-dressed sandal-scented young man that graced me on the day of my marriage was soon veiled by a black curtain for good.

One day my husband came to my bedside and said, 'I wouldn't lie to you anymore. It is me who ruined your eyes.'

I could sense that his voice was choked with tears. I held his hands with my right hand and said, 'You don't have to bother. You took what belonged to you. Would I have had any consolation if any other doctor destroyed them? No one would have been able to save my eyes since fate cannot be altered. The only silver lining that I can bask in is that it is you who took them. When Lord Rama fell short of a couple of flowers during his worship, he decided to offer his eyes to the gods instead. I hereby sacrifice my vision to my God—the shine of my full moon, the first rays of my dawn, the azure blue of sky, all the greens of my earth, I hereby dedicate everything to you. Whatever you find worth seeing, describe them to me in words. I shall accept that as your sacred offering.'

I could not articulate all of it; nor are words enough for that. But I have thought about this for many a day. At times when I felt depressed, when the light of my faith flickered, when I thought of myself as nothing more than a hapless, deprived, melancholic creature, I consoled myself with these words and tried to use my devotion and inner peace to rise above my sadness. The other day, I probably managed to convey what I really felt; some of it through words and some, through silence. He said, 'Kumu, the damage caused by my arrogance and stupidity cannot be reversed. But I shall be there with you to dispense the lack of your sight to the best of my ability.'

I said, 'That does not sound like a wise proposition. I shall not tolerate you making this household a hospital for the blind. You must get married again.'

My voiced choked before I could spell out the real reason behind why he should marry again. I coughed; gathered my thoughts and was about to say it, while my husband let his emotions overflow, 'Kumu, I might be stupid. I might be full of hubris; but I am not a heartless creature. I ruined your eyesight with my own hands. Now, if I forsake you and bring another bride to this household, then let me swear by our household deity Gopinath, may my sins tantamount to that of killing a brahmin and patricide.'

I would not have allowed him to make this vow. I would have stopped him. But I found it hard to suppress the tears that rose from the depth of my heart and clogged my voice and flooded my eyes, and speak. After hearing what he said I was overwhelmed with mirth, hid my face in the pillows and cried. I am blind, but still, he wouldn't leave me. He would keep me in his heart like the melancholy of a melancholic. I was not used to such great fortune, but I was too selfish to let it go.

Eventually when the first flow of tears passionately went by, I pulled his face close to my heart and said, 'Why did you have to make such a terrible vow. Did I ask you to marry for your own pleasure? I would have made my fellow-wife do all the things to you that my blindless prevents me from doing.'

My husband said, 'Even slaves work. Am I to marry a slave girl and put her in the same seat as my goddess?' He held my face and kissed me on the forehead. That kiss brought my third eye to life; I evolved into a goddess. I said to myself that it happened for the better. Now that I am blind, I cannot be a wife to this household. But I will be a goddess and rise above the family and look out for my husband. No more of telling lies, no further deceit; I hereby disown whatever that's petty in a wife.

I went through an inner conflict for the rest of the day. The joy that my husband took a vow to never marry again lingered obsessively in my mind. I couldn't get past it. The goddess that newly emerged within me said, 'There might come a day when it would be better for him to marry rather than stick to his vow.' On the other hand, the wife left in me argued, 'Doesn't matter. Now that he has vowed, I could always keep him to myself.' The goddess replied, 'So what? Which part of it makes you happy?' The mortal reasoned, 'Not that I don't understand. But now that he was vowed…' And so, it went on. The goddess finally shut up, but sternly raised an eyebrow. A sublime fear that something terrible would happen took over all my senses.

My repentant husband forbade all the servants to come near me and did all my chores by himself. At first, I liked how dependent I was on him for the most trivial of things because that allowed me to have him all to myself. Since I couldn't see with my eyes, I wanted to compensate by always keeping him at my side. The share of a partner's company that my eyes would have got was distributed among the other senses. When my husband used to be out on work for long, I thought I was suspended in a void, I was unable to grip anything, and everything was lost. Earlier, when my husband was late in returning from the college, I used to open the window facing the street and stare until he came. I used my eyes to tie myself to the world that he roamed in. Now, my body without eyesight craved for his presence. The bridge that connected his world with mine was burnt down. Now, there were miles of blindness between us. Now I had to helplessly wait for him to cross over to my side. Therefore, whenever he left me, even for a minute, my blind body tried to cling on to him and howled for his presence.

But so much of desire and dependence was not healthy. In any case, the burden of a wife on a man was enough; I couldn't let it be amplified by my blindness. It was entirely up to me to carry this enormous world of darkness on my shoulders. I promised to myself in utmost sincerity that I would not tie my husband to the disability of my lack of vision.

Within a short while, I learnt to do my daily chores with the aid of my other senses; hearing, smelling, and touching. In fact, I could accomplish them with finer skills than before. I began to understand that vision distracts more than it helps. The eye sees more than what should be seen. And when eyes take over the job of surveillance, the ears become lazy and do not listen as much they should have. Now, with the absence of my eyes, my other senses took over their job with utmost competence.

Now I did not have to let my husband do my chores and, like earlier times, I started running his errands too.

My husband told me, 'You're depriving me of the honour of atoning for my sins.'

I replied, 'I don't know why you need to atone, but why should I aggravate my sins?'

Whatever he might say, I realized that when I freed him from his compulsions, he breathed a sigh of relief. A man's duty is not to take care of his blind wife forever.

My husband finished his degree in medicine and took me along to the suburbs.

I felt I returned to my mother's lap after going back to the village. I left the village for the city when I was eight. In these ten years, the memories of that life became as blurry as shadows. When I had eyes, the city life of Kolkata stood in front of me by obscuring my other memories. At the first glance, I realized that Kolkata could dazzle one's eyes, but it never satiated the mind. After losing my eyesight, the memories of my childhood in a village flashed upon my mind's eye like visible stars in the dark night.

In the middle of December, we moved to Hasimpur. A new place; I couldn't see how it looked like, but its smells and touches engulfed my senses in the same way the village of my childhood did. The morning air rising out of dew-splashed ploughed fields, the sweet, enticing fragrance of mustard and golden paddy fields, the songs of the shepherds, even the sound of bullock-carts plying on dirt roads…there was no end to my delight! The memories of my early life with all its sounds and scents made their way from the past and greeted my present; my blind eyes could not resist that joy. I returned to my childhood, but I couldn't see my mother. Of course, I did see her in my mind at times; I saw my grandmother untying her hair, basking in the sunlight, as she laid out lentil balls to dry in the sun, but I couldn't hear her hum, in her old, broken voice, ballads on the carnal amour of Radha and Krishna sung by our village hermit Bhajandas. The festivities of the first reap manifested in a sky drenched in dew. But where did my old coterie of friends who ground the grains in the village mill go? I could hear the moo of cows coming back after sundown; I remembered my mother guiding them to the shed with an evening lamp. The smell of wet fodder and the smoke of burnt hay pervaded my senses as I heard the ringing of prayer bells coming from the house of the pandits beside the pond. Somebody seemed to have extracted the spirit and essence from the vast substance of the life of my first eight years and presented it to me like never before.

I remembered my childhood rituals of picking flowers at dawn and worshipping Lord Shiva. I must admit that, in the discursive rigor of Kolkata, one's sensibility undergoes a change. The innocuous practices of religious faith lose their innocence. I remember that once, after losing my vision, a friend from my old village came to me and said, 'Are you not infuriated, Kumu? If I were you, I would have refused to see my husband's face.' I told her, 'Dear, it's apparent that I can't see his face anymore and I do blame these wretched eyes for that. Why would I be cross with my husband?' Labanya was enraged at my husband for not consulting a doctor on time and tried her best to put me against him as well. I tried to make her understand that in the whirlpool of family life, a lot of things, pleasant or unpleasant, willingly or unwillingly, happen. But if one can retain their faith in spite of everything, then it is possible to attain bliss and inner peace. Otherwise, one has to spend their entire life in petty clashes, blame-games, and conflicts. It is indeed unfortunate that I have gone blind, but why would I add to my misfortune by fighting with my husband? Labanya was disappointed to hear these antiquated words and left with a shrug. But whatever I might have said, I knew that a few drops of the venom in her words had left their trace in my mind. A few flickers of her rage were left behind in my mind; I extinguished them promptly with my feet. Nonetheless, some scars remained. Which is why, I was saying, Kolkata is a city of arguments and rationalism; one's mind becomes twisted out of inhabiting that space.

After returning to the village, the smell of the fresh shiuli buds with which I worshipped Lord Shiva enlivened my senses as if childhood was reclaimed. The grace of God filled my life and my heart. I submitted myself entirely. I prayed, 'Dear God my eyes might have gone. But you are still mine.'

Alas, I was wrong. It is a dare to claim God as one's own. I only had the right to declare that I am still yours. One day my God would smother me and make me say that. Nothing might last, but I have to stay strong. I might not have power over others, but I do have power over myself.

A few days passed in happiness. My husband's practice consolidated, and we managed to save some money.

But money is not a good thing. It takes control of the mind. When the mind reigns by itself, it can create its own happiness. But when wealth takes charge of that, the mind becomes useless. Consequently, peace of mind is replaced by material luxuries; one can only procure more goods instead of happiness!

I cannot cite anything in particular. But, maybe because a blind woman feels more than she sees, or for some other reason, I could understand my husband's character change with the acquiring of wealth. At the beginning of his youth, my husband was sensitive to ethics and righteousness. Gradually, that was getting diminished. I remember that he used to say, 'It's not simply to provide a living that I have studied medicine; I can put my knowledge to the welfare of the poor.' He despised those practitioners who privileged their fees more than the urgency of treating a poor patient. I could sense that he was no longer the same. I saw him ignore a hapless woman falling on his feet to save her only son's life. Finally, I had to implore him to go although I realized that it was not what he wished. When we were low on money, I remember what my husband thought of earning money through corrupt means. Now, as we accumulated a lot of wealth in our account, I got to know that he conferred with a rich man's secretary for days in secret. I was not aware of what they talked about, but afterwards he would come to me gleefully and converse about other things, I realized with my special powers that he had fallen from grace.

I could no longer identify the man whom I saw for the final time before losing my sight. The one who kissed me between my eyes and awakened my third eye and hailed me as the goddess; I could do nothing to prevent his fall. Those that are suddenly overwhelmed by desire and fall have a chance of a fervid redemption. But those whose morality gradually decays, those that assassinate their inner goodness bit by bit, I do not know how they could be cured.

It didn't bother me that I couldn't see my husband; but it pained my soul to discover that we were no longer on the same page. I was blind; in the dark caverns of family life, all that I had to show for faith and devotion was the love of my early life. The dew on the flowers that I offered in humility to the god in my temple hadn't dried yet. But my husband had forsaken this shade of youthful amour and has trodden off to some distant, parched desert in search of more money. He seemed to stand far apart and scoff at everything that I believed in, all the tenets that I embraced as my religion, all that mattered more to me than material comfort. But this separation had not existed before. We had started our journey on the same path. He didn't realize when his path diverged from mine. Nor did I. Today I do not hear back when I cry out for him.

At times I thought that these things appeared larger than they should because I was blind. Perhaps, I would have been able to take family as it is if I had eyes.

One day even my husband demonstrated the same. In the morning, an old Muslim man called upon him to cure his granddaughter of cholera. I heard him implore, 'Sir, I am poor. But Allah will bring you good.' My husband replied, 'What Allah would do does not concern me. What you can do counts more.' Upon hearing that I thought why did god not make me deaf as well? The old Muslim sighed and left. Soon enough, I asked my maid to summon him at the back door and said, 'Father, here is a bit of money for your granddaughter's treatment. Please pray for my husband and call for Doctor Harish of our neighborhood.'

But I couldn't bite a morsel through the rest of the day. My husband woke up from his afternoon siesta and asked, 'Why do you look so depressed?' I thought of answering the way I used to: 'No, nothing happened.' But gone are the days of deceit. I said clearly, 'I have been meaning to say this for a long time, though I am not sure of how to put it. I don't think I would be able to explain properly but I believe you too realize that we have drifted apart.' My husband smiled and replied, 'Change is the rule of life.' I said, 'Yes, one's financial status and external beauty changes, but doesn't the core remain unaltered?' He replied gravely, 'Listen, other women are depressed by real reasons. Either the husbands do not earn well or they have fallen out of love. You create your sadness out of thin air.' At that moment I realized that my blindness had put special lens on my eyes and carried me out of this real world. I was not like other women. My husband would never understand me.

Meanwhile, one of my husband's aunts came to check in on his nephew from a distant village. As soon as we bowed to her and paid our respects, she said, 'Dear daughter, I say, you have lost your eyes by the turn of fate. Now how would our Abinash run a household with a blind wife? You should arrange for another marriage for him.' If my husband had jokingly remarked, 'Why don't you take charge of that, aunty?' then things would have been clear. But he replied with hesitation, 'Ah, aunt! The things that you say!' The aunt replied, 'Am I saying anything wrong? Come on, daughter-in-law, tell me.' I tried to laugh it off and said, 'You're asking for advice from the wrong person, dear aunty. Does the robber take his victim's consent before looting them?' The aunt replied, 'Yes, you are right. Abinash, we must conspire in private. But, dear daughter-in-law, the brahmin husband's repute depends on the number of fellow-wives his wife has. If our Abinash did not study medicine and married instead, he would not have had any shortage of money. These patients die at the hands of doctors. Dead persons never pay fees, do they? But, by the grace of god, a brahmin's wife never dies. Or as long as she lives, the husband profits.'

A couple of days later my husband asked his aunt in front of me, 'Aunty, can you find a girl of a decent household who could look after my wife like one's own? She cannot see. I would be relieved to have a companion by her side.'

This would have made sense just after I got blind. But now I wasn't sure how the lack of my eyesight had hindered my life or any household chore. However, I did not protest and remained silent. The aunt said, 'It wouldn't be difficult. One of my brothers-in-law has a daughter. Her beauty is as impeccable as her decency. That maiden is ripe enough for marriage. They would marry her off as soon as they find a suitable brahmin groom like you.' My husband was taken aback, 'Who's talking about marriage?' The aunt replied, 'Good gracious! How can you expect a girl from a decent family to stay here without marrying?' She had a point. My husband couldn't find an appropriate reply.

I stood alone with the closed doors of my blind eyes and looked up and prayed, 'Dear God, please save my husband.'

A few days later, as soon as I was done with my morning worship and came out, the aunt said, 'Daughter-in-law, the niece that I was referring to, Hemangini, has arrived from the village. Himu, greet your sister.'

Meanwhile, my husband appeared, saw an unknown woman, and was about to turn back, when the aunt said, 'Where you going, Abinash? This is my niece, Hemangini.' My husband was surprised and asked inconsequential details like when was she was escorted here and by whom, and so on.

I said to myself, 'It is not that I don't understand what's going on. But why add a layer of deceit on it? Why tell lies to cover up and play hide-and-seek? If you have to sin, then it is to give in to your temptations. But why am I being dragged into it? What is the need to tell me lies?'

I held Hemangini by her hand and took her to my bedroom. I ran my fingers across her face and body and realized that she was beautiful. She was not younger than 14 or 15.

The girl suddenly laughed loudly and said, 'Are you trying to ward off evil spirits from me?'

That innocent, hearty laughter instantly cleared the clouds that gathered in my heart. I put my arm dearly across her shoulder and said, 'I am inspecting you, dear sister.' Then I ran my fingers again across her soft, delicate face.

'You're inspecting me?' She smiled again, 'Am I an eggplant or a gourd in your garden that you have to touch me and inspect how big I have grown?'

Then I thought that probably she doesn't know of my blindness. I told her, 'Sister, I am blind.' Upon hearing that she was surprised and remained silent for a while. I could very well guess that she was gauging my sightless eyes and facial expressions with her young, curious eyes. Eventually, she said, 'Oh! Is that why aunt brought me here?'

I told her, 'I did not ask for you. She brought you of her own will.'

The girl laughed again and said, 'Out of mercy? Then I can safely assume that Her Merciful Highness would not be leaving soon. But I wonder why my father sent me here.'

Meanwhile, the aunt entered the room. She was done conversing with my husband. Hemangini promptly said, 'Aunty, when will I return home?'

The aunt replied, 'Good God! How eager you are to leave as soon as you have come. I have never seen an impatient lass like this!'

Hemangini said, 'Aunty, I don't think you would leave anytime soon. But they are your relatives, stay as long as you like. Let me tell you right away that I won't stay here for long.' Then she held my hand and said, 'You know what, sister? You are not that close to me.' I couldn't find an answer to this innocuous question and dragged her close to me. I understood that in spite of her best efforts, aunty couldn't fully control this girl. Aunty hid her anger and tried to appease Hemangini, who did not pay heed to it. The aunt tried to act as if she took it as another innocent joke of a young maiden and decided to leave the room. She paused for a while, thought something, and turned back, 'Himu, it is time for your bath.' Himu came closer to me and said, 'I shall go to the ghat with my sister.' The aunt unwillingly gave up. She knew that Hemangini would win if forced and that would expose their differences in front of me in a rather ugly way.

As we walked towards the ghat through the back door, Hemangini asked me, 'Why didn't you have kids?' I smiled and said, 'How am I to know that? God did not grace us with children.' Hemangini said, 'Then you must have sinned in some way.' I replied, 'That too, God only knows.' Hemangini tried to cite an example, 'Look at aunt. She is such a complicated woman that she cannot be impregnated.' I do not understand these theories of karma and sins; nor did I try to explain this to the girl. I just sighed and said to her in my mind: Perhaps, you are right. Hemangini hugged me right then and smiled, 'My goodness! You sigh at my words. At least someone takes me seriously.'

I noticed that my husband's medical practice had disrupted. He began to avoid calls from far-off places, even if he went nearby, he returned as soon as he could. Earlier, when he stayed at home during leisure, he came into the inner quarters only to take his lunch or a siesta. Now, the aunt asked for him whenever she wanted to; he too would come to ask after her with or without reason. When the aunt used to shout,. 'Himu, bring my case of betel leaves here,' I could feel that my husband was in her room. Initially, Hemangini used to deliver her case of betel leaves, a bowl of oil, her vermillion box, or whatever that was commanded. Soon enough, she did not move whenever she was called; instead, she would send over what the aunt wanted through the maid. The aunt kept calling, 'Hemangini, Himu! Himu...' She would cling on to me in pity and passion; she was engulfed by fear and melancholy. She would never mention my husband, even mistakenly, in front of me.

One day, my elder brother came to visit us. I knew that my brother was a close observer. It would be difficult to conceal what was going on. My brother had fierce judgments. He did not have the slightest mercy for the unjust. What I feared the most was that my husband would appear as the biggest culprit in front of his eyes. I tried to cover things up with excessive glee. I tried to uphold a festive mood in the household by being garrulous and constantly on my feet. I knew I overdid things and that, probably, aroused his suspicion. But my brother could not stay here for long. My husband showed his displeasure to an extent that it often translated into rudeness. He left. Before leaving, he placed his quivering hand on my head to offer his blessings. I could feel what he blessed. His tears would land on my tear-drenched cheeks.

I remember, on a late spring evening, people were returning home after a day in the village market. Storm and rain were imminent; one could sense the petrichor and humidity all over the air. Detached from their group, the people called out to each other in the dark field. As long as I stayed alone in my bedroom, I did not light the lamp. I feared if my drape would catch fire and cause some accident. In that dark, desolate chamber, I sat on the ground, joined my hands, and prayed to my god, 'My Lord, when I do not feel your mercy, when I do not understand your means, I try to clasp on to the reigns of this orphaned heart; blood often comes out of my mouth; I cannot hold on; how long would you keep testing me? How strong am I?' Tears came to my eyes. I put my face on the pillow and cried. I have to do all kinds of household work throughout the day. Hemangini clings on to me like a shadow. I do not get the leisure to shed the tears even if I need to. I got a chance to purge after a long time today. After a while, the bed moved; I could hear the sound of human presence in the room. Hemangini came to me, hugged me, and wiped my tears with her drape. I don't know when she came to the room and lay down. She did not ask anything, nor did I tell her what happened. Softly, she caressed my forehead with her delicate hands. Meanwhile, a storm raged outside with the roar of clouds and tumultuous rain. After a long time, a breath of cool air calmed my otherwise parched heart.

On the following day, Hemangini said, 'Aunty, if you do not leave, I will ask for my Kaibarta brother to take me home.' The aunt replied, 'Don't bother. I would be departing tomorrow; we can go together. Look at this, Himu. Our Abinash bought a pearl ring for you.' The aunt handed over the ring to her with pride. Hemangini said, 'Look at this aunt, how amazing my aim is, and tossed the ring through the window into the pond. The aunt was infuriated with grief and anger. She held my hand and requested repeatedly, 'Daughter-in-law, do not tell your husband of this frivolous act. Our Abinash would be disheartened to hear this. Promise?' I replied, 'I give you my word, dear aunt. I will not tell him anything.'

The next day before they left, Hemangini hugged me and said, 'Do remember me, sister.' I ran my fingers across her face and said, 'A blind woman never forgets, dear sister. I do not have sight; all I have is this mind.' I pulled her closer and kissed her forehead. My tears drenched her hair.

My world dried up after Hemangini's departure. All the light, laughter, scent and music that she brought along disappeared; I searched fanatically to find anything worthwhile around me. My husband was particularly delighted. He said, 'Now that they have gone, I can concentrate more on my work.' Curse me. What was the need of deceit? Do I fear the truth? Did I ever fear getting hurt? Does my husband not know that when I gave up my eyes, I embraced a fate of darkness?

Hitherto, there was a veil of darkness between husband and me. Now another obstacle was added to it. My husband never mentioned Hemangini's name in front of me, as if she had completely disappeared from his world of relations, as if she never existed in the first place. But I could totally realize that he wrote letters to ask after her. Just as the stalk of lotus feels a push whenever the flood water enters the pond, I could sense something had happened whenever he appeared more gleeful than usual. I was not aware of the days when he heard back about her or not, but I could not ask him anything. I was eager to know and talk about the bright, young and shimmering star that appeared in the darkness of my heart for a while. But I did not have the right to ask my husband about her. A wall of silence defined by speech and sadness emerged between us and stood strong.

On a mid-summer afternoon, the maid came to me and asked, 'Mother, I saw a lot of boats being arranged at the ghat today. Is the master going somewhere?' I could sense that some initiative was being taken. In the sky of my fate, there has long been the lull before the storm. Now the clouds of doom have appeared. The Destroyer Lord had orchestrated all his power at the wave of his finger right on me. I could feel that. I told the maid, 'Really? I have not been told anything.' The maid did not dare to ask me any more questions, sighed and left.

Long into that night, my husband came to me and said, 'I have been summoned from a far-off place. I have to leave tomorrow right at dawn. It might take me two or three days more than usual.'

I got up from my bed and said, 'Why are you telling me lies?'

My husband's voice quivered as he managed to say, 'Why would I lie?'

I told him, 'You're going to marry her.'

He remained silent. I stood motionless as well. There was not even a whisper in the room. At last, I said, 'I demand an answer. Admit that you're going to get married.'

His reply was almost an echo, 'Yes, I am going to get married.'

I said, 'No, you cannot do that. I must save you from this grave sin. If I fail then what kind of a wife am I? Why did I worship Lord Shiva for so long?'

There was again a bout of silence in the room. I fell on his feet and said, 'How have I harmed you? Where did I go wrong? Why do you need another wife? Swear on me. Tell me the truth.'

Then my husband replied slowly, 'Truth be told, I am intimidated by you. Your blindness has cloaked you from this reality. It is a world that I cannot enter. You are my goddess; you are my nemesis. I cannot run this household with you. I need a simple girl whom I can scold, fight with, buy her jewelry and make love to.'

'Look within me. I am a simple girl. My mind is nothing else but that of the young girl you once married. I want to learn how to trust, depend and worship you. Do not humiliate yourself by making me larger than what I am with your guilt. Keep me under your feet in all circumstances.'

I don't remember exactly what I said that night. Can the enraged ocean hear its own roar? Although I remember saying, 'If my devotion is true then let God be witness. You cannot break your vow. Before you commit that grave sin, may I be widowed or may Hemangini die.' I fainted soon after that.

When I came back to my senses, my husband had already left and the morning birds were yet to chirp.

I shut myself up in the prayer room and began my penance. I did not leave the room throughout the day. In the evening, a dreadful storm rocked the house. I did not pray, 'God! My husband is on the water, save his life' but asked, 'God. May whatever that is in my fate happen. But save my husband from committing that grave sin.' The entire night passed. I did not leave that room the next day as well. I do not know who provided me strength in spite of fasting and staying awake. I sat in front of the stone idol like a stone idol myself.

In the evening, people started knocking on the door. When they broke in, they found that I had fainted.

When I got back to my senses, I heard, 'Sister!.' I found myself lying on Hemangini's lap. As she moved her lips, her new bridal dress rustled. God, you did not listen to my prayers. My husband has therefore sinned!

Hemangini bowed her head and said slowly, 'Sister, I have come to seek your blessings.'

I remained stiff like a log for a while before gathering myself, 'Why would I not bless dear sister? It is not your fault.'

Hemangini broke into laughter with her sweet voice. 'Fault? If you getting married is not a fault, then why would my marriage be?'

I hugged Hemangini and tried to smile. I wondered if my prayers were ultimate in this world. Ultimately, His wishes would reign supreme. Whatever blows I must take I will; but I shall not let them destroy the faith in religion that still persists within the depths of my heart. I shall remain as I was.

Hemagini fell on my feet and bowed. I said, 'May you be forever happy; may fate be with you.'

Hemangini said, 'Not simply should your blessings work. You must embrace me and your brother-in-law with your pure, chaste hands. You must not be embarrassed. Now, if you allow, let me bring him inside.'

'Go on,' I permitted.

After a while I heard new footsteps in the room. I heard an affectionate question, 'Are you feeling better now, Kumu?'

I got up from my bed with haste and bowed down, 'Brother!

Hemangini said, 'What brother! He is your brother-in-law now!'

I could understand the entire narrative now. I knew my brother had decided never to marry. My mother tried her best but could not succeed. Now I seem to be the reason behind his marriage. Tears overflowed through my eyes. I could not hold them back. My brother ran his fingers through my hair. Hemangini kept smiling as she hugged me tightly.

I could not sleep that night. I was waiting eagerly for my husband to return. I was not sure of how he would deal with his shame and disappointment.

The door to my bedroom opened late at night. I sat up with alacrity. It was my husband's footsteps. I could hear my heart pounding.

He came to my bed, held my hand, and said, 'Your brother saved me from sinning. I was momentarily dazzled by lust. God alone knows the burden I carried inside me when I got on that boat. When the storm rocked our boat. I feared for my life. I also thought that I would be saved if I drowned. After reaching Mathurgunj, I learnt that your brother married Hemangini the day before. I cannot put in words with what delight and embarrassment I returned home. Over the past few days, I have realized that there is no happiness without you. You are my goddess.'

I smiled and said, 'No, I don't wish to be your goddess. I am your wife. I am a simple woman.'

My husband said, 'You must also keep my request. Do not unsettle me by gracing me as your god.'

On the following day, the neighbourhood came alive with the sounds of celebration. Hemangini pulled my husband's leg incessantly during dinner and repose, day or night. There was no end to her torture! But nobody breathed a word where he had gone off to or what had truly transpired.

Translated from Bengali by Debayudh Chatterjee

Asif Jahan's Daughter-in-Law

Rashid Jahan

Asif Jahan's husband was an affluent deputy collector and Nurul Hasan was her only son who survived after the death of many infants. Therefore, he was dear to everyone. There was no one in her entire clan who would not have gladly married their daughter to Nur, but it was Asif Jahan's wish to bring Kubra's daughter home. She was a righteous and devoted wife. She wanted Kubra's daughter as her daughter-in-law, because Kubra was not only her husband's younger sister but also married to Asif's brother. It was precisely for the quality of her farsightedness that she was loveable in her extended family. Had she chosen a bride from her own people, her in-laws would have expressed resentment, and if she had done so from among her in-laws, her own people would have felt displeased. Only if Kubra had a daughter, her selection as daughter-in-law would make everyone happy.

As God wills! Kubra bore a child every year, and hence at a young age of 25, she became the mother of five sons. Her good fortune was proverbial in her entire clan: 'May everyone get a bit of luck like Kubra's. Every time you see her, there is always a boy gracing her lap. One should not wish a daughter even to one's enemy.' Each time Kubra gave birth to a son, the entire world grew envious of her. If there was anyone who was saddened by this state of affairs, it was Asif Jahan. However, she used to certainly feel happy with Kubra's recuperation. After all, one is on the brink of death while delivering a baby. However, Asif Jahan could not help but cry when Kubra produced yet another son: 'Who do I blame but my stars. Only Nurul Hasan has survived out of my nine children, and I do not see my wish getting fulfilled for him. There are so many girls around us that people are unable to find grooms for them, but God refuses to send a bride only for my son.'

Kubra had been bearing birth-pangs for the last three days. Their family midwife was attending to her. The house was crammed with elderly women, sisters, sisters-in-law from both sides of the family and their offspring. There was such a commotion in the house that one could not understand a word. The whole scene resembled the festivities of a wedding. Women were discussing amongst themselves if it was advisable to send for a lady doctor. Despite the unrelenting throes of delivery, the baby refused to come out. 'After all, women produce babies all the time, but such a protracted labour pain is unheard of.' A lamb was sacrificed; grains were distributed among the poor; amulets and charms were used. No stone was left unturned but the baby showed no signs of popping out. Kubra was getting exhausted from the pain. Outside the labour room, on a prayer rug spread on a wooden seat, Asif Jahan's hands were raised in prayer. 'O Preserver of the universe! Have pity on Kubra's little children and free her from this calamity.

O, my Lord! Pay heed to my prayer this time and bless me with a daughter-in-law. O Provider! I have left disappointed five times from your court…fulfill my wish this time.' Asif Jahan prayed incessantly and fervently and the expectation of God's compassion was trickling from her entire visage.

Kubra's groans and screams were continuously reaching Asif Jahan's ears. 'Alas! Sister, My dear sister-in-law! I will not survive this time...Allah! Allah! Have mercy on my condition. I'll die…Hai, I'll die.'

'Oh Kubra! Don't utter such inauspicious words.'

'Water…get me some water.'

'Gulshabbo! Gulshabbo, where the hell are you? You wretch, can't you see that the bowl is empty,' a relative shouted from inside.

After a while, Kubra's screams multiplied accompanied by the increasing volume of women's chatter. 'Well done! Excellent! Push it…harder. That's it.' Then such a dreadful scream rent the air that it froze Asif Jahan's blood. The few seconds that elapsed appeared like years to Asif Jahan. Then the first cry of a newborn…Asif Jahan heaved a sigh of relief and completed her prayer. 'O Master of the world! Whether it is a boy or a girl depends on my destiny but I am grateful to you for saving Kubra's life.' After uttering these words, she bowed down in prostration, touching the prayer rug with her forehead. She had barely raised her head when a little girl came running with the good news of great joy: 'Hurray! It's a girl. Congratulation Begum Sahiba, you are blessed with a daughter-in-law!'

Asif Jahan began to exult while she was still in the position of prostration. As soon as she raised her head, she took out a wallet from her bodice and rewarded the messenger with one rupee, gladly walking towards the maternity room. The room was already thronged with so many women. Every married woman was present. Anxiety on the faces of women had subsided now. No sooner had Asif Jahan entered than a woman declared 'The navel string of the newborn child is yet to fall.'

Kubra's aunt, elder sister, and one of her sisters-in-law were sitting at the head of the bed, and the midwife sat at the other end with her feet placed against Kubra's thighs. The sister-in-law stood up to create more space for Asif Jahan to sit on the bed.

Addressing Asif Jahan, Kubra's sister said, 'Sister-in-law, this time Kubra has suffered a lot. But your luck has brought a girl into her house. It was a narrow escape from death.'

'God listened to the prayers of all of you. I had lost hope even this time. God showed mercy and thanked God the need to call a *mem* (a European lady doctor) did not arise.'

'O madam, don't even ask…you ladies confounded me for no reason. A baby will be born when God wishes it. What difference could the presence of a mem have made? She would have inserted all sorts of medical instruments (in delivery). You start shouting 'call mem, call mem' at the slightest delay. Did women not bear babies when these wretched mems were not around?' the midwife started mumbling irritably.

'There is a limit to the wait. She had been writhing in pain for two days and three nights and you couldn't even tell when the baby would be born. Haven't we borne babies? Don't we know the normal duration of birth pangs?' Kubra's sister Aisha Begum retorted.

'Now that you have talked enough, tell me when will the navel string fall?'

'O sister, matters of life and death are in God's control. No one knows the vagaries of Time. The baby is born but there is still movement in the umbilical cord. Look folks how it's trembling.' The midwife held the cord with one hand, which was covered with filthy and ragged silver rings and bangles, while she cleaned the blood with the other. Aisha Begum was pressing Kubra's belly very hard, for which she was famous in her entire extended family.

'O dear lady, do you feel the pain now?' the midwife enquired.

'No,' Kubra whimpered.

'The movement of cord has subsided now.' Having said that the midwife held it between her toe and left hand and began to clean it with her right. Kubra grew pale with agony.

'*Arrey* Masitan, don't cut the cord. The placenta has not fallen as yet,' a woman amongst the congregation of the standing women intervened.

'Oh dear, you are just a child and I assisted your entry into this world. Now you are teaching me the basics of midwifery. I have lots of experience. Badi Begum, I swear by

God, these wenches can fool anyone. Am I so stupid that I will cut the cord before the removal of the placenta?'

Masitan kept cleaning the placenta while other women narrated their stories—their experiences of childbirth and which midwife was called in their neighbourhood or in the house of their in-laws, and how a certain pregnant woman died immediately after giving birth to a baby and the placenta remained in the womb.

'Do you remember what happened to Ashiq Husain's wife? The placenta was stuck inside. Evening set in and the midwife used every possible means to no avail. She finally gave up declaring that the placenta was stuck in the liver. The mother was rushed to a hospital where mems removed it. But dear aunt, I heard that her liver came out too. She died in a couple of days leaving behind two little children...'

'The placenta of my sister-in-law was removed by a lady doctor too. She remained ill for a long time but at least she survived.'

The midwife could not keep quiet after the names of lady doctors and mems figured in the talk. She said irritatingly, 'Watch your tongue. Is this the moment to talk of such ill-omens? Do you have nothing to discuss except mems and doctors? Look Badi Begum...'

'Yes, she is right. Qaisera, leave this topic and start some other conversation at this time.' Badi Begum said.

'Yes,' the midwife said annoyingly. 'Aisha Bibi, press her belly hard. The afterbirth is about to come out.' Aisha Begum, who was already grasping the mother's belly in a firm grip, closed her fists, half rose on her feet, and began to clutch her sister's belly with her full strength. Kubra wriggled in pain and began to scream. 'Away! Sister, stop it for God's sake. I am about to die.'

'It's done.'

Having examined the afterbirth, the midwife said, 'Look Badi Begum. The whole placenta has come out and don't complain later.' After saying this, she moved the placenta towards Asif Jahan. All women present there analyzed it one by one and presented their opinions on it.

'Oh, lady! Don't loosen your grip on her belly as yet. She is bleeding profusely. Hold it firmly' the midwife instructed.

And Aisha Begum applied her whole strength.

'Let me cut the cord now. It will cease to bleed in the meantime.' Having expressed her intention, the midwife again clenched the umbilical cord between her toes and started cleaning it with her hands. She tied the cord with a thread that was lying near the bed and peered around. Then she picked up a rusting knife and cut the cord. She put the afterbirth in an earthen vessel. She took out rags from underneath the mother and cleaned it. Bleeding showed no signs of abating. Masitan got off the bed with the airs of a conqueror. Stretching her limbs, she said, 'Oh Badi Begum, please move aside. You will not be able to lift her. Sabira and Qaisera, come and help me pick her up.' Ignoring the mother's cries, Qaisera and Sabira put their arms under Kubra's waist and elevated her about eight inches so that Masitan could swaddle the lower part of Kubra's belly with a six-yard-long strip of cloth. The bleeding had somewhat ceased but due to the excessive discharge of blood from her body Kubra had grown pale and looked as frail as shreds. Now that the baby is born and the placenta has fallen, she will regain her strength by the grace of God.

Now Asif Jahan turned her attention to the baby girl and said, 'She has a dark complexion.'

'Sister-in-law, you must thank God that your luck has brought a girl in Kubra's house.'

'I would have chosen her as my daughter-in-law even if she was blind of one eye. Masitan, will you now give a bath to the infant or not?'

Masitan bathed the newborn child but refused to hand her over despite Asif Jahan's insistence.

'Dear sister, she was born after umpteen supplications. I won't hand her over unless I get my due.'

'Tch! Don't I know how much I owe you? I have already put your due in the earthen vessel of the afterbirth.'

Grinning, Masitan asked with curiosity, 'I swear by God, how much?'

'There are five rupees, what else?'

'Badi Begum, I swear by God, I will never settle for five rupees.'

'Have you gone crazy, Masitan. Do you know some people give only a paltry sum of one taka at the time of betrothal? Is this the time to distribute customary presents? Claim what you want at the time of her wedding.'

'Yes sister, you are right (ironically). I will certainly be alive at the time of her marriage. You ladies don't hesitate before spending lakhs of rupees, but you always cite customs at the time of paying our rightful due. You will give it to a female sanitation worker, to Gulshabbo. Whoever claims her due will get it. Sister, I will never be content with five rupees.'

Masitan was their family midwife. Almost all of them were born through her services. She had the right to haggle with them. Asif Jahan opened her purse and put two more rupees in the bowl. Masitan, who was expecting a further reward of five more rupees, was not very happy with the addition of mere two rupees. But she pursed the money. All the women present there gave something or the other to the midwife. Some handed out an eight anna coin, some a rupee. Picking up the earthen vessel, Masitan told Kubra, 'Dear, I swear, this baby girl is born after more supplications and prayers than are made for a son. I will not relent until I get a gift of gold bangles.'

'When did Kubra pray for the birth of a daughter? You ask your sister-in-law for whatever you want. She is the one who continued to supplicate for a daughter-in-law. We will give you what you usually get at the birth of sons in our family,' replied Aisha Begum.

'Are you listening Badi Begum?' Masitan appealed.

'Now relax. Go and wash your hands and face. Eat a paan. You are always obsessed with the word give.' Aisha Begum replied to Masitan angrily.

Aisha Begum was sharp-tongued. After getting free from her sister, she sent for *domnis*, the professional female singers.

The sounds of drums and songs turned the atmosphere of the house into a pandemonium. Amidst the pranks and commotion of the house, no one thought of the rest and sleep of the woman who had just given birth. All women teased Asif Jahan and played pranks among themselves. The professional female singers were told to sing *zaccagiriyan*, the songs for a newly-born child, and *Suhaggaliyan*, the obscene songs sung at the occasion of marriage. They parodied the situations of a maternity room by sticking their bellies out. 'O you, which month is this?' asked a domni who was playing the role of a husband. The female singer who played the role of wife answered, 'It's the seventh or eighth month.' The unmarried girls, who had assembled in a separate courtyard during childbirth, were now free to roam in the entire house. The lesser said about the ladies the better. Some boys also flocked into the hall. The twelve-year-old bridegroom was also sitting half-hidden in the gathering of children and was listening to everything. But he was spotted by one of his cousins. She pounced on him and drawing everyone's attention to him announced, 'Look here, the groom is quietly listening to every conversation.'

There was a burst of laughter.

The groom tried hard to free himself from the clutches of his cousin and pleaded, 'Elder sister, please leave me… let me go.' When he was escaping towards the entrance, his cousin shouted from behind, 'What kind of groom are you? Go inside and cast a glance at your moon-like bride.'

*Translated from Urdu by Mohammed Afzal**

* I am grateful to Dr Abdur Rasheed, Retired Professor, Department of Urdu, Jamia Milia Islamia for reading the translation and his invaluable suggestions.

The Plague-Witch

'Master' Bhagwandas

When the plague came to Prayag last year, and hundreds of poor as well as the kin of several moneylenders, landlords, lawyers, and representatives began dying almost everyday, people started to abandon their houses. Many doctors left town and went to other cities. In one of the local communities of Prayag, there lived a prosperous landlord by the name of Thakur Vibhav Singh. He, too, had planned to leave Prayag and shift to a different location, which was five miles away from the city. Except for his wife and a five-year-old boy, he had no other family in his house.

Early Sunday morning, they began preparing to leave the city. In her haste, his wife took a bath with cold water. But as soon as she did this, she contracted a fever. The local hakim was called and medicine was procured, but to no avail. By that same evening, a lump had appeared on her throat. This worried Thakur saheb and his servants. The doctor took one look at her and announced that she had been inflicted with the plague, and that it would be better for them to leave this house as soon as possible. Having said so, the doctor himself left the house immediately. Now Thakur saheb was caught in a quagmire; he could not decide whether he should stay back or leave. He reasoned with himself, 'If my staying did any good to Bahuji then I would stay and risk my life. But even medicine has no effect on this disease. Why should I then stay and lose my life?' But just when he had made up his mind to leave, his boy, named Naval Singh, started weeping seeing his mother's face and refused to budge. Thakur saheb became silent with love and pity and sat there helplessly.

Thakur saheb was a kind and courteous man. There had to be some reason behind his cold behaviour, which he was not sharing with anyone. However, he kept repeating, 'My wife's life is already ebbing away, I don't mind staying back, but my son's life should be spared. There is no justification for putting him in danger. At least my linage will not go extinct.' But how could that child understand these things? He was so attached to his mother that he stayed put by her side and cried through the night.

Next morning when Thakurain ji came to herself, her eyes welled up with tears. She said, 'Naval Singh, my son, do not grieve for me. You should go to another house. I shall meet you there as soon as I get well.' But the boy did not heed her pleadings, nor did he realize the dire consequences of staying at such a place. Bahuji lost consciousness once again while he sat there and wept. After a while, the doctor, vaidya and hakim came but their medicines had no effect whatsoever.

The morning turned to afternoon and by that evening her body had gone limp. The doctor saw her face from afar and pronounced, 'She is dead. Worry about carrying her out now.' The servants began to weep and the neighbours gathered around. Everyone said the same thing: 'Alas! Cruel death has claimed an innocent soul. Does it not care for her beauty, kindness and devotion? Is it unaffected by her virtues?'

A neighbour, who was also a poet, displayed his grief through a *savaiya*:

It shatters the brave in a moment, and destroys the coward too
it rips apart the wise, and picks clean the flesh of fools

Beauty cannot tempt it so, the ugly is swept away by its force.
No virtue or vice can dissuade cruel death and time from its course.

The women began to say, 'Look! How bitterly the boy weeps! Did death have no pity on his sorry situation? How will he bear the agony of separation from his mother? Ha! Such misfortune fell on this unlucky boy barely out of his childhood.' Thakur saheb had fallen to the ground in a swoon. The servants sprinkled rosewater on his face and brought him to his senses. None of his friends were present there. His neighbours, who had gathered around, advised him to carry his wife's body to the Ganga ghat and cremate it with due rites. But doctor saheb, who had just returned, said that they should leave the house immediately and go elsewhere; rest of the mess can be handled later on.

Thakur saheb found his advice agreeable. He had wanted to escape since the night before but his son's pleadings had held him back. Would the boy now leave easily? No, he refused to move away from the side of his mother's dead body. Several times he fell on her body, looked into her half open eyes and called out crying, 'Mother! Mother!' The sight rent the heart of onlookers and tears fell from their eyes.

Finally, Thakur saheb picked up the child in his arms and left for the other house. Albeit, as the vehicle began to ply, Thakur saheb did look back at his wife one last time and said something in English; I recollect only one word from it, 'Farewell.'

All the servants left with him, except for one old attendant who stayed back to guard the house. The neighbours too returned to their homes having witnessed the sad turn of events. One of the neighbours was so affected by what had transpired that he sat on the very spot and began to reflect on his duty as a neighbour. The law of the land prevents anyone from eating and bathing till the corpse remains in the community. Only when the arrangements are in order and the body taken away that people can return to their daily routines. The state of affairs here worried him greatly and he wondered what would become of the body, if Thakur saheb continued to stay in his new location out of fear? Would the corpse of this pious lady be carted away ignominiously? He expressed his anxiety to the old attendant. The attendant replied that they should wait for Thakur saheb and see what his orders were.

That neighbour understood that this is the way things were and reflected on the vanity of the world and the infirmity of love between living beings. He reminisced a verse by Nanak, 'Everything here is treatment for living…' and another by Soordas, 'Who is you friend in hard times?' He thought it inappropriate to sing the songs at that moment and so hummed the tunes in his head. Just then, two of Thakur saheb's servants returned and informed the old attendant that they had been sent to guard the house while he has been summoned by Thakur saheb himself. He should make haste; Thakur saheb was lodging at Mattan merchant's house. The old attendant was called Satya Singh.

When he reached Mattan merchant's house, he found that Thakur saheb's friends—who were lawyers, moneylenders, and suchlike—were all advising him that he should go to the safe house, 'Do not get into the mess of cremation rites and rituals. If you live, you'll retain your Dharma.' Thakur saheb turned to the priest for his opinion. The priest also thought it prudent to agree with everyone else. He said, 'According to the scriptures, it is possible. Let someone else perform the final rites for now; when a more agreeable time arrives, you can make an effigy of the dead and cremate that instead.'

'Here, take these thirty rupees,' Thakur saheb offered the money to the priest as soon as he heard the priest's verdict, 'Take eight of my servants to perform the crematory rites and allow me to leave for my safe house.' Saying so, he took the boy, bid farewell to his friends and left for his destination, while the priest arrived at his house with Satya Singh and his eight servants. By the time they bought the shroud and got the bier-ladder made, evening was upon them. When the *nayin* (barber's wife) began to wrap *bahuji* in the shroud, she exclaimed, 'Her body has not gone cold yet, and her eyes are still half-open. I feel scared.' The priest and the servants rebuked her, 'Your mind is playing tricks. How can a corpse be alive? Wrap her up quickly so we can take her to Ganga ghat and get done with it. It is getting dark, should we also die as this woman? When Thakur saheb abandoned his post, why should we get embroiled in this mess. We only need to burn the body somehow and get back to our lives. Do you want us to be cremated along with her?'

Satya Singh protested, 'If the nayin says so, perhaps we should take another look. Maybe Bahuji is not dead yet. Thakur saheb abandoned her, the doctor announced his verdict from afar, in such a situation it is prudent to do a proper check at least.'

The servants chided him, 'Satya Singh, you have become senile. What you say is impossible. Don't delay anymore and help us carry her out.' Having said so, they placed the body on the bier, put the bier on their shoulders, pronounced the word of Satya Singh false and affirming the name of God, '*Ram naam satya hai*!' made their way towards Dashashwamedh Ghat. Along the way, a servant protested, 'It is already seven o' clock, by the time we are done with the rites it will be midnight.' Another said, 'No doubt the cremation will take the entire night.' The third responded, 'It would have been better if Thakur saheb had asked us to leave the corpse unburnt.' The fourth opined, 'I say, those who die of small pox, plague and suchlike should be set a float on the river.' The fifth enquired, 'If the priest agrees, we could still do so.' The priest himself was afraid of venturing into the cremation grounds after dark. He said, 'If the jury has come to this decision, then I agree; since Thakur saheb will perform the rites on the effigy anyway, we aren't required to double it by performing them here as well.' The sixth and the seventh servant announced that it is best if we abandon the body and inform Thakur Saheb that we burned the body. Satya Singh, true to his name, refused to comply, 'I don't think this is the right thing to do. It is our duty to follow our master's orders and properly cremate the body. If you don't agree with me then I'll return to my home. You can do as you please and tell Thakur saheb what you wish; but if he asks me, I'll tell him everything truthfully.' His words made the servants anxious. They tried to bribe him and said, 'You can take the largest share from these thirty rupees but don't tell Thakur saheb of what transpired here.' Satya Singh was adamant, 'I am not a traitor. I cannot do this. I'll go home now; you all may do as you please.'

Watching the old attendant leave, the other servants got scared and turned to the priest, 'What should we do? That oldie will spill the beans and send us packing.' The priest pacified them, 'Do not fear. It is a good thing that the old man has left us. Now we can do what we want. I shall speak to Thakur saheb and tell him that we burned the corpse. He trusts me more than the old attendant. Of those 30 rupees, seven have been spent on the shroud and ladder; each of you should take two-two rupees each and leave the remaining nine for me as auspicious almsgiving. Thereafter, immerse the corpse in the Ganga and go around chanting 'Ram-Ram' through the streets so all the neighbours know that the corpse has been properly cremated. Only then return to your houses.' Everyone was happy to hear this. They divided 23 rupees amongst themselves and took the corpse to a remote ghat where neither a *dom* was present who could ask for the shroud, nor a *mahabrahman* who could ask for alms. Once there, they made such haste of the job that they dumped the body into the river along with the ladder and climbed back up to the bank chanting 'Ram-Ram' in unison. They did so because firstly the darkness of the night scared them and secondly because they feared that a government sentry would catch them red-handed since the government had banned disposal of unburnt bodies. Thus, those unfaithful servants, having disobeyed their master's orders, returned to their houses alongside the untrustworthy priest.

Now, hear the tale of the corpse.

The bamboos in the bier-ladder were thick and lightweight like the scull of a boat and the woman's body was so emaciated that the bier did not sink under the weight but floated on like a raft on the river. Had it been daytime, such a sight would have upset the people on the river bank and the crows would have certainly created a ruckus. But since the night was dark, that body bearing raft slowly floated on past Triveni and went at least five miles hence. This, however, was no wonder. The miracle was that the body, which others had thought lifeless, now anointed by the cool waters of the Ganga came alive again and Bahuji regained her senses. She was startled to find herself in such dire straits. Her body was still weak; although the fever that had threatened her life had ebbed away, the lump in her neck caused her such spasms that she fainted again and again. But, with the almighty's blessings, new ways of rescue come about.

Eventually the raft floated towards a river bank where a gigantic karaunda tree stood with one of its branches dipping in the water and offering its fruits and flowers to the river goddess. The bier bumped into that branch and got entangled into it. A thorn from that branch cut through the lump on Bahuji's neck like a knife punctures a boil. The lump burst open and the pain inducing plasma poured out, bringing Bahuji back to her senses. She looked around and found herself gently rocking in a cool and calm embrace of the green bough, resting in its hammock like a way-weary traveller.

With the rising sun the riverside lotuses blossomed and the birds on the trees began to chirp. For a moment Bahuji forgot her physical pain in the middle of this beautiful scenery and thought, 'Am I in heaven? Or is this a dream? Oh Lord! Even if I have come here upon my death, let me remain in this happy state forever!' But happiness is momentary in this world:

Happiness seldom falls in showers;
Clouds of sorrow pour in heaps.

This is the land of dead, my dear
Joy is costly; sorrow, cheap.

Soon the birds flew away and the waves scattered the lotuses. The bier-raft rocked roughly on the water and brought back the jabbing pain in her body. Bahuji was distressed but equally helpless. She didn't have enough strength to swim to the shore; although, there was a small and beautiful ghat only four yards away or so away. She thought—Perhaps, my husband thought I was dead and so dumped me in the river. But he should not have been so quick about it; he should have done a thorough examination first. It is fine if he left me; he'll find several other women. But what of my child? How would he survive without me? Oh! How he must pine away in my absence! Where will he find an unwavering mother like me? And a stepmother will only cause him more sorrow. O Almighty! If I am in the kingdom of death, then grant peace to my son and give me strength so I may leave this state and meet him.'

She only had to say this when a wave fell upon her with such force that she swallowed several draughts of water. The holy water of the Ganga brought tranquility in her body and filled her up with great passion to meet her son. She used her hands as oars and rowed the boat towards the shore, but by the time she reached land, her strength ran out and she fell unconscious on the ground. When she gained consciousness, she believed she was in heaven, once again. The light reflecting off the waters of Ganga seemed like the

Akashganga Galaxy and the blooming lotuses on its shore appeared like stars in the night sky—

The water-born blooms on the dainty neck of Ganga dazzle
Like a blue cotton dress on ivory pale skin

The shore was lined with ashok and kadamb trees that went far into the distance. The woods 'enraptured by spring' was so serene that it captivated the beholder. Karaunda, kauraiya, indrabela perfumed the air with the scent of their flowers. The branches of chameli, ketaki, champa, all laden with flowers were so entangled that they appeared like beautiful maidens standing hand in hand with garlands around their dainty necks. Among them the dhak trees, burdened with red blooms, appeared as ascetics amidst a crowd of householders.

On the one hand, the ascetic's image reminded Bahuji of her own state, on the other hand, the cuckoo's call filled her heart with such longing that she pined for her husband and started to say, 'It is far better to throw myself in the Ganga rather than slowly drown in the sea of sorrows. But first I must ascertain if such a choice is even possible for me. How can death touch me if I have entered a portion of heaven? But this cannot be heaven, since there is no place for mental or physical agony there; and here I am besieged by both. Besides, I am hungry too. No doubt, death has claimed me in such a state! But if I still inhabit this human body and have not yet become a ghost, then it is my duty to seek out my adolescent son and embrace him. But I am helpless and weak, who will hear my call in this secluded place? Where would I go? O pitiful Light of the World! Seek me out! You have heard the cries of Draupadi, Damyanti, women in need, now heed my cry as well!' Saying so, she turned her face to the Ganga and sat admiring its beauty.

Just then a woman arrived from the south-side carrying a pot in her hands to fill water from the river. When she saw that a woman, clad in a shroud, is sitting silently all by herself, she became suspicious. When she noticed the bier floating idly nearby, fear took root in her heart. She was convinced that a dead woman, newly turned as a witch, was sitting by the ghat. Upon hearing the maid's footsteps, Bahuji turned around and began pleading in a pitiful demeanor. Finding her voice faint and her eyes red and swollen, the maid screamed 'Witch! Witch!.' She dropped her pot in haste and ran for her life. Bahuji screamed after her at the top of her lungs, but the maid did not stop till she had reached her village. When the other women enquired after her fearful state, she narrated her entire ordeal. All the while she kept looking towards the ghat for fear that the witch might follow her here.

A few men from the village had left to harvest the crops, others were accompanying Thakur Vibhav Singh on his walk. Only the children and womenfolk were left behind in the village and none of them could muster up enough courage to verify the maid's story by going to the ghat. The mention of a witch had scared them to such an extent that they began locking up their boys in their houses, lest the witch finish them off. At that time, Thakur Vibhav Singh's boy, Naval Singh was also roaming about lost in the thoughts of his deceased mother. He had lost the desire to play with the other kids and only wept for his loss. When a woman advised him to hide in his bungalow or the witch would get him, he looked at her innocently and asked, 'What does a witch look like? And why would she take me if she comes here? I have done her no harm.'

While this commotion was taking place in the village, Bahuji in her misery, began to question her state, 'It is certain that I am dead but have I really been reborn as a witch? Like what that woman screamed as she ran away from me? There has to be some truth in it; how else should I end up in such a remote place with a white shroud draped over my weak limbs and my hair disheveled and rutted into serpentine coils. O! Writer of Destiny, what sin have I committed that you granted me the birth of a witch? Is this the reward for having followed with devotion the role of a dutiful wife? How will I find my son in this state, and if I find him, how will I embrace him? He will flee at the sight of my face. But come what may, I will find him, and if he refuses to accept my love then I will try and convert him into my own state.' With these thoughts she took the path that the maid had taken and started dragging herself slowly towards the village.

Her body shook with weakness, but what could be done? Hunger compelled her to move forward somehow. Soon, having crossed the woods, she came upon an orchard where several fruit bearing trees, such as that of guava, tangerine, lychee, berries and oranges, were arrayed in neat rows alongside bowers of both native and English flowers. 'I see a small bungalow standing south of the orchard, one quite like my own house.' She observed. 'Has God brought me to my own garden? Oh! Aren't these the same flower boughs where I fed my son, Navalji? When I had come here first, the village women had told me that the Ganga ghat is nearby. I had sought Thakur saheb's permission to bathe in the river, but he had denied it. Is this punishment for that, that I have been reborn like this? But how could that be my fault? It is a wife's duty to follow the will and command of her husband. This must be the punishment for sins I once committed in another birth.'

With such dreadful imaginings, Bahuji sat under an orange tree and plucked one orange from a hanging branch. She was about to assuage her hunger pangs when she laid her eyes on Navalji who had strolled into the orchard just then. Her hunger and thirst disappeared and like a lost deer who has just found its kid, she ran to embrace her son. She pulled him into a hug and calling his name repeatedly, 'Navalji! Navalji!' started kissing his face. Naval Singh found himself in an unusual position. Looking at his mother's scary visage he wanted to run away, but then he reminisced his mother's face and amid tears asked her innocently, 'Mother, have you returned from the dead as a witch? We had left you back at home. How did you manage to find us here?' Bahuji replied,

'Son, I do not know how I came to be like this. But if I have turned into a witch, believe me, my heart is still the same. It is for you that I have dragged myself all the way to this place.'

Here was a moment of affection and exchange, but there the village women saw the scene and raised a cacophony. They shouted, 'Hey! The witch has got hold of Navalji! Gather around! Run! Save him! Oh, it's a catastrophe! How could we know that the witch was squatting in the orchard! Or else we would never have allowed Navalji to wander into it.' They made a clamour from afar, but none of them had the courage to go near the boy.

Meanwhile, Thakur Vibhav Singh and his companions, who had gone for a walk, came back. They were surprised to see the confusion. Having heard the entire tale from the maid's mouth, Thakur saheb said, 'I don't believe in the existence of ghosts. But God works in mysterious ways. It might just be true.' He brought out his pistol from the bungalow and rushed towards the orange tree where the witch had held Navalji. The villagers followed him, wielding sticks in their hands. On seeing his father approach, the boy wanted to leave his mother and run to his father with the good news. But his mother wouldn't let go of him. Thakur saheb saw this struggle from afar and understood that certainly the witch has got his son. He roared, 'Don't be afraid, son! I am coming!' Once within range, he wanted to shoot the witch down, but his son intervened, shouting, 'Don't shoot! Mother! She is my mother!' In the moment of confusion Thakur Saheb could not understand the boy's warning. He had already taken aim, and so he fired his pistol. With the loud thunder, Bahuji fell to the ground and the boy sat down, shocked. Thakur Saheb picked him up in his arms and said, 'You are safe now, my son. Tell me, who is she? Is she really a witch?' Finding Bahuji unconscious, the villagers began shouting, 'The witch is dead! The witch is dead!' The women gathered around to see the spectacle. The maid spoke up, 'This is the witch who sat on the ghat and now tried to swallow Navalji whole.' Others joined in, 'We had heard that witches have huge teeth and claws. She has neither. What sort of a novice witch is she!'

Someone opined, 'She is a witch's baby. Her teeth would've grown with her.'

While jokes and laugher abounded here, there Navalji, believing that his mother had been shot and now lay dead, fell down unconscious. The villagers stared at him, afraid. Someone said that the sound of the pistol had shocked him, another said that the witch had possessed him. Eventually the boy regained his senses and began to cry, 'This is my mother; I warned you, why did you kill her?' 'Your mother is no more, my son.' Thakur saheb consoled, 'Only yesterday I received the priest's letter where he informed me that he had cremated your mother's body on the Ganga ghat. How can this witch be your mother?' The boy replied, 'Go and see if you can recognize her.' Thakur saheb stepped closer to examine the body. He removed the cloth from her head to reveal a face similar to his wife's. The mole on her forehead was the same, and so were the two dark spots on her bosom.

'How strange! This is indeed my wife!' Then he turned to the boy and said, 'Don't you worry son, I did not shoot her. I heeded your warning and fired into the sky thinking if this is some evil, the gunshot will be enough to drive it away.' The boy replied, 'Look! She has a gun-shot wound on her neck and you say you did not shoot her.' Thakur saheb said, 'This is the wound from the lump on her neck. My bullets became a star in the sky.'

After that Thakur saheb removed everyone from the scene and standing at a distance himself, ordered the nayin, 'You know every inch of her body. Examine her thoroughly and find out if this really is my wife, or some other woman.' The nayin inspected the body, her eyes wide with fear. Bahuji came back to her senses, but just as she began to get up, the nayin ran away, afraid. Bahuji recognized her and called after her, '*Aree* Badamiya! Where is my child? Quick, call him here or I won't live long. Thakur saheb is after my life. He abandoned me in Prayagji, even though I was sick. When I reached here somehow, he tried to shoot me. I don't understand what crime I have committed. If I have died of plague and have returned as a witch, I will still serve him even with this ghostly shell. But if he finds my current state disgusting, then I too cannot bear this insult. I shall drown myself in the Ganga. Just bring my child to me, let me hug him one last time. How can I live without him? Oh Almighty! Take me with you.' Having said this, she began to weep loudly.

Thakur saheb could not bear those words filled with love's longing and the agony of separation. His heart was overwhelmed with excitement and tears poured from his eyes. He rushed to embrace Bahuji and said, 'Please forgive me. I did not abandon you intentionally. If you are my wife then I do not care if you come to me as a human or a ghost, I shall accept you in all forms. Although I am still doubtful, but with time everything will become clearer. From now on, I accept you as my dear wife. If closeness to you may inflict on me the torment of plague or the horror of ghosts, I shall not flinch from the challenge at all.' He picked Bahuji up and lead her into the bungalow along with Navalji and asked them what had happened.

Just then, the old attendant, Satya Singh also arrived from the city. When he heard the miraculous tale from the villagers, he figured what must have happened. He approached Thakur saheb and said, 'Maharaj! Remove all doubts from your mind. This, indeed, is Bahuji; there is no doubt in it! When the nayin was wrapping her in the shroud, she had said that her body is still warm. I wanted to examine her claim myself, but the evil servants would not listen to me. They dumped her into the river without cremating her. Such luck! or she would have been a pile of ashes by now. I am certain that she was not dead and, by the grace of Gangaji, she floated on to this shore and came back to us. Praise your fortune, accept her as your wife and sound the celebrations!'

All doubts left Thakur saheb when he heard this. He embraced Bahuji and shed loving tears. Overwhelmed with love, Bahuji too sat crying with her head on the shoulders of her son. The village folk celebrated the resurrection of Bahuji by dancing to the beats of Magh, Manjira and Phag. The women brought paan, fruits and flowers to worship her and asked for her forgiveness. Bahuji only said, 'You people are not at fault. It was my fate to suffer such a time. May God grant good days to all as he has returned me mine.'

Translated from Hindi by Abiral Kumar

The Stranger

Ashok Vasishth

'He is indeed a stubborn man! I have told him countless times that Madam cannot meet but he just does not want to listen…on the contrary, he says: "No problem, she will meet me when she can… You can get back to your work." Tell me, what am I supposed to do?'

'Maybe, he is in deep trouble! No issues. You can ask him to wait for some time,' the madam responded in an empathetic manner.

'Well! I have told him this thing almost fifty times, but he refuses to listen!'

'Do not lose your mind on these trivial issues…You can leave now. I will handle him myself,' Doctor Madam explained to her and sent her outside.

'Shalu, he looks like some old, adamant, and stubborn lover who is sitting out and waiting endlessly,' commented the familiar voice of the woman patient sitting right next to her.

'Well, everyone amongst us is torn by some sorrow, some trouble or misery…This poor lady is troubled by the fact that someone has been sitting outside and waiting.'

'And this "poor man" seems to be only troubled by the fact that he cannot meet you,' the familiar voice of Shalu's acquaintance said once again, before the former could complete her sentence.

'Well, whether he is troubled or not I can't say that. But maybe, he is caught in some tricky situation, because of which it is necessary for him to see me,' Shalu spoke earnestly in an attempt to stop the conversation from going in another direction.

Shalu further discouraged the conversation by asking the lady patient who was sitting right in front of her: 'Forget him, you tell me what has bought you here?'

'Well, they say, one shouldn't hide anything from mother or doctor: from the last few days, I have been facing an unbearable stomachache…I have been seething in pain,' the lady described her misery.

Shalu asked the lady patient a couple of questions, investigated her thoroughly, and began to write down the names of some medicines. She further said with a sense of objectivity: 'These are some medicines…you could show this slip to the pharmacist…it is one week's course…there is no need to worry...it is just a case of mild infection.'

After finishing with this routine investigation, Shalu rang the call-bell to call the patient who had been waiting for a long time. The female attendant entered and informed hastily (even before Shalu could ask her): 'Madam, he has just left.'

Slightly perplexed by the information, the doctor thought: What a strange man! He was getting so impatient to meet otherwise. She further investigated: 'Did he say something to you before leaving?'

'Well, he just mentioned: "I don't know when your Doctor Madam is going to find time…I will come at some other time,"' the female attendant replied.

'No problem, the next time he comes, do send him straight away to my cabin,' the doctor replied and asked her to leave.

'I do not know when your Doctor Madam is going to find time', the words of the stranger echoed in her ears once again. She began to reflect upon it, and all of a sudden, a face—an image flashed in her mind. He was exactly the same! He could not wait even for a single extra minute; he respected punctuality and if someone could not keep time, he would walk away. Recollecting from the deepest layers of her consciousness, she stepped out of her cabin.

At that very moment, one of her close friends of yesteryears entered the cabin. In a rather playful tone, she teased affectionately: 'Where are you heading to?...I have just come.' Dr Shalu replied in an equally warm and affectionate manner: 'First you make yourself comfortable… have something to drink…then we shall move onto other issues.'

Shalu's friend took a seat right in front of her, picked a glass of water for herself, and asked her: 'Now tell me, what is the secret?'

'There is no secret as such…this happened in my life years ago.'

Shalu's friend annoyingly observed: 'Years ago...and yet you did not share it with me!'

'There is no secret really...it is just that in life when you meet different people or are drawn to them due to their individualities…often, in some situations, you are reminded of them. Our past becomes a reflection of our present position,' the doctor responded in a contemplative tone.

Shalu's friend insistently asked her the details of the person that she was talking about and why he had such a deep impact on her life.

The Doctor began to narrate the incident in a nostalgic as well as contemplative manner: 'This goes back to the days when my career had just started. Since a lot of things were new to me, I quite often took help from my seniors. They were very good to me and helped me see through the depth and complexity of different situations in life.'

'Were they all boys?,' asked the friend with a sense of keen interest in the doctor's life.

'No, there were girls too…whether girls or boys…we were all tied by a common bond of friendship and empathy towards each other…though all my friends were extremely considerate to me, one amongst them still stood out.... He was of a cool and calm temperament…he was also extremely introverted...spoke only when it was required, but was quite polite and well-behaved. Though reticent, lacking a good sense of humour, and slightly reserved, he was very good-looking. I was immensely attracted to him. I wanted him to be with me all the time…to spend moments, exchange a laugh or two, share conversations…but he usually stayed in a world of his own…'

The friend, once again, intervened in her typical intrusive manner: 'If you liked him so much, why did you not express your feelings?'

'I did try many times…but was unable to do so…then, one day, he came and sat right next to me. When I saw him quiet and confused, I asked him: "Do you want to say something?" He looked at me dismissively; moved a little away, and replied, "No, nothing. You can continue with your work".

I was a little taken aback by this response, wondering if there was nothing to say, then why did he come to sit beside me. His introverted and reticent nature had begun to affect me deeply.

The friend jumped in again: 'Then what happened?'

'On that particular day, he did not talk to me. But when he met me the next day, I asked: "You wanted to say something yesterday, but you did not say it. Anything of specific interest?"'

"It was certainly a matter of specific interest," he replied subtly.

"What was it?" Shalu could not contain her excitement.

Expectedly though, he cut short her excitement once again and said: "Leave it! Why are you so bothered about the specifics?"

'By now, I was clear that he would never confess anything to me…even beforehand, many-a-times, I had witnessed him in a similar state of mind...I…'

'Madam,' before Shalu could finish her sentence, the female attendant intervened—almost in a manner of giving her a reality check.

'What is it?' Shalu asked.

'Some people are sitting and waiting outside. Should I send them in?'

Shalu told her old friend, 'I shall continue the story next time.' She then asked the female attendant to send in the patients one by one.

'Let me take your leave. But I would definitely want to hear the complete story next time,' Shalu's friend said before leaving.

***

'It has indeed got quite late,' the female attendant said suddenly, before Shalu could call in the next patient.

'Look at the time,' the attendant said while pointing towards the clock hanging on the wall. 'You really care for me,' said Shalu, as she got up from her chair.

The attendant, suddenly remembering something, 'Madam, that stranger...'

'What about him? Did he say anything?,' Shalu asked with a sense of nervousness as well as excitement.

'No, he did not say anything...he just sat calmly and looked at the clock twice or thrice. He then, seemed to remember something, stood up, and left.'

Shalu murmured something in response to his expected behaviour. When the female attendant enquired about the murmuring, Shalu diverted the issue and left the clinic.

The next day arrived and Doctor Shalu's clinic witnessed only a few patients. Shalu wanted to enjoy her free time, so she attended to the patients promptly, and then sat in a deep, meditative state, reflecting upon her past and the present, witnessing them merging into a beautiful and seamless whole.

This happened many years ago when she was a medical student. She was sitting in her classroom and the teacher had not arrived. All the students were sitting in the classroom. Amid all the frenzy and mild laziness that was setting in amongst the students, the teacher entered the classroom. She did the customary roll-call and began with the lecture. There was pin-drop silence in the class and everyone's complete focus was on the discussion in the class. Shalu was sitting on the last bench, and out of a sudden, she became ill. The attention of the entire class shifted to Shalu. The students began whispering among themselves.

The teacher hurried towards Shalu's seat. She examined Shalu's condition and said: 'This appears to be a case of dehydration. There is no need to worry. Bring her to my room and we shall call upon the doctor.'

She gave some instructions to a few students and proceeded towards the principal's office.

***

'Do not repeat this mistake,' Sameer said as they stepped out of the dispensary.

'Nothing serious. Just a little bit of giddiness.... However, I have never experienced this before,' Shalu replied in her defence.

'I am glad that it did not turn out to be anything serious. We were quite stressed. However, even the doctor said that it might be a case of change in weather...,' Sameer said while expressing a sense of relief on seeing Shalu's improved condition.

As some work for the practical exams was pending, both of them proceeded towards the college laboratory. Though Shalu's condition improved considerably since morning, she wasn't looking completely fine. This prompted Sameer to ask her why she resumed work so soon. To this, she replied in an objective tone: 'I will take leave as soon as I finish my work.'

Sameer did not cross-question her at this juncture. He quietly followed Shalu to the laboratory. He hardly had any work, but what mattered to him was Shalu's company. He was concerned about ensuring that she finished everything on time.

Today, at the present moment, years later, the reflections of the past unfolded one memory after the other. Shalu realized that her most treasured and precious memories in the depth of her consciousness were of the time that she had spent with Sameer during her medical school. Sameer, a distinctive and unique person—extremely supportive, compassionate, and selfless.

While diving deep into the recesses of her consciousness, she was reminded of another incident from the past.

One day, she had to travel far due to some urgent work. It was quite late when she was returning home. The bus reached the bus stop of her locality; she alighted the bus, and just as she was about to proceed towards her home, some goons surrounded her taking advantage of the darkness. Somehow she managed to escape from them and ran towards home. However, the next day, when she narrated the incident to Sameer, he not only got angry but also, from that day, he accompanied Shalu to her home every night.

Apart from that incident, there were countless other occasions when Sameer extended his help to Shalu. After the completion of their medical studies, they were destined to be separated from each other. However, in spite of the passing years and increasing responsibilities as a medical practitioner, Shalu could never forget Sameer's unconditional love. His memories were still close to her heart.

***

Shalu was busy examining her patients. She did not get a single minute to ease herself. The patients were coming continuously one after another. She had become almost like a non-stop machine that runs without any break. She took a two-minute break, and to divert her mind from the banal humdrum of her everyday life, she shut her eyes for a few moments. At the same time, the female attendant suddenly came in and interrupted her meditative state of mind.

'That stranger has come again.'

Well, he must be in serious trouble since he has come to see me again! 'Send him in,' Shalu responded. She did not want to see any other patient at this moment except him. The only thought that lurked in her consciousness was that the patient has come to visit her for the second time.

'Can I come in?' the patient standing outside, asked.

'Well, you are already in…any specific problem?' Shalu queried without looking at him.

'There are certainly some problems. The great medico whom I have been struggling to meet for such a long time… she hasn't even looked at me.'

She was overwhelmed by nostalgia and a sense of familiarity as she looked at him. The gentleman entered and said in a subtle tone: 'Doctor Shalu, no actually, even Shalu is enough…Many years ago…you and I…'

Doctor Shalu was shaken with a sense of disbelief by the familiarity in the voice. She saw Sameer standing right in front of her; she replied: 'Yes, many years ago… in this town…a gentleman studied with me…my constant companion in all the thicks and thins of life. I don't know where he went off after the completion of the studies…but at every single moment of crisis, self-doubt, or confusion, I searched for this stranger…'

Overwhelmed by nostalgia, she hugged Sameer. And at this moment, when the past and present came together in a seamless whole, she could identify that the foundation of her present strength was Sameer's love and care and the beautiful memories that enabled her to confront the gravest doctor-patient challenges at some of the defining moments in her life. The time that she had spent with Sameer helped her to redefine her life, and persuaded her to help people around her, particularly her patients.

Translated from Punjabi by Guntasha Tulsi

Heartless

Annie Zaidi

Once upon a time, there was a city where the hearts of its citizens were taken away before they turned thirty.

That was the law and, significantly, it was not an unpopular measure. By the time a thirtieth birthday rolled around, people would grow sick of their hearts. It would heat up and grow noisy, like a second-hand latte. Skeins of muscle would start writhing under the skin like fish caught on a hook. People would lose appetite and fail to show up at bakeries and meat shops. In the cold months, it was worse. Even the bakers and butchers would throw off their aprons and declare that they were done with this blight called life.

Before the Heart Law was enacted, several citizens left home without the courtesy of even a goodbye note. Their families would be distraught. Other citizens would go drinking every night and would drink until they ran out of credit, and then they'd fight like wolves.

There were also those who tried to cut down trees in public parks because they had once carved into the bark a misshapen heart with the name of their beloved. Worse, some citizens strung themselves up on trees. Others went out walking, then vanished near the lake.

The rulers had been watching these events with concern. Public misery was sure to trigger revolt. Or elections. Some such manner of unpleasantness. So, they funded research at the university and asked scholars to develop a happiness meter to get a measure of citizen grief. Next, the rulers ordered that annual happiness reports be published in the newspapers. The reports concluded that though the state was amongst the top happy states in the world, it must strive to be happier yet.

They gave out medals for positivity. Suicide was already punishable by law. Survivors were awarded three years of solitary confinement. Now weeping in public places like parks, cafeterias and school grounds was an offence that attracted stiff fines. Repeat offenders could be sent to jail for anywhere between three nights and three months.

Citizens grew cautious but their hearts did not. They wept and scuffled and made scenes in public bars. They scribbled messages on the walls of the High Court. They attacked trees with flame torches. In prison, they curled up on the bare floor, turned their faces to walls stained with the piss and spit of robbers and murderers of yore, and they did not complain. Nor did they appear to be in any hurry to leave. There were cases where citizens who were awarded a fine, simply threw their wallets at the magistrate as if to say: Take it! Take it all, damn you! Some of the magistrates had even written to the newspapers, questioning the purpose of such laws. Then came the night when everything changed.

It started with a student called Ray. He was fined for weeping in public when in fact, he had not been weeping. He had only laid his head down on the table of an empty bar. The ache in his chest was replaced with rage, and after he had finished paying the fine and signing a no-repeat pledge, he went home and cut out his heart with a kitchen knife.

As he lay back in bed, he thought, 'Well, that's that!' Well, it wasn't. Ray woke up the next morning. He opened his eyes and found that he could sit up. He was surprised, but not displeased. He wrapped up his excised heart in a blue bath towel and hid it under his pillow. After a few days of rest, he decided to go back to work.

Life went on much as before. When he went for a swim, people noticed a scar but there was no evidence of a missing heart. Ray smiled if someone cracked a joke. He no longer snapped at his mother. In fact, he was unfailingly courteous. His friends found him quieter. He no longer burst into song, but since he was quite tuneless, they were relieved rather than concerned.

Ray would have died with his secret under his pillow, if he had not met Nayan at a friend's birthday party. When he first saw her, he thought that there was something familiar about her. And yet, she was a stranger. All evening, he looked at her. She too kept glancing at him. He moved closer to the spot where she was dancing until he brushed against her.

Perhaps he did so from old habit rather than with any sense of purpose, but before he could move away, Nayan turned and looked him full in the face. The hollow where his heart used to be started to throb. For the first time since the excision, Ray felt as if he could not breathe. He fled.

Nayan was puzzled. She was convinced that Ray wanted her. The look in his eye, the heat of his skin. It was unmistakeable. He was a shy man, she decided. Perhaps, he was too decent for his own good. There were men like that. So she decided to follow him.

She waited until the moon had disappeared behind a cloud, found an open window and squeezed in. She tiptoed up the staircase and into the room where Ray was curled up in his bed. She did not whisper his name nor sought his permission. She kicked off her shoes and lay down beside him. But the moment her head touched the pillow, she felt a great throbbing underneath.

Nayan sat up in confusion and Ray was terrified. Now his secret would be out. He would be announced a freak. Yet he dared not stop Nayan as she slipped her hands under the pillow, drew out the throbbing bundle and unwrapped the towel. She saw the quivering heart and in sheer terror, she dropped it.

Ray snatched up his heart at once, snarling at Nayan to go away and mind her own business.

Nayan went home shaking. She did not tell anyone but she could not get the thing out of her mind. Days passed, then months. She felt as if her palm was still wet and warm from holding the heart.

Nayan took to watching Ray discreetly as he went about his life. She scanned his face for signs of sickness. Was he too pale? Was his skin yellowing? She watched him as he drove his mobile around town, danced at parties, swam in the pool. Except for the scar on his chest, he looked fine. He even went out with other women. In fact, he seemed utterly content.

Summer turned to winter and Nayan's fascination did not wither. The nights grew longer. The wind howled and the trees seemed to catch its mood and screeched in sympathy. Finally, a night came that was so dark, so cold, Nayan could no longer bear it. She had battled such nights before but this time, she felt her heart to be a festering wound. She thought of the man who had the gumption to cut out his heart. What a sad useless thing, she thought. And a jelly heart like hers? What a terrible imposition! What did it do that a pump couldn't? Ugly piece of machinery. Vile, vile, vile!

A storm raged inside her and, before it could subside, Nayan too had carved out her heart. She was prepared, as Ray was, for the end when she collapsed on the bed. The bleeding heart continued to pulse where it lay on the floor.

In the morning, it was discovered by the maid who let out a long shriek. Nayan sat up in bed in confusion and at this, the maid stopped screaming and fainted.

There was no hushing it up. The maid told her man, her man told his mates, his mates told their wives, and it was all over town until at last the State heard, and the rulers ordered an enquiry.

Nayan hid away her heart but it was too late. She had to suffer the fools who came to gawk, and policemen who came to question her. They wanted to arrest her for attempted suicide but they couldn't because a large team of doctors waited to examine her. They poked and prodded. They made her jump and run and swim, and when it was time for rest, they strapped her down.

When the tests were done, Nayan was given a year in isolation. Jail authorities petitioned the rulers to send her to the islands, for she unnerved everyone else—the way she calmly took orders, ate well, slept well, and did not beg to be taken out of her isolation.

Meanwhile, researchers from the university urged her to donate her heart to science. She refused. The amazing thing was how easy it was to say, 'no.' All decisions were easy. It was as if she observed people at a slight remove. Still, she could not help being annoyed when people turned to stare.

Notoriety made her defiant. Nayan began to openly preach the virtues of getting rid of the heart. She swore she'd never felt better. She did as she pleased and suffered less. She ate, drank, smoked, and went out with a new man every week. Her friends said she was an inspiration.

It was not long before one of these friends decided that she too had had enough and must cut out her heart. The trouble was, she lacked the courage to do so herself. So she went to the hospital and demanded that a doctor do it. The doctors looked sombre and made dissuasive noises. Secretly, they were glad. They had been itching to get their scalpel on a volunteer and witness this miracle for themselves. So, after making the citizen sign a no-culpability pledge, they did the needful—removed the heart.

Barely a week had passed when another man showed up. He had heard about the woman who survived and he wanted the doctors to perform a similar surgery. Thus the doctors discovered that it was true. One could not just survive but work, play, conjugate and give birth without a heart.

Then they came in droves. Teenagers, students, lovers, divorcees. Excised hearts were placed in neatly labelled glass boxes at the hospital. Their health was monitored. Soon researchers noted that people without hearts participated in fewer crimes of passion, nor did they join strikes or political movements. As soon as the rulers were informed of this observation, they declared that any citizen who wanted his or her heart excised could get it done free.

Over the years, researchers began to notice patterns. If a heart was removed after the age of 40, the chances of the owner surviving were slender. But those who cut out their hearts by the age of 30 were likely to live another 20 years. After that age, the heart in the glass box began to shrink rapidly. It would turn a shade of blue, beat slower and then it would stop. The owner would keel over.

The rulers received this observation with great enthusiasm. Fifty was the average age when citizens began to lose their jobs to youths in their twenties. At 55, many citizens would lose all hope of finding jobs and would descend into sickness and despair. They were staring into the yawning maw of 40 years of no income, no work. This fuelled discontent even among younger workers. Now here was a solution, perfect in every way. If everyone had their hearts taken away at 30, nobody would live much beyond 50. Nobody would suffer. Everybody would have jobs.

The rulers decided that, for the maintenance of law and order and greater social amity, henceforth all citizens must excise their hearts before the age of 30. The young did not utter a word of protest. It was only the elderly who wept and cursed in the streets. Past 50, they swore, one's whole body flowered into one giant heart. That was when life started to beckon with intense beauty and calm. They loitered outside the university, whispering about rebellion.

Some of the young couples believed them and refused the excision. They fled on boats to the south, or through mountain passes in the north. Some even walked across a frozen river in the deepest winter, saying they'd rather die of frostbite than of boredom. Such people, however, were in the minority. Of them, the rulers said, 'Good riddance!' Most citizens thought the Heart Law was good. They were able to do the jobs assigned, able to eat and drink without complaining, able to resign themselves to death without kicking up a fuss. The ringing slogan of the time was: Heartfree is Carefree.

There were others who did not approve of the Heart Law but kept their doubts to themselves. It had been noticed that babies born to heartfree couples were given to self-harm. To be honest, there were very few babies. Once the heart inspector came knocking, the instinct to make babies seemed to dissipate. Even this, the rulers said, was a positive outcome.

The rulers themselves were, naturally, exempt from the Heart Law. As rulers, they declared, it was their duty to try and live for as long as possible. The official line was that it was a national security imperative. Research had not yet shown the impact of excised hearts on policy making, international trade and diplomacy. The magistrates also sought exemption. Research had not yet shown the impact of excised hearts on rationality, morality and judgment. Then there were senior bureaucrats who wiggled out of the mandatory excision on the grounds that they need to function as a reliable bridge between rulers and citizens. Therefore, they must mirror the qualities and abilities of the rulers.

For a few years, the state was full of good, heartfree citizens. They were neither happy nor sad. They thought taxes were avoidable but they did not resist paying. They thought life was dull but were comforted by the knowledge that it would soon be over. They knew the rulers were liars and the magistrates unfair, but they did not trust in their own ability to overthrow the regime. There matters would have rested.

But then came a night when Ray lay awake in his bed and started wondering how close he was to the end. He had been very young when he had excised his heart. So far he felt no tremors, no fatigue, but he was turning 50 soon. How much longer? A year? Two? Most of his friends were already gone. His mother was still alive, of course, but hers was the generation before the Heart Law came into force. She would outlive him. Just as well, he thought. She seemed to enjoy living. As for him, he would be glad to keel over. There wasn't much to live for.

As soon as he had had this thought, Ray's heart set up a great knocking. He sat up in surprise. All these years he had been careful to avoid thinking about Nayan. He knew, of course that she was famous as the Heartfree Pioneer. He did his best to avoid reading about her in the newspaper. Just hearing her name caused distress. The thought that he would soon cease to exist and would never see Nayan again had shaken his drowsy heart. It wanted something more. Something still within reach, hidden in a drawer.

That night, Ray cut himself open once again and put his heart back in place. Each nerve jangled as if touched by lightning and all night he whimpered, clutching his hands to his chest. At dawn, he fell asleep and then he slept a whole day and a whole night. When he finally woke up, his first thought was to find Nayan and persuade her to replace her heart. He rushed out, forgetting to eat or bathe or change into a clean shirt.

He did not know where Nayan lived, so he paced the streets, conjuring up scenario after scenario. There was no time to lose. She must be nearing 50 too. What did she look like now? He fretted. He could walk right past her and not recognize her. The colour of her hair, her posture, her dressing style would be different.

Indeed, it was different. Nayan, after the first flush of notoriety passed, had slid into dispassion in a way that confounded those who knew her. Before the excision, she changed her job every few months. Now she had worked steadily at the same desk for decades. She rarely accepted invitations to parties. She went out with men very rarely and if she did, she never had anything amusing to say afterwards. It was so unlike her that her friends began to cross the street when they saw her.

As for her heart, she had wrapped it in an old tea towel and hidden it inside a shoebox on the topmost shelf of her wardrobe. She never looked at it, not even on nights when her fingers and toes stiffened, when her ears rang with songs that nobody was singing and the hollow in her chest pumped with the faint echo of a beat.

Ray sought out the friend who had hosted the party where he had first seen Nayan. He learnt where she worked. He waited outside the office and when he saw her stepping out, he called out her name. She turned.

His face was familiar and yet, she didn't know him. His eyes had been cool when she had first seen him; now they were a fierce amber. Since she showed no sign of recognition, Ray had to introduce himself again.

Nayan stared hard. What had made her go to his house that night and put her head on his pillow with its bloody secret tucked underneath? She had forgotten why she suffered so intensely, why she strove to become like him. Here he was now, hands folded, saying that she must listen, that it wasn't too late.

Once she understood what he was suggesting, Nayan turned away. No, she did not want to do this. On the contrary, she was quite looking forward to the end. She was 52 and she was done. It drove him mad to see her placid, determined face.

That night, Ray followed her home as she had once followed him. He waited until the street was empty and the house was dark, then he searched for an open window to squeeze through.

He found her awake in her room and again he pleaded. He begged her to tell him where her heart was stored. He promised that he would go away if her heart did not respond to him the way his own had responded the first time she held it in her palms. When she refused to tell him, he began to search the room, pulling out drawers, peeping under the bed. Minutes passed and a slow, soft thud began to pulse through the room. It echoed in his ears and he traced the beat to a box sitting on the top shelf of the wardrobe.

Nayan's heart had shrunk to half its size. It was already turning blue, but it was beating. When Ray took the heart in his hands, an echo started up inside Nayan's hollow chest. She began to weep and told him to leave her alone. She tried to snatch her heart out of his hands but he held onto it firmly. He argued. How did it matter, if it truly did not matter? If she was indeed ready to die, then why not run the risk of a few days with him? Half the night she wept and railed but at dawn, Nayan agreed to cut open her chest and put her heart back.

This time, they knew enough to keep both joy and pain hidden under a mask of dull contentment. They told no one about what they had done. Still, word slipped out. After all, Nayan was well known as the Heartfree Pioneer. When she did not die that year or the next, and was always seen at Ray's side, the rumours started.

The old rejoiced and exhorted the young to follow her example. The middle-aged began to grumble. Why did the same rules not apply to the rulers and magistrates? Some people even suggested a forced excision of the rulers' hearts. It was only a matter of time before the hospital was stormed.

Many glass boxes were damaged. Many lost their labels. The rulers did not hesitate to order the destruction of all hearts kept in storage. It was a short, bloody revolt, squashed within a week. But despite arrests and the restoration of order, the state was transformed. The rulers no longer sat easy in their chairs. Fewer people submitted to the Heart Law voluntarily. More armed policemen had to be pressed into service. The young had to be dragged out of their homes and taken to the hospital. There were sullen faces on street corners but spilling over the walls of the jailhouse were thumping songs. Whenever this happened, even without their hearts in place, many citizens would feel the echo of a beat inside their chests.

As for Ray and Nayan, they lived a few more years.

The Final Test

Amar

Twenty pairs of eyes gazed with rapt attention at the Professor of Operative Surgery who was demonstrating a delicate abdominal operation on a dead body, in the anatomy dissection theatre of the Medical College, to a batch of final-year students.

To an outsider, the scene would have appeared to be forbidding—perhaps, even macabre: a long, high-roofed hall flanked by tall glass windows; at one end of it, a line of porcelain wash-basins, and at the other, a row of five or six human skeletons, dangling from iron hooks bored into their skulls; along the entire length of the room two columns of wooden trestle-tables topped with metal sheets; on each table, sprawled in some fantastic attitude, a shrunken cadaver, which had been the living body of some destitute or derelict of society, and had now become an assemblage of 'parts' for the student of anatomy or the budding surgeon.

The operative surgery class came to an end, and the students straggled out of the musty hall in small groups into the sunshine. 'Operation successful, though the patient was already dead,' observed Ashok, who had the reputation of being the wag and wit among the final year. His cliche was greeted with a chorus of laughter from his listeners; but one of them, a tall earnest-looking young man, said in a serious tone, 'Really, Professor Kadlekar is a marvellous surgeon! If I were to possess a fraction of his skill, I would feel proud of myself.'

'Why so modest, my dear Gopal,' inquired Ashok sarcastically. 'When you have already won the gold medal in surgery awarded by Cuddly himself!' 'Gopal is Cuddly's curly-haired boy, and they can form a mutual admiration society,' said Shankar, who had been a close second to Gopal in the surgery prize examination. Ashok glanced over his shoulder, and whispered warningly, 'Shh! Here comes Cuddly!'

Professor Kadlekar overtook and passed the students with quick, short steps, his head cocked a little to one side, and his eyes fixed to the ground. He was a short, compactly built man of about 55, with a bulbous head sparsely covered by greying hair. His eyes were small, almost beady, but they shone with the light of an acute intelligence and could almost emit sparks when he was angry—as his students often found out to their cost. Though they referred to him familiarly, amongst themselves, as Cuddly, they regarded him with awe and respect; but even at those whom he most lashed out with his stinging tongue knew that his words were without malice and admitted that he was scrupulously fair as an examiner.

He nodded vaguely in response to the students' greetings as he passed them, but when he happened to catch sight of

Gopal he smiled slightly, raised his hand, 'Hello, Gopal!' When the professor was out of earshot, Ashok exclaimed, 'You see! Gopal is the only name he knows; all the rest of us are merely numbers on the surgery answer papers!' Shanker turned the topic saying, 'Let's go to the canteen and have some tea.' The other two agreed with alacrity, and they strolled towards a large zinc-roofed shed, which served as a cafe, as well as an unofficial common room for the 500 students of the college.

It was almost deserted when the three friends entered it. They chose a table in a secluded corner, and ordered tea and fresh, hot buns for which the canteen was noted. Shankar munched a bun and murmured wistfully, 'I shall miss this greatly when I leave college for good, next month.' 'Cheer up!' exclaimed Ashok. 'Perhaps you will have to stay a bit longer!' And then as if to atone for his unkindness, he added, 'For my part, I don't expect Cuddly will ever give me a pass in surgery.' Shankar said reflectively, 'He is not really a bad chap, you know. The hardest of him is the crust, just like this bun…As a matter of fact, I heard from our surgery tutor a few days ago, the story of Cuddly's private life and his family history. It is a tragic tale, and it provides the explanation of his cynicism and irritability, and the general moodiness of his temperament.'

Shankar paused to find out whether he was holding the attention of his audience. Being apparently satisfied on that point, he continued, 'Cuddly was married when he was still a medical student, and a couple of years later his wife bore him a son, who proved to be their only child. Cuddly was deeply attached to the infant and hoped he would have inherited his intelligence and would grow up to become famous in some field of knowledge. He was severely disillusioned when he discovered that the child was differently abled, almost an imbecile. When the boy, (whose name was Ganesh), was eight or nine years old, he began to display criminal propensities—stealing things, wilfully destroying other people's property, and assaulting younger children for the sadistic satisfaction of watching their distress. On one occasion, when he was trying to stick a penknife into another child's face, the instrument injured his own cheek, leaving a permanent scar, which gave him a grotesque appearance. You can imagine how much Cuddly must have suffered, but he bore his cross bravely, and lavished his love all the more upon his half-witted son.'

Shankar interrupted his narrative to sip his tea. He selected another bun and resumed. 'One day, when Ganesh was about 15, a wealthy merchant visited Cuddly's place, accompanied by his wife and seven-year-old daughter. The lady happened to be wearing a valuable platinum ring set with three diamonds, and at Cuddly's wife's request she took it off her finger and offered it for inspection. The ring passed from hand to hand and was somehow forgotten for a while in the course of the conversation. When the merchant's wife asked for it, it was nowhere to be seen; but the little girl remarked that Ganesh had held it last. Cuddly searched the lad immediately, and on failing to recover the lost article, he insisted upon the visitors to make a systematic search of the house and all its occupants. But the ring was not found, neither then nor later. When Cuddly called for Ganesh to question him again, the boy had also disappeared. The police were informed, and rewards were offered, but Ganesh never returned.'

Shankar ceased talking. The others had finished their tea; so, he drained his own cup, grabbed the last bun, put it into his pocket, and then rose to his feet. As they left the cafe, Ashok said in a subdued tone, 'No wonder Cuddly is so crabbed and vicious at times!' and added 'Perhaps he still hopes his son will turn up someday.' 'I don't think so,' said Shankar, 'for it is now 15 years since the boy vanished, and it is hardly likely that such a disfigured and mentally deficient individual could have survived for so long even if he begged for a living.' Gopal kept silent but it was evident from the expression on his face that Shankar's strange story had moved him profoundly.

A fortnight passed, and the final-year students were engaged in frenzied study and last-minute speculations for the qualifying examinations, which were less than a week away. Gopal also studied late into the nights. He knew he had no cause to fear a failure, for he had always managed to secure one of the top three places in the periodical class tests. What he was trying for, now, was to achieve the first rank in the final examination—not for its own sake, but because it would help him to obtain a scholarship for higher studies abroad. His parents were poor, and his college education had been made possible only because of the scholarships he secured year after year.

The great ordeal commenced at last, and for 10 days Gopal and other students went through a gruelling series of tests—written papers, practical, clinicals, and orals—having to appear, in turn, before six examiners in each of the three final-year subjects. On the morning of the last day, as Gopal walked towards the anatomy dissection theatre, he felt reasonably certain of his ambition being fulfilled; he had done very well in all the subjects so far, and the only one that remained was operative surgery practical—his strong point.

On arriving at the dissection hall, he was gratified to know that Professor Kadlekar would be his examiner. When the slips of paper, each containing the name of an operation, were distributed among the candidates, Gopal's heart leapt with joy at his good fortune. He had to conduct the operation related to removal of the appendix, a procedure in which he had assisted Professor Kadlekar on several occasions at the hospital, besides having practiced it on the cadaver. He was assigned a table near one end of the hall, and he was slightly relieved to see that the dead body on it was a fresh one, with supple skin and elastic tissues, which would enable him to perform the operation almost as neatly as on a living subject.

Processor Kadlekar came to Gopal's table to watch him make the skin incision and the separation of the underlying structures, and then he wandered away to inspect the progress of the other candidates. Gopal worked quickly, deftly, with precision and confidence. And, as his forefinger dipped into the abdominal cavity, feeling for the appendix, there rose in his mind a vision of himself sailing to distant lands, working with world-renowned surgeons, and returning to dedicate his knowledge and skill to the service of his own country.

His cogitations were cut short suddenly, when his probing finger touched something round and hard, in the region of the appendix; something that should not be there at all. He palpated it carefully, through the thin wall of the intestine. It was smooth and circular, like a narrow metal band. Gopal's memory jerked, and his eyes turned involuntarily towards the face of the corpse, which was covered, as usual, by a piece of cloth soaked in oil, in order to keep the skin and subjacent tissues in good condition. The dead body was that of an emaciated man of about 30, with a rather small head. Gopal lifted the cloth a little, and he saw, running obliquely across the right cheek, a huge scar, which gave the face a repulsive, almost hideous appearance…Instinctively, Gopal knew beyond doubt that the dead man was Ganesh, the professor's son, and that the object lurking in his appendix was the ring which he had stolen, and evidently swallowed, 15 years ago.

Gopal's mind raced against time…. In a few moments, Professor Kadlekar would be coming round to see the completed operation, and he would of course want to examine the appendix to find out whether it had been correctly removed. If the ring was still inside, he would certainly cut down on it, and discover the identity of the corpse. On the other hand, if Gopal were to open the appendix himself, without revealing to the professor the reason for having done so, his action would surely appear to be an operative blunder, which would be unpardonable in an academic examination. Gopal's choice was limited to two alternatives—securing a first class for himself, while breaking the professor's heart; or sparing the professor, at the cost of a downright failure for himself. Because the operative surgery part of the examination required a separate minimum of marks for a pass in the whole subject and Gopal knew that Professor Kadlekar was too rigidly conscientious to give him any grace-marks basis his past record.

Gopal looked across the length of the hall, and saw Professor Kadlekar turning away from a table at the far end and walking slowly towards him. Professor's face was sternly-set, lined, and careworn, but to Gopal, it seemed, somehow, strangely sympathetic, serene, and graceful, and he could not bear to think of the change it would undergo at the sight of the platinum ring, or the scar on the cheek of the corpse. He knew he had only to dispose of the ring, for the professor would not raise the cloth from the dead man's face, nor would he visit the dissection theatre again until the next term, by which time the whole cadaver would have disappeared under the hands of the second-year anatomy students... Gopal picked up his knife, and slashed at the appendix. From within the cavity of that organ, three lustrous diamonds, set in a slender hoop of platinum, sparkled and winked at him. He extracted the ring and put it into his pocket.

When Professor Kadleker came to his table a minute later, Gopal did not look up at him. The professor seemed to sense that something had gone wrong, for he did not begin with the customary questions. He glanced at the loop of intestine lying on the dead man's abdomen, and held out his hand for the appendix. Gopal placed it on his palm. The professor spoke, without lifting his gaze from the mutilated organ. 'Have you any explanation to offer for performing an appendicectomy in this manner, Gopal?' he asked, in a low, vibrant tone. Gopal made a slight gesture of hopelessness and said, 'No Sir, except that I couldn't help it.' Professor Kadlekar put the appendix down on the table and said, 'Then you may go. I have no questions to ask you.' He turned away, and with his face still averted from Gopal, he added, 'Please see me in my office at two o'clock this afternoon.'

***

At the appointed hour, Gopal entered Professor Kadlekar's private office in the college, and found him standing at an open window overlooking the lawn. He turned around and greeted Gopal with a smile, and then seated himself at his desk, motioning Gopal to do likewise. In a calm, level tone, he began. 'I have not called you, Gopal, to admonish or to question you regarding your performance in the examination this morning. I am sure you know what it's only possible consequence could be, and I shall not be revealing any great secret in telling you that I have given you a zero in your operative surgery practical.'

Gopal found himself trembling at this abrupt announcement, even though he had anticipated and mentally resigned himself to such a result. The professor rose from his chair and paced up and down the room, while he continued, 'I can understand how much this failure will hurt you, and I sympathize with you, deeply. But I want you to understand that it is not mere sympathy which actuates the suggestion I am going to make to you…I have watched your career in college, and I feel convinced that your talents, industry, and strength of character mark you out for the greater achievements of life.' He stopped in front of Gopal, and said, 'I have no children; and I have more money than I need. I would be very happy, Gopal, to enable you to go abroad for a couple of years to complete your education, and to obtain experience, as well as higher qualifications, in surgery.'

Gopal wondered whether he was dreaming: his thoughts and emotions were in a chaotic state. He managed to say, 'I am very grateful to you, sir, but I would like to consider your offer for a day or two.' 'Of course, my boy,' said the professor, 'You can come and see me whenever you like.' Gopal got up and walked towards the door, but stopped suddenly when he heard the professor say. 'Oh, Gopal! If you have brought the ring with you, will you please give it to me so that I may return it to its owner?'

Gopal stared in astonishment and consternation at the professor, who went on, 'When I visited the dissection theatre early this morning, to inspect the arrangements for the practical, all the cadavers were uncovered, and I noticed, on the face of one of them, the scar that I knew so well. Later when I saw the apparent mess you had made of your operation, I guessed that you must have found the ring inside the appendix and removed it. I am aware that the circumstances of my unfortunate son's disappearance are commonly known among my students, and no doubt you wished to spare me any added distress…Yours was a noble self-sacrifice Gopal; and even though it happened to have been unnecessary, I am sure God will reward you for it.'

Professor Kadlekar turned again to gaze out of the window. Gopal took the ring from his pocket, placed it on the desk, and went out of the room.

Works Cited in the Introduction

Alavi, Seema. *Islam and Healing: Loss and Recovery of an Indo-Muslim Medical Tradition, 1600-1900*. Palgrave Macmillan, 2008.

Arnold, David. *Colonizing the Body: State Medicine and Epidemic Disease in Nineteenth-century India*. University of California, 1993.

Chakrabarti, Pratik. 'Covid-19 and the Spectres of Colonialism,' *India and the Pandemic, the First Year: Essays from The India Forum*. Orient BlackSwan, 2021.

Charon, Rita. et.al. 'Literature and Medicine: Contributions to Clinical Practice,' *Annals of Internal Medicine*, 1995, Vol. 122, No. 08, pp. 599-606.

Defoe, Daniel. *A Journal of the Plague Year*. Penguin Random House, 2003.

Desai, Prakash. 'Indian Religion and the Ayurvedic Tradition,' *Oxford Textbook of Spirituality in Health Care*. (eds.) Mark Cobb, Christina Puchalski, and Bruce Rumbold. Oxford University Press, 2012.

Duffy, Thomas P. 'Agamemnon's Fate and the Medical Profession,' *Western New England Law Review*, Vol. 21, 1987, pp. 21-30.

Every Man's Bible NIV, Deluxe Journeyman Edition, p. 153.

Foucault, Michel. *Abnormal: Lectures at the College de France, 1974-75*, edited by Valerio Marchetti and Antonella Salmoni, translated by Graham Burchell. Picador, 2003, p. 47.

Foucault, Michel. *Discipline and Punish: The Birth of the Prison*, translated by Alan Sheridan. Vintage Books, 1995.

Foucault, Michel. *The Birth of the Clinic: An Archaeology of Medical Perception*, translated by A. M. Sheridan. Routledge, 2003.

Gawande, Atul. *Complications: A Surgeon's Notes on an Imperfect Science*. Profile Books, 2007.

Jewell W. *Historical Sketches of Quarantine*. TK and PG Collins, 1857.

Katz, Jay. *The Silent World of Doctor and Patient*. Johns Hopkins University Press, 2002.

Khatri, Prashant and PC Joshi. 'Bio-medicalisation and Gandhi's Vision of Health: Observations from Sevagram.' *Economic and Political Weekly*, Vol. 50, No. 10 (March 7, 2015), pp. 53-58.

Landon, William J. *Lorenzo Di Filippo Strozzi and Niccolo Machiavelli: Patron, Client, and the Pistola Fatta Per la Peste/An Epistle Written Concerning the Plague*. University of Toronto Press, 2013.

Leslie, Charles. 'The Ambiguities of Medical Revivalism in Modern India.' Charles Leslie (ed.), *Asian Medical Systems: A Comparative Study*. University of California Press, 1976, pp. 356-367.

Mukharji, Projit Bihari. *Nationalizing the Body: The Medical Market, Print and Daktari Medicine*. Anthem Press, 2009.

Steel, David. 'Plague Writing: From Bocaccio to Camus.' *Journal of European Studies*, 1981, 11 (42), pp. 88-110.

Stiedenroth, Kira Schmidt. 'Introduction.' *Unani Medicine in the Making Practices and Representations in 21st-Century India*. Amsterdam University Press, 2020, pp. 11-33.

Wood, Jane. *Passion and Pathology in Victorian Fiction*. Oxford University Press, 2001.

Notes on the Authors

Annie Zaidi (b.1978) is the author of *Bread, Cement, Cactus: A Memoir of Belonging and Dislocation*, *Prelude to a Riot*, *Gulab*, *Love Stories # 1 to 14*, *Known Turf: Bantering with Bandits and Other True Tales*, and the co-author of *The Good Indian Girl*. A series of illustrated poems, *Crush*, was made in collaboration with artist Gynelle Alves. She is the editor of *Unbound: 2000 Years of Indian Women's Writing*, and *Equal Halves*. She is the recipient of the Nine Dots Prize (2019) and The Hindu Playwright Award (2018) for her play, *Untitled 1*. Her work has appeared in various anthologies and literary journals including *The Griffith Review*, *The Aleph Review*, *The Massachusetts Review*, *The Charles River Journal*, *The Missing Slate* and *Out of Print*. She is also a screenwriter and filmmaker and had made several short films and the PSBT produced documentary film, *In Her Words: The Journey of Indian Women*.

Ashok Vasishth (b. 1949) is a Punjabi short-story writer and journalist. At present, he is the Assistant Manager of Punjabi Bhawan, New Delhi, and founder member of Punjabi Sahit Sabha. His interest in politics, educational and literary activities has given new dimensions to his personality.

Bhabendra Nath Saikia (1932–2003) was an important short-story writer in Assamese literature. He started writing from the 1950s and continued well on to the late 1990s. He was a novelist, poet, short-story writer, journalist, playwright, and film-maker. He was also the editor of a well-known Assamese fortnightly called *Prantik*. He also wrote extensively for children. His two prominent novels *Antorip* and *Ramyabhumi* are set in pre-Independence Assam. His short stories reveal his penchant for details and his plays include many one-act plays. He was associated with the two widely known theatre troupes in Assam, namely, Kohinoor Theatre and Abahan Theatre. He directed most of his plays by himself that have been subsequently made into films and have received critical acclaimtion. In recognition of his abilities, he was awarded with the most prestigious 'Srimanta Sankardev Award' by the Assam government in the year 1998. He also received the Padma Shri in 2001.

Basant Kumar Satpathy (1913–1994) was an eminent short story writer from Odisha. Born in a remote village in the princely state of Mayurbhanj, Satpathy obtained MA in English from Ravenshaw College. In 1948, he led a delegation to Delhi to plead unsuccessfully with Sardar Patel for the autonomy of Mayurbhanj. He wrote extensively in Odia, mostly short stories; but also translated and adapted plays, wrote literary criticism and Ramya Rachna (a form of belles lettres). He was the recipient of numerous prestigious literary awards. He was a professor of English at Utkal. His stories have been translated into English and published as *The One-Eyed Chick and Other Stories*.

Bhagwandas 'Master' was Born in Mirzapur, Uttar Pradesh. He was a writer and critic who contributed to the second wave of the rise of Hindi prose. His story, *Plague ki Chudail* was published in *Saraswati*, the first Hindi monthly magazine, in 1902. Ramchandra Shukl, in his history of Hindi Literature, included *Plague ki Chudail* amongst the first original short-stories published in Hindi. His other popular writings include *Urdu Begum,* a satirical biography of Urdu.

Bibhutibhushan Bandyopadhyay (1894–1950) was an Indian writer in the Bengali language. His best-known work is the autobiographical novel, *Pather Panchali* (The Song of the Road), *Chander Pahar*, *Aranyak*. With the release of this literary work, he became one of the leading authors in the field of Bengali literature. One of the best-known Bengali film makers, Satyajit Ray, made a film on this novel. In 1951, he was posthumously honoured with the Rabindra Puraskar.

Jeelani Bano (b.1936) is an acclaimed Urdu author. She was awarded Padma Shri by the Government of India for her contribution in the field of literature. She has received the Andhra Pradesh Sahitya Akademi Award in 1960, followed by the Soviet Land Nehru Award in 1985. She received the Qaumi Haali Award from the Haryana Urdu Academy. She has 22 books to her credit. Her major works include *Aiwaan-e-Ghazal, Baarish-e-Sang, Roshni ki Minar* and *Sach ke Siwa*.

Kartar Singh Duggal (1917–2012) wrote in Punjabi, Urdu, English, and Hindi. His works include short stories, novels, dramas, and plays. He received the Padma Bhushan in 1988, and was awarded the Sahitya Akademi Fellowship in 2017. His writings have been translated into Indian as well as foreign languages. He has also served as Director of All India Radio.

Rabindranath Tagore (1861–1941) is the greatest known Bengali poet and intellectual whose extensive plethora of work ranges across genres from poetry to novels, short stories to drama, essays to songs, political treatises to satires, and so on. Tagore was awarded with the Nobel Prize in Literature in 1913. He was an educator, a philosopher, a painter, and a philanthropist who left his mark in almost every path he traversed. Tagore's poems have gone on to constitute the national anthems of India and Bangladesh.

Rajinder Singh Bedi (1915–1984) was an Urdu writer from India who was associated with the Progressive Writers Movement. He wrote fiction and plays. He also worked in Hindi cinema as a film director, screenwriter and dialogue writer. His masterpiece *Ek Chadar Maili Si* has been adapted into a Hindi movie.

Rajshekhar Basu (1880–1960), better known by his pen name 'Parashuram' was a Bengali writer, chemist and lexicographer. He was chiefly known for his comic and satirical short stories, and is considered one of the greatest Bengali writers of the 20th century. Though born in Bengal, he spent much of his childhood in Darbhanga, Bihar, where he became proficient in Hindi. His first book of stories, *Gaddalika*, was published in 1924. His dictionary, *Chalantika* (1937) was an attempt to modify the Bengali orthography. Basu was awarded the Padma Bhushan in 1956.

Rashid Jahan (1905–1952) was a doctor, writer of short stories and plays and a pioneer of radical writing about women. She is believed to have written around 25-30 short stories and 15-20 plays. She was a prominent member of the Communist Party of India and one of the founders of the Progressive Writers Association. The common themes were exposing private injustices within Muslim households to the public, foregrounding women's experiences within a variety of social milieu, and on how patriarchy impacts relationships between women.

Saadat Hasan Manto (1912–1955) was an Urdu writer, playwright and author born in Ludhiana, India. He has written 22 collections of short stories, a novel, five series of radio plays, three collections of essays, and two collections of personal sketches. He is famous for his short stories depicting the human condition.

Shanker Raina (1939–1979) was a trained doctor (cardiologist) who also wrote short stories and radio plays in Kashmiri. He has a collection of short stories titled *Zietni Zool* (Fireflies) to his credit. He has also scripted *Harud* (Autumn), a popular play for Radio Kashmir, Srinagar.

Sheeba EK (b. 1975), a prolific writer from Kerala, has published extensively in the Malayalam language. She has won several prestigious awards including Ponkunnam Varkey Story Award, Sahithyashree Award, Suvarnarekha Award, Thulunadu Novel Award, Pravasi Shabdham Award, New Age Riyad Kamala Surayya Award amongst other. Her works include *Dhuniya* (2013), *Manjanadikalude Suryan* (2017), *Rithu Marmarangal* (2012), short story collections *Y to K* (2004), *Neela Lohitham* (2013), *Kanalezhuthu* (2016), novelette *Vasanthathil Tharishakunna Poomaram* (2018) and a memoir *Azhichukalayanavathe aa Chilankagal.* She has also translated Qaisra Shahraz's *Typhoon*, Anjali Joseph's *Saraswathi Park*, Thich Nhat Haan's *The Novice*, and Fatema Mernissi's *Beyond the Veil* to Malayalam.

Shirin Shashikant Valavade is a practising physician who has worked in different hospitals across India. She writes short stories in Marathi, Hindi, and English, and has published five collections of Marathi short stories. Most of her stories are based on her experiences as a medical professional. She has also published a couple of horror short stories in Hindi.

Premchand (1880–1936) was an Indian writer famous for his modern Indian literature. He is one of the most celebrated Urdu-Hindi writers of the Indian subcontinent, and is regarded as one of the eminent Hindi writers of the early 20th century. His novels include *Godaan*, *Karmabhoomi*, *Gaban*, *Mansarovar*, and *Nirmala*. He published his first collection of five short stories in 1907 in a book called *Soz-e Watan*.

Zakia Mashhadi (b. 1944) is an acclaimed Urdu short story writer and translator. After an advanced degree in Psychology from Lucknow University, India, she worked in its Demographic Research Center for some time and also taught Psychology for six years at Loreto College. Her marriage to Shafi Mashhadi, a bureaucrat, and later the birth of their two children obliged her to put her writerly ambition on hold. She has published four collections of short stories so far and several books of translated fiction. Her major works include: *Paray Chehre* (1984), *Naqsh-e-Natamam* (2008), *Ye Jahan-Rang-e-Bu* (2013). She has translated Jeelani Bano's Urdu short stories into English.

Notes on the Translators

Abiral Kumar is a doctoral fellow at the department of English, University of Delhi. His work focuses on early Hindi novels. He has taught at the department of English, Miranda House and Sri Venkateswara. His published works include a novel *The Lost Pearl of Paradise* alongside poems and short stories featured in *The Pacific Review* and other magazines and anthologies. His team was awarded second prize for their graphic novel '*Fragrance of Time*' in the international Hamzanama contest.

Aditya Nayak is a journalist, photographer, movie freak, and a translator. He is currently working at Sahitya Akademi, New Delhi as an editorial assistant. He translates from Odia to English. He is known for his English translation, *Fragments of a Diary* (Diaryra Kiyadansha) of the 110-year-old Odia travelogue written by an eminent essayist and short story writer Jalandhar Dev. He has translated two critical essays in Odia into English. His English translation of Gopinath Mohanty's *Utkalamani* (The Gem of Utkal) has been accepted by Odisha Sahitya Akademi for publication.

Amit Julka is a Postdoctoral Fellow at the Asia Research Institute, Singapore. He is currently working on a co-authored manuscript, tentatively titled *The Evolution of Indian National Identity*, 1950-2010. Apart from this, he is also working on another project that explores the Gramscian concept of mass common-sense as a lens to analyze foreign policy decision making. This project is based on his doctoral research, which looked at the role of Indian mass common-sense in Hindi and Urdu and its impact on the country's foreign policy in Jammu and Kashmir from 1947-50. His research is thus situated at the intersection of critical theory, International Relations and South Asian area studies.

Debayudh Chatterjee is a doctoral candidate at the Department of English, University of Illinois at Urbana-Champaign. A published poet having three titles to his name, he translates extensively from Bengali into English and vice versa.

Dhurjjati Sarma studied at the University of Delhi for his MA (English) and MPhil (Comparative Indian Literature) degrees. He earned his PhD degree in English Literature from the English and Foreign Languages University, Shillong Campus. Presently, he is an Assistant Professor in the Department of Modern Indian Languages and Literary Studies, Guwahati University, Assam. He engages himself in teaching and research activities in literary criticism, literary history, comparative literature and cultural studies, with special emphasis on Indian Literature.

Guntasha Tulsi has done her B.A. and M.A. in English from Hindu College, University of Delhi and M.Phil. and

PhD from the Centre of English Studies, JNU. She has been teaching English Language and Literature from last ten years with experiences of teaching at Delhi University, JNU and Guru Gobind Singh Indraprastha University. She has also finished a Post Graduate Certificate Course in ELT and Post Graduate Diploma in Teaching English from EFL-U, Hyderabad. She has presented papers at various national and international conferences, published numerous research papers, newspaper articles and book reviews and is also experienced in Corporate Training Programmes across MNCs and has conducted workshops and short-term courses in English Proficiency and Communication. Currently, she is working as an Assistant Professor at Maharaja Agrasen College, Delhi University.

Haris Qadeer teaches at the department of English, University of Delhi. His areas of interests include Muslim Women's writings, Modern British literature, Postcolonial literature and translations. He has translated short fiction of Rokeya Hosain Sakhwat, Krishan Chander, Joginder Paul, Anis Rafi, Saadat Hasan Manto, Balraj Menra, and Tarannum Riyaz. His articles have appeared in popular publications such as *The Hindu* and *Hans*. He has co-edited the special issue of *Thesis Eleven* on Postcolonial World Literature and *Sultana's Sisters: Genre, Genre, and Genealogy in South Asian Muslim Women's Fiction* (2021). His forthcoming projects include *The Silence That Speaks: Short Fiction by Indian Muslim Women* (2022) and a English translation of a Hindi play. He was a UGC-

DAAD visiting fellow to Department of English, Potsdam University, Germany in 2019. He has also received the Charles Wallace Visiting fellowship to King's College, London (2022).

Kanupriya Dhingra an Assistant Professor, JSLL, OP Jindal University. She has earned her PhD from SOAS, University of London. Her research on the parallel book markets of Delhi is supported by Felix Scholarship Fund. She writes and translates in English, Hindi, and Punjabi. Her creative and critical writing has been published by *The Caravan*, *Scroll.in*, *Indian Literature*, *Muse India*, *Guftgu*, *Aainanagar*, and *Anti Serious*, among others.

Keerti Ramachandra has been a teacher of English, a translator of long and short fiction and nonfiction from Marathi, Kannada and Hindi, and has edited over 75 books from all the leading publishers. She has won the Katha A K Ramanujan award for translating from two languages and her translation of a Marathi novel *A Dirge for the Damned* was shortlisted for the Crossword award in 2016. Three of her translations appear in *Land Lust* (Joginder Paul). Currently, she is a visiting faculty at Mount Carmel College, Bangalore, where she teaches post graduate courses and Communication Skills.

Mohammed Afzal is an Assistant Professor of English at Zakir Husain Delhi College, University of Delhi, India. His PhD thesis is a sociological study of the early Urdu novel with special reference to the emergence of the Muslim service-class in late 19th-century colonial India. He has made many academic presentations on the Urdu novelist Deputy Nazir Ahmad in many international and national conferences. He is the author of the book *Relocating Jane Eyre: Religion and Politics in Victorian Britain* (2019).

Neerja Mattoo taught English at Government College for Women in Srinagar, from where she retired as principal. She is a writer/translator, and apart from contributions to anthologies and academic journals, she has three books of Kashmiri short stories in English published: *The Stranger Beside Me*, *Contemporary Kashmiri Short Stories*, and *Kath—Stories from Kashmir*. She was awarded an HRD Ministry Senior Fellowship to work on four Kashmiri women poets. She is the chief editor of the quarterly journal *Miraas*, which is devoted to Kashmiri culture.

Rajorshi Das is a PhD (English) student at the University of Iowa. Das relied on her *Bangal* parents, Lipika Das (born in Bangladesh) and Bhaskar Das (of Sylheti origin) to understand the nuances of the Bengali words, that are so integral to the original story.

Swetha Antony identifies herself as a generalist whose fingers are dipped in multiple fields of literature and humanities. Though her academic and professional routes did take her away from her roots momentarily, she has never left Kerala behind. She has a PhD in English Literature from The English and Foreign Languages University, Hyderabad. Her doctoral research work on the poetry of Kamala Das is broadly oriented towards postcolonial theory and literatures, with special focus on the language question and the theories of Cosmopolitanism. Her ongoing research is on the larger impact of Portuguese colonialism and the origin and evolution of the Latin Catholic community in Kerala. She works as an Assistant Professor in the Department of English, Faculty of Arts, University of Delhi.

Zakia Mashhadi (b. 1944) is an acclaimed Urdu short story writer and translator. After an advanced degree in Psychology from Lucknow University, India, she worked in its Demographic Research Center for some time and also taught Psychology for six years at Loreto College. Her marriage to Shafi Mashhadi, a bureaucrat, and later the birth of their two children obliged her to put her writerly ambition on hold. She has published four collections of short stories so far and several books of translated fiction. Her major works include: *Paray Chehre* (1984), *Naqsh-e-Natamam* (2008), *Ye Jahan-Rang-e-Bu* (2013). She has translated Jeelani Bano's Urdu short stories into English.

Acknowledgements

I was a student of Master of Arts (English) at AMU, Aligarh, when Tauheed Ahmed, a medical student from Jawahar Lal Medical College, AMU, introduced me to the fascinating area of Medical Humanities during one of our casual conversations. He told me that 'Medical Humanities' was already an established field and was being taught in different American and European universities. He also informed me about his efforts to persuade the medical fraternity to understand the importance of introducing literature in the curriculum of medical colleges in India. Though I don't know whether he was successful in his efforts, the idea of exploring the relationship between medicine and literature has remained with me since then. I profoundly thank Tauheed Bhai for drawing my attention to this mesmerizing field of studies. It won't be a gainsaying that the inspiration to bring together an anthology of short stories on disease and cure comes from my friends who are doctors. I have always cherished my friendship with them, and I offer my thanks to each of them: Dr Shafi Imran, Dr Nityanand Pandey, Dr Saif Ahmad, Dr Zafar Iqbal, and Dr Syed Naved Zahid. Dr Ali

Atif and Dr Rabab Tarin are my favourite people! Prof. Abrar Hasan, Jawaharlal Nehru Medical College, AMU, has always inspired me with his dedication and discipline. Thank you much, Abrar Sa'ab! I also offer my thanks to Dr Namita Kaul and Dr Ankur Gupta, both brilliant doctors and amazing human beings. More power to each one of you!

I fondly remember my young and dynamic friend Dr Khursheed, who unfortunately passed away soon after his postgraduation in ophthalmology. Dr Haneef Tarin, my kind neighbour, has gone but his memory remains: the memory of his many good deeds and of his exemplary life and conduct. I also remember Dr Yusuf Ansari, my friend who left us during the first wave of the pandemic.

The book wouldn't have been possible without the generous support of the contributors. I thank all the authors and translators for their contributions. I thank Annie Zaidi, Neerja Mattoo, Keerti Ramachandra, and Zakia Mashhadi for allowing me to use their published pieces. Zaidi's 'Heartless' was first published in *The Aleph Review*, Mattoo's English translation of Raina's story was first published in *Contemporary Kashmiri Stories* (Sahitya Akademi), Mashhadi's English translation of Bano's story was first published in *Alien House and Other Stories* (National Book Trust), and Ramachandra's English translation of Valavade's story was first published in *Stree*. Amar's 'The Final Test' was first published in the Sunday edition of *The Indian Express* on October 5, 1947. The story has been taken from Dr Kiran Kumbhar's fascinating blog, 'Caring for India.'

I also thank the following for their help at various stages of the anthology: Dr Animesh Mahapatra for suggesting Basant Kumar Satpathy's story; Prof. Sumanyu Satpathy for allowing me to include his father's story; Dr Imran Ahmad, Director, Jamia Makhtab, for permitting me to include Rajinder Singh's Bedi's story; Dr Renuka Singh (Navyug Publishers) for allowing me to include KS Duggal's story; Dr M Ashraf Peer for sending Mattoo's translation; Archit Nanda for reading the translation of Manto's story, and Dr Bodhisattva Chattopadhyay, University of Oslo, for recommending Parshuram's 'Chikitsa Sankat.'

Niyogi Books has been an encouraging and efficient host of this book. Trisha De Niyogi has been very supportive of this project right from its inception. I have immensely benefitted from her suggestions. I also offer my sincere gratitude to Mr Nirmal Kanti Bhattacharjee, K.E. Priyamvada and Arani Basu.